THE ULTIMATE

THE ULTIMATE

James Lund

JOHN CALDER
LONDON

First published in Great Britain in 1976 by
John Calder (Publishers) Ltd., 18 Brewer Street, London W1R 4AS

© John Calder (Publishers) Ltd.

ISBN 0 7145 3595 8
ISBN 0 7145 3596 6

Photon typeset in 11pt Baskerville by Specialised Offset Services,
Liverpool
Printed by M & A Thomson Litho Ltd., East Kilbride

CONTENTS

Chapter One

The Quiet Irish-American

Conshohocken, Montgomery County, Pennsylvania
November 19, 1975

He had woken about an hour earlier and tried to get back to sleep, but the techniques taught at the Farm had failed him. He was restless. The supreme confidence in the mission of the Company, with which he had been indoctrinated as a J.O.T. at Camp Peary, had evaporated. He could hear the welcoming words of Colonel Horden but only like an echo from a past life. 'You have enlisted in the Junior Officer Trainee Program and if you pass out you will be joining an élite group of dedicated men, dedicated to protect America against the enemies of our democracy; enemies who will stop at nothing to destroy us. We are the first line of defence against that attack.' For nine months he had sweated at the classes learning about KUTUBE – the operation to find out the real intentions of foreign governments, and KUDESK – the counter intelligence operation which tries to protect CIA secrets from detection by the enemy – and learning about weapons, including the most valuable weapon of all – himself. Was it all worth it? He sometimes thought he knew less about himself now than then – twelve years ago.

He turned to look at the luminous hands of his watch – still only 5. He could not wake Kathy yet, sleeping soundly as though she did not have a care in the world. 'That's the trouble with marriage,' he said to himself, 'even ours which has been as successful as most. How can I tell her my anguish about the collapse of morale in the Company. She never wanted me to enlist, would have preferred me to be a humdrum executive working out sales charts or computer programs. I persuaded her with my enthusiasm. How can I bare my disillusionment now after her loyal acceptance of my decision for all these years?'

Lately he had been sleeping badly and this was a disturbing new experience. They say everyone has dreams but only some people remember them. Once he could never remember having dreams at all and assumed he never had them, but during the last couple of months he woke almost every night with a vivid dream still in his mind.

And now he had just emerged from a nightmare, and the memory made him shudder physically in the dark. He remembered:

He was in a troop plane with army men, all total strangers. The windows were opaque and he couldn't see whether it was night or day, or where they were. The plane was primitive, had no seat belts and was lurching all over the place as though the pilot didn't know where he was going. Men were vomiting and the stench was overpowering. He tried to walk up the aisle to the cockpit to see the crew but the scene was so confusing he could not tell the front from the rear.

Now awake, he was still shaking with feelings of disgust and hopelessness. And he was worried; his self-control had definitely deteriorated. The nightmare must have some deep meaning but he could not fully comprehend it.

Once he could have put himself to sleep in five minutes, without pills, and pre-determine the time he would wake up. Only rarely could he still do it and only when he was relaxed. The nagging doubts about his own role – and the state of the nation – played on his mind and disturbed that disciplined quietude which had been his mainstay through many a crisis. Everyone regarded him as the most balanced member of the team – equable, good tempered and never prone to excessive anxiety. Something was eroded inside, and as there was nothing much wrong with his personal life he thought the cause of his distress must be his attitude to the Company. Or was it his deep concern about the decline of the country? What had gone wrong?

The rot had probably started with Watergate. Or was it Vietnam – that hopeless war against peasants with so little to lose that the great United States could not frighten them. The real enemies had been the Soviets, who provided most of their weapons, and the Chinese Communists who had cunningly smuggled in the Cannabis and heroin which had gotten half our men hooked on drugs. He felt sick thinking about it: the tragedy of all tragedies, that America, which thirty years before had saved Britain from its inevitable final defeat by the Germans, and had crippled Japan after overrunning half of Asia, should be humiliated by a bunch of gooks.

The decay in America could be traced straight back to Vietnam: the insane shootings on the campuses, the mass demonstrations at the Lincoln Memorial, the drug problem with the veterans even spreading to the schools, the freakouts, the weirdos and Jane Fonda. It was all because of the stupidities of the U.S. policy in South East Asia where we had no serious strategic assets anyway. Not even much oil. Was it the vanity of leaders which put us in that mess? McNamara with his regular briefings, as Secretary for Defence, telling us that the military solution was just on the horizon. False optimism from intellectuals who overreached themselves and then poured hundreds of thousands of American boys into the battle to try to prove how right they had been. Politicians, and pseudo-politicians like McNamara, were a bigger threat to the integrity of America than the KGB. The thoughts whirled about in his now fevered brain: sleep was out of the question.

It was maddening that not a single Russian had been killed in all the years of Vietnam. They had their surrogates to fight their war for them. And probably not a single Chinese Communist killed either. How crazy. But we, he thought sadly, had lost more American boys than in any foreign war – except for 1941-45. And the tough South Koreans and the Australians had lost some men too. The British had funked it, which was hardly surprising.

Will America never learn? How can a great democracy – the greatest ever – fight against the powerful forces of Communism if our own leaders take us into foolish wars and then, as a salve to their own consciences, start dismantling the very institutions which can save America.

No wonder morale in the Company was lower than he had ever known it. Why did the Senate Committies have to pick on them? No one in the Company could understand it, unless they were the scapegoat for Watergate. That Senator from Idaho – Church – was obviously ambitious: suppose he is doing a Nixon in reverse? Instead of Hiss he picks on Helms. Where would it end? He felt like a powerless cog in a machine going nowhere fast. It was pointless, desperate and depressing. Where were the ideals on which the Company was based: the sturdy defence of American values? The nagging doubts assumed a pattern of reiteration in his mind until they became a strange lullaby. He fell asleep.

Kathy was shaking him vigorously.

'Wake up Rick.' He stirred from a deep and apparently dreamless slumber.

'What time is it?'

'It's 7.30 already, you'll be late for that 9 o'clock appointment.'

'Okay, I'll get up.'

He slouched into the bathroom, dropping his pyjamas on the way. Time for a quick shower but only just. The yoga will have to go by the board today except, maybe, for some deep breathing exercises on the balcony. He ran the Remington over his stubble, whisked the shower hose – tepid turning to cold – over his taut body, splashed his face and neck with Brut from the big flask Kathy had bought him for his birthday in October and stepped back, a changed man, on to the comfortable thick pile of the bedroom carpet. The mirror on the bedroom wall did not show the tension of the night. He still looked handsome, clean cut and purposeful and not a month older than his thirty-four years. The night thoughts disappeared. There was a lot to do today.

He opened the door and stepped on to the balcony. The cold morning air hit him like his cold shower. He must ask Kathy to turn down the central heating; it was too high, and, anyway, they should be thinking, patriotically, about energy conservation. The day was crisp and healthy with barely a cloud in the sky. He lifted his arms slowly outstretched to touch fingers as high as he could reach, breathing in slowly to fill his lungs to capacity. Then he gently breathed out again, bringing his arms down gradually until all the air was pumped out. He almost had to gasp at the intake of glorious fresh cool air which came flooding back to reoxygenate him.

The exercise took only a few minutes but made all the difference; he could even skip the press-ups. He felt fit; glad to be alive. The view towards the Eagle Lodge golf course always made him feel good in the mornings. There was something basic and beautiful about the countryside and although these suburbs of Philadelphia were hardly country, they had, at least from his angle, enough of the green to give the illusion.

The Fall comes late in Pennsylvania, tentatively and reluctantly creeping over the horizon from the North. It was quite unlike New England where, in his youth, the Fall seemed to drop like a shroud as soon as the summer was over.

No time for reminiscences now for he could not fail to be at the office by 9. Fernandos must be convinced about the cover, and if he was not properly installed in the office or appeared to take his sales problems too lightly, it might be too obvious to an intelligent and perceptive man like his customer. Even after nine years operating as a salesman for the Penn Tubular Stacking Company, he was still sensitive about making the right impression on the occasional foreign buyer who visited the Stacking Company headquarters in downtown Philadelphia.

Fernandos was a systems consultant to a group of supermarket owners in Caracas and Rick Collins wanted to use him as a respectable and thoroughly safe contact on his next visit to Venezuela. He had no intention of recruiting Fernandos but he did not want anyone in the Venezuelan Government to suspect that he was not just an ordinary American salesman, and Fernandos himself must have no suspicions.

Perhaps he was hyper sensitive, but he did not think so. At the Farm they had been taught never to underestimate the perspicacity of others. Better to perfect the cover to the point of boredom than to have it blown by overconfidence or silly indiscretion.

Venezuela was not a banana republic by any means and it was in nobody's pocket. The Venezuelans felt powerful and indeed were powerful since the Arabs had increased oil prices eight-fold. Venezuela was not a shy, reluctant member of OPEC although they were not Moslems and had about as much in common with Arabs as Esquimaux with Turks. Common material interest is a great unifier: countries the world over moved on the axis of self-protection and self promotion, producing strange and unexpected alliances.

Rick put on his blue button-down shirt, pulled on his gray trousers, adjusted a not too flamboyant tie, pushed on a pair of dark brown shoes, grabbed the gray coat, brushed back his tousled light brown hair and bounded down the stairs to see the children. They were already in the kitchen tucking into waffles and lashings of maple syrup. Deidre invariably got in first.

'Good morning, Daddy: you're late again.' She was very pert and serious for all her eight years.

'Morning, darling,' said her father with a kiss on her rosy, tubby cheek.

'Morning, Mark, ready for that school adventure again?'

'Sure am, we've got a movie today.'

'Lucky,' said Deidre, who mostly felt like a little mother to her brother who was only two years younger, although she could not help being a little jealous at times when his youth or male sex seemed to give him privileges.

Rick had just time for orange juice – always insisting it came out of a bottle rather than a can – black coffee and buttered toast. He seldom had waffles; they would not be consistent with his 170 lbs weight stripped. And he had learnt in the Company to keep fit and lean; a sluggish body is a sluggish mind and in the big stakes of espionage, an alert mind will win every time.

He edged the Lincoln convertible out of the garage, closed the garage doors, dodged back to the house to collect his files and to say goodbye.

'Back tonight early darling, but remember I must go to New York tomorrow and drive back on Friday afternoon. We should be able to take the kids to Harrisburg for the weekend; I'm still hoping to keep it free.'

Kathy gave him a knowing look. She knew the chances were worse than 50 per cent but over the years she had resigned herself to the sudden trips that Rick had to make.

She watched him gently ease the car out of the drive. It was an awkward exit, obscured by conifers, and he did not want a repetition of the petty accident when an irate neighbour threatened a civil claim. The Company insisted that its officers avoided the courts at all costs – whether for criminal or civil actions. The Company was very particular and even pernickety. Rick could think of several students at Camp Peary, sometimes among the best qualified, who were suddenly dropped after minor incidents which had led to a mention in their neighbourhood newspapers. Two of them had gone on to become career officers in the State Department. The standards there were not so high.

He turned from Barren Hill into Ridge Pike. From here he would take the Bells Mill slip road through Fairmont Park, joining up with route 422 into town. He loathed these early morning starts. How could these hundreds of drivers streaming down from Norristown and the North West suburbs do this every day? They were locked into a technological trap, automated to leave their homes like robots at a set time to join the crush of other robots on to the predictable route and then into the overcrowded mäelstrom that was Philadelphia. Thank heavens he was not sentenced to that daily struggle against his fellow human beings. For him it would also be a struggle against ennui.

Perhaps it was the opportunity of freedom the Company gave which had attracted him to forsake an ordinary life. Freedom to decide his own timetable, freedom to make his own decisions and the freedom to travel – at least in his

Caribbean and South American region – whenever he chose.

He had to make regular reports to his head of unit in Washington but apart from that he was free; not like all these drones with their daily routine.

As Rick drove down Germantown Avenue he caught his own thoughts. 'What is that expression from Shakespeare?' he asked himself. 'Methinks you do protest too much.' Maybe. He could not disguise from himself his growing concern. The CIA was getting a bad name and, in reality, he was personally frustrated. The car was stopped suddenly at an intersection and he recalled, with a feeling of cold horror, his recent dream.

'This is no good,' he thought, 'I must find a way of snapping out of this. They might detect my doubts.' For a dedicated Peary graduate it would be a grave dishonour.

Chapter Two

The Square Mile of Westminster

Across the Atlantic at two o'clock in the afternoon, at the same time as Richard Collins was on his early morning journey towards downtown Philadelphia, the British Prime Minister Harold Wilson was putting the final touches to the speech he was due to make shortly in the House of Commons. It had not been an easy few days for him. Over the weekend he had been in Paris in conference with Presidents Giscard d'Estaing of France and Ford of the USA, Chancellor Schmidt of Germany, Prime Ministers Mikki of Japan and Moro of Italy. They had talked about the world economic problems which had caused a disastrous decline in international trade and high unemployment in most countries. The official communique exuded confidence.

Returning to London he faced the realities of running a country in crisis and yet another hectic week of frenetic activity. President Julius Nyerere, the diminutive and lively leader of Tanzania, had arrived on a State Visit the day before, but due to a stomach upset the Prime Minister could not be at Victoria Station to meet him. He sent his deputy Mr. Short in his place. The Royal Family, however, had been well represented by the Queen, the Duke of Edinburgh, Princess Anne and others. It was an impressive turn-out for the modest ex-school teacher from a poor country which, although bigger than France and Germany combined, had an average weekly income of only seventy-five pence for its eight million people.

For the Prime Minister, Tanzania was an important factor in the ten year old struggle to bring the rebel leader of an illegal regime in Rhodesia to heel. He needed Nyerere's cooperation, as the training camps for most of the black guerrillas operating in Rhodesia were in Tanzania.

Tanzania was an enigma on the African scene. The general liberal philosophy which flowed from the philosopher President himself was coupled with Socialist ideas in administration and massive Chinese support in building the long railway link with Zambia into the interior of Africa. In Zanzibar Nyerere still had the nauseating problem of African persecution of the Arabs, which had not been ended by the assassination of his brutal Vice-President Karume. On the mainland he could be more constructive and had embarked on a remarkable programme aimed at bringing the benefits of progress to the peasants in the rural areas through the creation of a whole network of community villages. Nyerere did not want to make the error of other newly developing countries, concentrating progress in the towns and thus creating listless and potentially dangerous urban populations. Furthermore Nyerere had proved that non-racialism could work in Africa because in the recent elections a European, who had once been a farmer in the White Highlands of Kenya, and an Asian were both elected against Black opponents in overwhelmingly Black constituences. Prime Minister Harold Wilson wanted the philosopher President to help work that oracle in Rhodesia where the white minority had become dangerously entrenched in the middle of a sea of restless blacks. Hence the special attention of the State Visit and the political talks at No. 10 Downing Street which went with it.

Although the Prime Minister had to forgo some official engagements because of his indisposition, he did not miss the annual party for all his Ministers which he held on the eve of the Queen's Speech to Parliament. That speech, which gave the Government programme for the coming year and was not written by the Queen at all, was always unveiled at this gathering. It gave the Members of the Government the feeling of being one united team and was actually the only occasion in the year when all the

Ministers – however junior – were together in one room.

The party was held, as usual, in the large reception room on the first floor of No. 10 Downing Street between the drawing room, in which the Prime Minister received his guests, and the large official dining room. To reach it guests climbed the surprisingly narrow stairs at the rear of the building just beyond the hall to the Cabinet Room. Along the stairway walls were the photographs of all past Prime Ministers, including the string of post war incumbents: Attlee, Churchill, Eden, Macmillan, Home, Wilson – from his first time round – and Heath. On each step the visitor, although awed by the aura, was given a distinct impression of the impermanence of office. To some of the middle aged Ministers it was a spur rather than a deterrent. Indeed within a few months six of them would be competing for that office.

Insipid drinks were served by the waiters from the Government Hospitality Department whilst those present warmed to the bonhomie of the evening. The Speaker of the House, Selwyn Lloyd, still looking distinguished despite the absence of his full-bottomed wig, was present by tradition, and so were the two backbenchers from the Labour side who had been chosen to move and second the Commons reply to the Gracious Speech. Always hovering in the group was the Prime Minister's personal secretary, Marcia Williams – now elevated to Lady Falkender – who, although not a member of the Government, knew the contents of the speech long before the Ministers themselves, and was invariably present to hear it presented.

In due course the Prime Minister called for order and the hubbub of cocktail conversation died down. 'For better accuracy I have obtained a copy,' he quipped, taking the words usually used by Mr. Speaker himself when he read a Statement. And then he read:

'My husband and I look forward with great pleasure to visiting Finland; and also to our visit to the United States of America to celebrate the two-hundredth anniversary of American independence. I am confident that the long standing friendship and cooperation between our peoples will continue to flourish.'

He went on through the preamble which all present knew would not contain any of the new legislative proposals.

'My Government will maintain their efforts to bring about a just and peaceful constitutional settlement in Rhodesia.'

And his voice became firmer as he continued

'My Government will continue to strive for a constitutional solution to the problems of Northern Ireland. They will maintain determined efforts to eliminate terrorism, and attach particular importance to dealing through the courts with all those responsible for violence.'

The Speech went on longer than usual detailing the measures for setting up separate Assemblies in Scotland and Wales, public ownership of the aircraft and shipbuilding industries and a dozen other measures. 'It will be a tough session' said the Prime Minister, 'but we are determined, as a Government, to carry through the full programme on which we were elected. A big responsibility rests on all Ministers to help our Party maintain its unity – and its voting strength – in Parliament. It will be a testing year for all of us.'

There were no other speeches and the party returned to its chatter while the non-Cabinet Ministers who had just heard the detailed measures for the first time, exchanged comments on them. One by one, intoxicated more by the heady atmosphere than by the drinks, the Ministers crept away to their homes or to other engagements. For the ninth time Harold Wilson had introduced a Queen's Speech to the Ministers, the office holders that he alone had appointed. He was becoming, some thought, the longest serving Prime Minister in Britain's history. If dexterity and longevity (or survival) were the prime political values, the statistician from Yorkshire might go down in history as the most successful Prime Minister of them all. It was indeed a supreme achievement to have ridden so many storms in recent British history. But one crisis, Ireland, had proven to be the most intractable. It received only a cursory mention in the Queen's Speech and yet for four years it had given rise to a mounting horror both in Ulster and here in Great Britain itself. The horror, unbeknown to the participants in the deceptively soothing rituals of democratic pageantry, was to get unbelievably worse.

When the Members of the lower House of Parliament gathered in the Commons Chamber soon after eleven o'clock on the following morning, few of them had the problems of Ireland uppermost in their minds. The annual ceremony, summoning the Commons to the Upper House was absorbing enough. There were about twenty-five Labour and thirty-five Conservative Members standing in their places as the Speaker advanced into the Chamber from the Inner Lobby. As he entered, the Speaker and the Members bowed to each other once and yet again after he had advanced six paces. The Speaker was dressed in customary knee breaches and wig, which added to his commanding presence. The Chaplain accompanied him to the Learned Clerks' desk in front of the tall Speaker's Chair and they knelt to say Prayers.

'Almighty God in whom all wisdom resides grant us strength.

'Let the people praise thee, O God, let the people praise thee and the earth shall bring forth her increase.'

The Chaplain intoned similar prayers for four minutes and finished, whereupon the cry went up from the attendants guarding the doors, 'Prayers are over'. The Members took their seats on the green benches to await Black Rod, the Messenger from the Lords who had, by custom, to knock on a Commons door shut in his face to show the independance of the lower House from the aristocracy.

The Messenger stepped forward.

'Mr. Speaker, the Queen commands the attendance of this Honourable House in the House of Peers.'

Lead by the Speaker, who was followed by the Prime Minister and the Leader of the Opposition, the Members paired off two by two to walk through the Members Lobby, the corridors, the great domed Central Lobby and on to the Chamber of the House of Lords, there to crowd around the bar of the House.

What they saw was a magnificent and colourful scene. The Queen, radiant, was seated on the throne with her husband, the Duke of Edinburgh, by her side; her children Princess Anne, with her ladies in waiting, and Prince Charles with his aides, were seated on each side. To her right, in the Chamber itself, were the Ambassadors and High Commissioners accredited to the Court of St. James, crammed together on closely packed seats, while immediately in front of her the law lords were huddled in their wigs, and all around the benches were the peers in their cloaks of ermine, and the peers' ladies in their fine dresses and sparkling tiaras. The MPs in their workaday lounge suits were dowdy in contrast.

The Queen read the Speech prepared by her Ministers in a strong clear voice ending with the time honoured conclusions:

'I pray that the blessing of Almight God may rest upon your counsels.'

Parliament had been launched for another session, another year, but it was a year in which, unlike all others before, the fates would be gathering to threaten the continued existence and the hallowed traditions of the oldest democracy and of Parliament itself. As the Members ambled back to the Lower House few, if any, were conscious of the looming threat hanging over the ordered pattern of their lives.

By the stroke of noon Labour Members had collected for a Parliamentary Party meeting in the Grand Committee Room number fourteen, overlooking the stately River Thames. The attendance was small – only some sixty members out of over two hundred – and apart from the Prime Minister, only five Cabinet Ministers were present. It was a desultory meeting and no credit to the opening of a new session of Parliament.

Sitting on the platform at the end of the long room the Prime Minister listened as the Chief Whip, the cockney Robert Mellish from Bermondsey, complimented the Party on the achievements of the previous session – seventy-three

Bills passed into Acts and one thousand hours of work in Standing Committees. He seemed to be oblivious to the obvious criticism of such bald figures, voiced by some leader-writers and the more independent members of the House, that what mattered to the people outside was not the quantity of legislation produced by the parliamentary treadmill, but the quality of Government affecting their lives, and that too many new laws could be counter-productive as the complications of yet more legislation clutter up the administrative machine and produce a nightmare of hideous confusion for the ordinary citizen.

Immediately behind the Prime Minister and the Foreign Secretary who was also present, was a plaque seldom seen by the rushed participants in the processes of Party participation, but coldly confirming the mortality of even the greatest in the land. In this room it read, "Field Marshall Earl Kitchener, K.G., Secretary of State for War, spoke with Members of the House of Commons on Friday, July 2nd, 1916. On Monday, July 5th, 1916 he died at sea."

Harold Wilson, smoking his pipe, followed the points raised by Members in speeches, before he replied to the short debate: the fishing dispute with Iceland, the need for legal aid at Tribunals, comprehensive education, the lack of apprentices which was destroying the building industry, and backing for the measures to abolish pay beds in National Health Service hospitals. The meeting was hardly vibrant with socialist enthusiasm; on the contrary it was deadened by the atmosphere of unthinking complacency; and not a single speech referred to the subject which would engulf all those present and many others within the coming twelve months. Ireland was on nobody's lips and in nobody's mind.

But the walls were pregnant with meaning. Huge paintings dominated the room: The Flight of the Five Members in 1642 who took the course which prudence dictated, The Last Day of Parliament in 1629, which was followed, said the caption, by eleven years without a Parliament and then civil war and, most ominously and dramatically of all, a massive painting of five figures from antiquity entitled boldly The Burial of Harold.

The meeting broke up without ceremony and Members dispersed to the dining room, the tea room, the library or to their individual rooms scattered around the square mile of Westminster. Harold Wilson was among them; he had his speech to check. James Callaghan, the Foreign Secretary, also returned to his room. He did not know that five months later he would be taking over the job of Prime Minister and with that mantle an awesome and sinister destiny. By the time both the present and future Prime Ministers had returned to the Commons Chamber for the opening day of the debate on the Queen's Speech, another man in a seemingly other world had turned his large American car into a parking lot on Locust Street and was walking briskly to the offices of the Penn Tubular Stacking Company.

Chapter Three

Meeting on Locust Street

The offices of Penn Tubular Stacking were not particularly ritzy or ostentatious and this pleased Rick Collins, who was convinced they gave just the right impression to his contacts. Too much luxury – or too little – would not convey the image of solid respectability which was the essential requirement of the cover.

Tube Stack was genuine enough, set up in 1938 as a back shed venture by one William Adams, engineer, who had conceived the then ingenious and original notion of constructing shelving from lightweight tubing which slotted firmly together to form a stable structure. The success of the idea was in its simplicity: the customers could built it themselves to suit exactly their own requirements. Even a child could construct it. The business took off in 1942, a year after the war started and the real breakthrough had been the first Army contract. As the material was easily transportable, and could be put up in a matter of an hour or so, it became extremely valuable in the efficient use of storehouses for Army equipment. Civilian uses were also innumerable, especially as warehousing costs were climbing and Penn Stacking meant better utilisation of space.

Craggy Bill Adams – as he became known to his associates – was a canny businessman; after the war he made his fortune by keeping his feet firmly on the ground. At the time of the Korean war he had been offered a twelve per cent share in an aircraft company which had big Pentagon contracts. But it would have meant allowing his own creation – still a privately owned concern – to be swallowed up in a conglomerate and he was not having any. After a spectacular boom in its share price the aircraft/engineering conglomerate collapsed from the burden of its own excessive expansion and the fatal underestimating of a Navy plane contract. The Government refused to bail it out and it went to the wall. Bill Adams always held that the manufacturing profit was in the nuts and bolts and the relatively straightforward operations; high technology and the delusions that went with it had no attractions for him. Why get involved in the ulcer generating game of the Boeings and Lockheeds when you can make more money selling them stacking, he used to say. He lived long enough to see his decision to remain independent vindicated, but the sudden heart attack robbed him of the retirement he had been planning. He died, only sixty-three, at his desk in his second-floor office in Locust Street. The tensions he had suffered had inexorably taken their toll although he had never really noticed them.

His widow – they had no children – had no interest in retaining control and decided to sell the concern, lock stock and barrel; a New York Trust made the appropriate offer. She understood, vaguely, that it was some family investment completed through nominees and neither she nor her lawyers were interested enough to inquire any deeper. The payment, $2.4 million in cash, came through without a hitch and the lawyers, who pocketed their easy – and inflated – fees, passed on to other such transactions where, whatever the outcome for clients, the monetary interests of the legal profession is always safeguarded.

Bill Adams, had he known, would have been horrified. His creation had in fact passed into the control of the Central Intelligence Agency and would, henceforth, be used for its covert operations. Most of the employees – and even two of the Directors – would remain oblivious of the fact that Tube Stack had become a Government company. It was ironic that the Agency most opposed to Communism needed, in the course of its work, to imitate Socialism. The Controllers of policy in the CIA agreed with the

Communists at least on one point of philosophy: that the end justified the means. The idealogical opposition to State ownership crumbled in the face of the practical necessity to have vehicles of operation.

Rick Collins had joined Tube Stack two years later. As far as he knew only the President of the concern, a shadowly figure who appeared from New York only four or five times a year, the Vice-President (Personnel) and the Vice-President (Sales) knew of his attachment to the CIA. Rick had never inquired into the organisation of Tube Stack, as one of the basic lessons of the Company was that its operatives acquired information solely on a need-to-know basis. The Vice-President (Sales) expected him to turn in a miminum amount of business to justify his designation as a Senior Salesman but, of course, allowed him every freedom to perform his real function as a member of the Company. Rick had been instructed to keep references to the Company to the absolute minimum in Locust Street as it was paramount that legitimate employees should have no suspicion of the real nature of the operation. He did not know that one of the switchboard operators and a stenographer, who often worked for him, were also on the CIA payroll and had the job of reporting independently on his activities. Four other Tube Stack salesmen, on the international beat, were also Company operatives but in Tube Stack only the two senior Vice-Presidents knew this. Secrecy was a credo.

Rick shared an office with two other salesmen, one of whom handled the Phillipines and Indonesia and the other Peru, Chile and Ecuador. The latter had been with the Company five years but Rick never suspected he was such a close colleague.

Fortunately, as international visits were so frequent, the office was usually available for one or other of the salesmen to use exclusively, and if not, an important client could be received in a Vice-President's office. On that November morning Rick was on his own and as he sat at his desk waiting for Fernandos, he skipped through the daily memo from the Vice-President (Sales) and checked the new

catalog. The salesman side of his work did not really
interest him, but he had found over the years that as it was
a necessary part of his profession, he did it willingly and
even enthusiastically, and succeeded in turning in some
creditable sales figures. Even if they had been dismal, the
Vice-President (Sales) would have found some way of
bolstering up his results, but Rick's effort made this
unnecessary.

He had met Fernandos at the Supermarket Operators'
Convention at Atlantic City in September and had sold him
a small quantity of tubestack merely from a catalog and
without a sample. It had gone out by airfreight, at the
expense of Tube Stack which had impressed the customer
and led to the prospect of a reorder. His knack of putting
the customer at ease had also helped; he had studied the
psychology of salesmanship and considered that his relaxed
attitude, created by his involvement with a more embracing
and stimulating career, was the secret of his success. He
always felt sorry for the legitimate salesman who was so
wrapped up in the product and so anxious to clinch a sale,
that he almost perspired with nervous excitement, thus
creating an unconscious barrier between him and the
prospective client. Salesmen, Rick had concluded, should
develop a studied nonchalance, just short of indifference,
and should aim the conversation or salespitch at the client's
actual need, creating a vacuum in his current inventory
which the product would naturally fill Too many salesmen
concentrated on the specifications of the product boring the
client almost to tears; sometimes even this won sales
through sheer pressure. But the other way was more
satisfying and effective; it usually resulted in more
recommendations as the customer had reached the buying
decision of his own volition to fill an obvious need, and felt
proud of himself for finding such a solution. It was
immaterial that before meeting the skilful salesman he had
often not been conscious of any such requirement.

Rick picked up the *New York Times* and the *Inquirer* to use
up the few minutes before Fernandos was due to arrive. The
Times front page showed a photograph of protest marchers

in lower Manhattan demonstrating against cuts in the anti-poverty programmes. That was hardly new: there were always protests in New York, not a good advertisement for America. The city was bankrupt due to its corrupt overspending and the unions and the banks were getting a hand in its government because they were putting up the money to keep it going. Rick thought cynically that Socialism was arriving in America by default and he did not like the idea. Then his eye caught another news item: "Packed Restaurant in London Bombed; 2 Killed, 17 Injured." He read rapidly with a fatal fascination. "Terrorists threw a bomb through the window of a packed restaurant in the Chelsea district last night killing two persons and injuring 17 others, five of them seriously. The restaurant, Walton's, was crowded with about 70 people when the three pound bomb containing ball bearings was hurled from a passing car shortly before 10 pm."

Rick could not conceal his excitement. They have done it at last, he thought. As an Irishman he had subscribed for many years to IRA funds and he well knew that his money had gone to buy arms for the war in Northern Ireland against the occupying British troops. He did not believe his support for a United Ireland, and his opposition to the occupation of part of Ireland by the British colonists, conflicted in any way with his loyalties as an American. Had not the War of Independence been fought against the stupid mercenaries of German/English George III and had not the persecuted of Ireland fled to the new lands to be free of the English. It was imperative for the true Irish-Americans to contribute to the cause of their fellow Irishmen and women even if they did so only passively.

For the past year or so he had followed with increasing disgust the news from Northern Ireland. The terrible shootings of Bloody Sunday had shaken him, the siege of the bogside in Londonderry had moved him, but the relentless and daily killings of Irishmen by Irishmen which had followed, had given him a deep sense of despair. He had never participated in the American-IRA Committees, although some of his best friends in Boston had been

members of them and one, Michael O'Halloran, was very
senior in the American command. He had therefore never
been in a position to influence IRA policy: if he had been he
would have advised them to take the war closer to the
English to get results. Irishmen being killed by Irishmen or
even killing the occasion English soldier, would not do it.
Only if the English suffered directly would they take the
decision to pull out of Northern Ireland.

Rick was delighted that his ideas were now apparently
being paralleled in the ranks of the IRA hierarchy in
Dublin. The war would end sooner if the IRA acted
decisively in London itself. He read further: Dr. Laurence
Martin, consultant in charge of the casualty department at
St. Stephen's Hospital said, 'We have been involved with
nine bomb incidents in the past two years but this is the
worst.'

Rick was sorry innocent people were killed or injured but
soon dismissed his remorse; death always came with war
and some sacrifice had to be paid if a greater good was to be
achieved. Of course some Americans might be among the
dead or injured – there were always tourists around in those
expensive restaurants – but more fool them, they should not
go to London while the war was on. It was good that the
Times showed a photograph of the restaurant's bloodied
guests. That would help put off those tourists who went to
England and bolstered up the economy of the enemy.

The pert little receptionist called on the internal
telephone.

'Mr. Fernandos to see you, Mr. Collins.'

'Show him in,' said Rick, momentarily shaken out of his
reverie. He put the *Times* and *Inquirer* on his desk and went
to the door; Fernandos was already coming down the
corridor, sharply dressed in an Italian suit and looking
younger than his thirty-eight years.

'Good morning, Carlos,' said Rick. 'How is Caracas?'

'Good morning, Richard,' replied Carlos who could never
get used to the North American custom of using Christian
names immediately after the first meeting, and he used
Rick's proper Christian name instead of conceding to the
vernacular.

'Caracas is as hot as ever. When are you going to forsake these cold climes and deign to visit us again?'

'Soon, soon,' replied Rick. 'You know I was in your delightful country this summer, and it was certainly hot then. I aim to come again in January.'

'Still very hot,' said Carlos. 'In Venezuela we have a permanent summer. That is why we are such a happy people'.

'Coffee?' asked Rick.

'Yes please,' said Carlos smiling, 'We must give some support to our Brazilian neighbours.' They had settled down on the easy chairs and Rick produced a Tube Stack applications folder.

'This is what our people think is the best way to tackle your supermarket requirement. You will get the maximum value from the material and Tube Stack will enable the owners to make the most efficient use of their old buildings which they still have to use.'

'Well,' said Carlos, 'I've compared your systems with others and I grant you it is cost-effective. But some of our members are not anxious to dispose of the existing equipment they have.'

'That is a reactionary attitude,' said Rick, 'Look at it this way: Tube Stack will pay for itself in two years in better utilisation of space and in better stock control; after two years it's sheer profit.' The little blonde receptionist brought in the coffee. 'Will that be all Mr. Collins?' she asked, demurely. Rick could think of a great deal more but curbed his feelings. 'Yes thank you, Susan. If anyone comes I'm engaged, and ask switchboard to put all my calls through to the Sales office.' Rick was not expecting any callers but wanted Fernandos to have the impression of Tube Stack activity.

They talked for two hours on the economics of warehousing and stock control, during which time Rick had called in the Tube Stack expert on supermarkets – a lively thirty-five year old who had spent ten years with A & P before their decline. At half past eleven they broke up.

'Can I pick you up for lunch?' asked Rick.

'That would be a pleasure,' said Fernandos, who by now

was fully convinced of the virtues of Tube Stack and only wanted to talk about the financial arrangements. He did not want to do such a delicate thing in the office, where his conversation might be bugged, but the restaurant might be a suitable place.

'Okay,' said Rick. 'I'll pick you up at your hotel in an hour's time. It's the *Benjamin Franklin*, isn't it?'

'Yes' said Fernandos. 'I'll wait in the foyer by the flower shop.' Rick walked Fernandos to the reception area. 'Be seeing you,' he said. 'Look forward to that,' said Fernandos, well pleased so far with his reconnoitre.

Rick returned to his office to hear a buzz on the intercom. It was the Vice-President (Sales). 'Say Rick, could you come into my office, something important has cropped up.'

Hal Warren had been with Tube Stack since the Company took it over and Rick knew he was highly regarded in Washington. Every few months Hal disappeared on a sales mission and Rick knew that, invariably, such trips were on Company business. Chile, for instance, had not produced any orders for Tube Stack except for the one for the U.S. Embassy, and that did not really count. It could have been a put up job – the Company buying from itself. And yet Hal had been to Santiago de Chile at least five times during the last year of Allende and had spent an unexplained week in Valparaiso, probably talking to the Chilean Navy. Rick was amazed by Hal's capacity. He handled his security assignments efficiently without, apparently, it affecting his cover work for Tube Stack. Some of the other salesmen had remarked on Hal's absences but the rumours that he had girlfriends in strange places provided sufficient explanation to their shallow intelligences.

'How'd it go with the Venezuelan?' asked Hal as he reached for his second Jamaican cigar of the morning.

'Fine,' said Rick. 'We're going to wrap up the order. Can I talk frankly?' he indicated quizzically.

'It's secure,' said Hal. He knew the room was sound-sealed and that very morning he had used his anti-bugging gadget to check for any surveillance devices. The window panes had been specially installed to prevent listening devices stationed outside the building from penetrating.

'I'm aiming to go to Caracas in January,' said Rick.

'You'll have to advance that,' said Hal. 'Washington want you to go in December. There's a report that a section of the Army are plotting a coup and that they have Cuban connexions. It may be a false alarm; you know how the local Station is often taken in by informers who will say anything for a hundred dollar bill. We must have an independent assessment. It would be a devastating blow if we lost Venezuela: a hundred times worse that losing Chile to Allende. Chile we could break economically, Salvador Allende didn't stand a chance once we applied that pressure but it wouldn't work with Venezuela. It's too rich with oil. See how impotent we are with the Arabs. A communist coup in Venezuela! It's unthinkable. What's more: Brazil could follow if the peasants were organised and with Venezuelan money they could be. I'm telling you Rick, it's dangerous. This may be a false story but we must check it out without delay.'

'What do you want me to do?' asked Rick.

'Washington want at least three reliable agents in the Army – medium rank people who know their way around – and some fresh agents in the Navy. The local Station have links which we suspect are stale and might in fact have been infiltrated by double agents with the Cubans or even the KGB. As usual Washington need you to work quite apart from the local Station. They must not know you are there. This exercise will also be a test of their effectiveness.'

'Do you want Fernandos recruited?'

'Heavens, no!' said Hal. 'Keep him as your respectable cover, you'll need him. He may have some useful University and schooldays contacts. But he must never know you are with the Company.'

'Right,' said Rick. 'To every man his role and Fernandos will have his. I'm seeing him for lunch and will cement the relationship.'

'Good,' said Hal. 'But make sure you get to Caracas in the first week of December without arousing suspicions.'

Rick returned to his office; he picked up the *Times* to re-read the London restaurant bombing report. Venezuela might be important to America but in his bones and especially in his blood, he knew Ireland was more important to him: Ireland, where – to his shame – he had never been; Ireland where his grandfather had been born; Ireland where his distant relative, Michael Collins, had helped organise the Easter Rising with Eamon de Valera in 1916; Ireland which Michael Collins had helped to free and which was now still suffering under the yoke of the English, fifty years after Michael Collins had paid the supreme sacrifice at the too early age of thirty-two. But, Rick thought, the spirit of Michael Collins lives in the IRA which he had founded. The English can be defeated yet.

Chapter Four

Lunch at the Bookbinders

Rick Collins strolled into the foyer of the *Benjamin Franklin* five minutes late but Fernandos was nowhere to be seen. It was not until a quarter to one that the tall ebony man sauntered across from the elevator.

'Did I keep you waiting? I did some shopping on the way back to my room and it delayed me longer than I expected.'

'No worry,' said Rick, feeling a bit annoyed all the same. He had booked a special table in the corner of the Old Original Bookbinders on Walnut Street, and did not want to lose the booking. He thought, ruefully, there was a time when coloured gentlemen would not be allowed anywhere near Bookbinders but now they used the restaurant without compunction. Even so American negroes still had a slightly self conscious air about them, especially the older ones. Not so Fernandos and other foreign coloureds; they sailed into the most unlikely places with aplomb. Having so many black foreigners in the States – particularly in New York at the United Nations – had given the American blacks much more confidence. If Ghana, Nigeria, Senegal and even tiddly places like Gabon could have their independence, no one could blame the people descended from the slaves originating from those countries wanting a bit of the action too.

Although Rick had never regarded himself as colour prejudiced he could never get on well with blacks. There were a few on the course at Camp Peary and the white trainees had mercilessly, behind their backs, called them the regulation coloureds. Every agency has to have a number, he was told, even the CIA and the FBI; but that did not mean one had to mix with them socially.

Rick never had the same hesitations about foreign blacks. It was part of his job to get associated with them and subconsciously he felt they were no threat to his way of life. Domestic blacks posed a sort of danger which he never tried to articulate, least of all to himself: it was an area best left alone. Venezuela was, anyway, quite different from the United States. It was thoroughly mixed up after years of intermarriage and generations of bastards from every kind of cross-race union. Racially it was a coffee-coloured paradise. Rick approved of it there but did not want that sort of society in the United States. Already a third of Philadelphia was coloured and year by year they were making inroads. There had to be a stop to it if the basic quality of American culture was to survive. Herbert Hoover, he thought, had been right to keep close tabs on Martin Luther King but he was less sure about the assassination. Americans should stop short of killing one another for political reasons.

Rick broke off from his thoughts as he walked Fernandos along the busy side walks of Walnut Street.

'This is America's second most historic city,' he said.

'And the first?' asked Fernandos.

'Boston of course' said Rick. 'Boston was the cradle of the American Revolution two hundred and two years ago when the Bostonians threw the Englishmen's tea into the harbour and started the protest against English rule.'

'How do you remember your dates so well?; asked Fernandos as a compliment.

'Well, I was born in Boston,' said Rick, 'and the independence struggle has always inspired me. Did you know,' he added, 'that Benjamin Franklin came from Boston to Philadelphia to found the nation's first free library and its first hospital? Philadelphia could not have made it without a Bostonian.'

'And America could not become rich without Philadelphia's industry,' said Fernandos.

'You are well informed,' said Rick.

'I studied economic history at University,' said Fernandos.

'Well, there's a lot for you to see here if you like history. You should certainly see Independence Hall where the Declaration of Independence was signed.'

'Don't you have your bicentennial next July?' said Fernandos, more to parade his knowledge than ask a question.

'Sure do,' said Rick.

They reached the Old Original Bookbinders and were shown to the secluded corner seat Rick had requested.

'Will you have a drink Carlos?'

'Yes, a Pernod will do me fine.'

'Where did you learn to drink that stuff?'

'I did a postgraduate course at the Sorbonne. I lived in France for nearly two years. What do you prefer to drink?'

'Whiskey. Irish whiskey,' said Rick.

'Why not Bourbon?'

'I'm an Irish-American and I have an emotional attachment to the land of my people although, to be honest, I've never been there.'

'I see. Ireland is to you what Africa is to me.'

'Do you trace your family back to Africa?'

'Yes, my great, great grandfather, or it may have been my great, great, great grandfather was shipped from Luanda by the Portuguese to Brazil. After freedom the family moved to Caracas. My grandfather became a successful trader, my father a lawyer – in fact he is still practising, has a prosperous partnership – paid for my education.'

'Do you still speak Portuguese?'

'Only a smattering. Spanish is my mother tongue and I speak near perfect French as well as English. Do you speak Gaelic?'

'Hardly a word.'

'Well, I suppose your Gaelic would be equivalent to my forbears African dialect.'

Rick did not answer him and turned to study the menu and so Fernandos remained oblivious of the insult he had just uttered.

They both ordered steaks but Rick, ever conscious of his

diet, had melon as starters to Fernandos shrimp cocktail.

'Are you a Roman Catholic?' asked Fernandos.

'As a matter of fact I am,' said Rick. 'But is it wise,' he countered playfully 'for us to discuss religion or politics?'

'I think we can be more open than you,' said Fernandos, daringly. 'We do not carry the burden of guilt which Anglo-Saxons must carry.'

'But I am not an Anglo-Saxon,' protested Rick. 'I am a Celt. We were also oppressed by the Anglo-Saxons. We have no guilt, on the contrary we have suffered.'

'The Europeans plundered Africa,' said Fernandos, 'and they used religion as the handmaiden of domination. When my ancestors were being transported from the West Coast of Africa, a Portuguese bishop stood on the quayside and baptized whole ship loads before the journey.'

Fernandos sensed from Rick's reaction that perhaps the conversation was going a little too far. Celt or Anglo-Saxon his host was still sensitive. White men generally, he had found, could not fathom the iniquity of their race. For generations they had been so indoctrinated with a sense of superiority that a collective mental block prevented them from grasping some of the most elementary facts of racial relationships. He changed the subject.

'Why is this restaurant called Bookbinders?' he asked.

'This was the centre of our culture: Franklin started the Philosophical Society here. There were printers and publishers and bookbinders all around this area. Two hundred years ago there were over twenty printers and newspapers in Philadelphia, although the population was only thirty thousand'.

'Fewer newspapers now!' said Fernandos.

'One morning paper for a population of two million,' said Rick. 'And even New York now has only one. That's progress: more bigness, more conformity.'

They had reached the steaks: Fernandos had his well done, Rick's medium rare. Fernandos wanted to broach the subject of commission before they were carried away on other themes. He found Collins an interesting man, extremely cultured for a salesman, and for a moment wondered why he had not chosen another profession. He must be doing it for the money, he concluded; money explained a lot.

'Richard, do you have any agents in Caracas?'

At that point Rick was chewing a morsel of steak, otherwise his flicker of surprise at this blunt question might have shown. Surely Fernandos did not suspect, he had to assume not.

'Tube Stack never felt the need to appoint any in Venezuela because we have been selling direct to specialised users like yourselves.'

'But if you had a reliable contact he could drum up a lot more business with you,' said Fernandos. 'It would be worth your while.'

'Do you have anyone in mind?' Rick replied, knowing full well what Fernandos was edging towards and willingly throwing him a line.

'I suppose I know as much about Tube Stack as anyone in Venezuela,' said Fernandos, 'couldn't I volunteer?'

'That,' said Rick with emphasis, 'would make an intriguing idea.' His plans for Fernandos' future role were developing nicely but he could not concede too quickly. 'I'll have to check it with my Vice-President,' he said. 'But he will agree if I recommend it. What could you do for us?'

Fernandos then showed his hand. He wanted ten per cent on all orders – including the current supermarket contracts – and would use his friends in the Government to make Tube Stack an officially specified material for use in the service. That would cost something extra, he confided, for no Government official did anything for nothing, but once in the Government inventory Tube Stack could not be dislodged.

Rick could not believe his luck. This could provide him with an entry into Venezuelan official circles and Fernandos having himself suggested it, would never suspect his real purpose. Strictly speaking it was hardly legitimate of course – bribery never could be, but without bribery and corruption normal business would never be carried on in South America. Life, mused Rick, as he chewed his steak and sipped his whiskey, is layer upon layer of illegitimacy – every action covers another which is even more clandestine.

Over lunch an agreement was made. Fernandos would set up a nominee company using his father's legal office for the formalities. It would be appointed as the official Tube Stack agents for Venezuela and would receive ten per cent commission on all orders. On special contracts Fernandos would be paid five per cent and for this he could open an account with a Cayman Islands Bank.

Rick looked at the smart negro who, having achieved his purpose, was very relaxed – the half bottle of Bordeaux wine had also had its effect – and thought, every man has his price. Who would have thought two months ago that I would be recruiting black power. This man will suit my purpose very well.

'Carlos, you should see more of our city before you leave tonight. Let me fix a car for your sightseeing. Elfreth's Alley is a must. It is the oldest inhabited street in the United States; there are still thirty old houses there. You must see that. And the Edgar Allan Poe house on 7th Street and 'A Man Full of Trouble Tavern' which is now a very good museum of decorative art. There's lots to see.'

Fernandos was a bit confused and wanted to do nothing except curl up in bed with a woman. Anyway sightseeing was the same in every city: he was sure he had seen an Edgar Allan Poe house in Baltimore.

'Don't worry about a car, Richard. I'll fix one at the hotel.'

They walked back to the hotel and parted at the swing doors of the *Benjamin Franklin*.

'Have a good trip. See you in Caracas,' said Rick.

'Au Revoir and thanks for everything,' said Fernandos.

Rick returned to the office, ill at ease. He could not understand why he felt disturbed. The encounter with Fernandos had gone extremely well and there was every likelihood that his own mission to Venezuela in December would be successful. He knew that Warren thought highly of his work and that OCI (the Office of Current Intelligence) had no complaints about his reports. He was probably in line for promotion and could get to be the head of a local Station if he wanted it. No, it was not the prospects of his personal career that worried him; it was something more fundamental than that.

When he reached the office block he bounded up the stairs, two at a time. It pleased him that he could still do it, even after lunch. Susan, the cute little receptionist, was doing her nails, holding her left hand fingers outstretched with the nails hovering like deep red talons. He paused. 'Any calls, Susan?'

'No, Mr. Collins,' she answered with a seductive quaver in her voice.

Perhaps it was a woman he needed. It was six months at least since he had had another woman and that was the profoundly unsatisfactory affair with the English girl in Barbados. She was a right bitch, wanting her sex hard – and getting it – but always giving the impression, ever so subtlely, that her partner was not quite as good as he could have been. She had been submissive in her way but never completely so, and she always retained that prissy English dignity. Her attitude to Americans was influenced by the ingrained superiority she had to anybody who was not English. How did I ever get into that relationship, Rick chided himself, and to think it lasted six weeks. Perhaps he should lay Susan to get it out of his system. She, at least, would not try to be superior.

He quickly dismissed the thought. Susan was too close to home, it would be against all the regulations and, anyway, she would probably be as fragile as a china doll and he could do without that.

He passed through to his office, closed the door firmly and sat at his desk to complete the notes on the Fernandos interview. There were two reports to do: one on Tube Stack prospects including the appointment of new agents in Caracas, and the other, for the Company, he recorded on a special tape which he kept locked in a security cupboard. By four o'clock he was finished and he decided to drive out of town to try to shake off his restlessness.

'Goodbye Susan, see you tomorrow.' He waved his way

out of the reception area.

'Goodbye, Mr. Collins.'

She was still doing her nails, right hand this time.

He collected the car and headed west along Walnut Street, not knowing where to go. The traffic, outward bound, was already building up so Rick decided to double back through Fairmont Park. There he parked the car so he could walk around Wissahickon Creek. The beauty of the place was quite breathtaking, but Rick, slouched with both hands in his pockets, could not immediately appreciate the splendour of it. His mind felt like the grating of glasspaper on a rough surface; not like a normal headache, for it was a throbbing of bitter intensity as the jabs of glass found the crevices of his brain.

The sun was still visible in-between the scattering clouds and every now and then it would light up the vivid green of the shrubs and the dull browns of the trees. This is a beautiful land, though Rick at last. Where else in the world could one leave an overcrowded city and be in such solitude within minutes. And still within city limits. For all its faults there is a lot to be said for America – land of the free.

But are we so free, he asked himself, when the very people who are working to protect American interests are undermined. Kennedy was shot because he stood up for America and the mystery of that killing hadn't yet been solved. Most people thought the Warren commission was a white wash job anyway. Rick could not entirely approve of JFK; he had been much too indiscreet in his sexual liaisons. Rumours credited him with hundreds of women, some said even more than a thousand. Whatever the figures he had been rash and greedy. It certainly wasn't justice, Rick thought, that government servants like himself could imperil their whole careers by having an affair with a receptionist or a stenographer in the office, but the President could not only get away with having film stars and models, he even had girls on the government payroll as secretaries. Some of the boys down in Clandestine Services in Virginia had told him that during the crucial skybolt talks with Prime Minister Macmillan in the Bahamas,

Kennedy had taken two girls along for his bedtime amusement. The secret service had called them fiddle and faddle. What a crazy thing for the President to do. Dangerous to give the English such a titbit and certainly *their* secret service could have found out. It had not been good for America that the Head of State had a reputation for womanising only exceeded by that of Sukarno of Indonesia. For all they'd said against Nixon, his morals hadn't been that bad.

Rick walked for nearly an hour skirting the golf course and returning to the car along the other side of the creek. He felt better for the exercise and the fresh air and the effect of the whiskey at lunch was wearing off. He turned to head home, only ten minutes away, and switched on the radio.

'This is KYW bringing you the news, stay tuned for station identification.' Rick turned into Ridge Avenue behind a line of cars, moving at a steady pace towards the suburbs.

'Francisco Franco, the Head of State in Spain is dead and the President has sent condolences to the Spanish people.' Disgusting the doctors left him alive so long, thought Rick; he had been a good man in his later years giving Spain the stability she needed after the bloody civil war. The last of the Fascist dictators, some of those clever liberals had said, but how could a man who had allowed Spain to re-emerge so much and who had never indulged in external aggression be dismissed like that. Had not de Gaulle been a dictator? The Frenchman was as authoritarian as the Spaniard. The news droned on and then Rick pricked up his ears.

'William E. Colby, the Director of the Central Intelligence Agency, today made a rare public appeal to the Senate not to reveal the names of twelve individuals who are alleged to be involved in CIA plots against the lives of foreign heads of state. Speaking at the CIA headquarters in Virginia, Mr. Colby said he was opposed in principle to the publication of the report on CIA assassination plots. He said he was concerned about the safety of the individuals concerned. Meanwhile, Senator Frank Church, the

Chairman of the Senate Select Committee ...' Rick turned the radio off in a sharp reaction of disgust, nearly swerving his car into a Cadillac in front.

Why must our state security be paraded in public for all the world to see? he thought. Neither the KGB nor the British MI6 would do that; why must the men who sacrifice their personal lives to protect America now be so vulnerable; why can't the President use his executive powers to stop the Senate releasing confidential information? Rick was getting more exasperated. The trouble was that since Nixon, the President had no executive power, and the Senate and the House Committees all play up to television to get re-election. He turned off Ridge into Barren Hill – he could almost see the house from here. At least he would be home early as he had promised Kathy.

Chapter Five

A Breakfast in London

The grey morning was the same as so many in London in late November, neither autumn nor winter, with the sun hardly penetrating the heavy blanket of cloud. It was a sombre day with little to alleviate the atmosphere of gloom pervading most of the British scene.

Graham Commin, a youngish stockbroker, who had been elected as a Tory Member of Parliament for one of the seaside resorts in the 1974 February election, was having breakfast with his wife. They lived in fashionable Wilton Crescent, near Hyde Park and almost within division bell distance of the Houses of Parliament. Commin, only thirty-two, had been somewhat surprised by his sudden elevation to Parliament nearly two years before, and for a safe seat too. Provided he did not upset the local Tory ladies who were the backbone of the constituency party, he could expect to be in Parliament for life. He was young enough to become the Father of the House one day if Parliament lasted that long. He had had the luck of the devil winning the selection with two ex-MPs on the short list; he presumed they had chosen him as the lesser of evils – at least they did not know his faults. Not then.

'How did it go in the House yesterday, darling?' asked Valerie still dressed in the Indian Kaftan which was her favourite dressing gown.

'Pretty dull stuff, although Margaret put up a relatively good performance. Harold was dismal – too long and repetitious. I think the man looks ill. He's got worse since I've been in the House.'

'Does he take that much notice of you darling?'

'Don't be silly. I meant the responsibility of Government again is getting him down. He wasn't expecting to win in February last year and, in all truth, Ted should not have lost on the Trade Union issue. If we'd have won Harold would have retired within six months as Leader of the Opposition; he couldn't have faced another five years slogging it out.'

Valerie spread a little more course cut marmalade over her toast. 'He's still only sixty odd isn't he?' she asked.

'Yes and he has this new ambition to be Britain's longest serving Prime Minister. As his only interest in politics is survival I suppose that explains it. He seems not to care what the Government actually does, provided it stays in office with him as PM.' Commin had a peevish disdain born of long standing distrust of pragmatic socialists. He preferred the left-wingers in the Tribune Group, recognisable political enemies who could be isolated, not like the so called moderates and careerists who occupied the centre of the Labour Party.

'What do you think he'll do when he does retire? Become a don again?'

'Hardly likely! Do you think modern undergraduates will listen to him? I expect he'll write more memoirs and make his money easily like that'.

'I heard he's already made his fortune. Cecil King says in his diaries that he received £250,000 from the Sunday Times for his last lot. Is that true?'

'Yes, it's true. Thomson was sorry he forked out so much for them.'

'What did he do with the money?' asked Valerie, innocently.

'Who knows? It's a mystery.'

'Did Harold go into politics for the money?'

'No, he wanted prestige and power but once he got power he didn't know how to handle it. He's been thrown in every direction by every prevailing wind. The prestige is still very important to him though. I expect he'll choose to take a peerage when he retires and go to the House of Lords.'

'But Churchill and Macmillan didn't,' said Valerie.

'You mark my words: as an ex-Prime Minister, Harold could have a peerage at any time and although Winston and Mac both refused them, Harold will want one. He'd take an hereditary Earldom if he could.'

Commin poured himself another cup of coffee from Great Aunt Maud's silver coffee pot, wishing Valerie would not keep using it and added, 'Anyway, I think Harold's losing his grip over the Parliamentary Labour Party. Yesterday there were only about thirty back benchers in the Chamber to hear his speech and some of those walked out half way through.'

'Don't they have to attend the Chamber to hear the PM?'

'No, there is no such discipline. Once upon a time I used to think so myself but since being in the House my respect for the place has evaporated. No one wants to listen to anyone's speeches unless they want to speak themselves.'

'What do you do all day then?'

'Some members are in Committees but most are just lolling around the place. It's very listless you know, if I didn't have my job in the City I'd be as bored as hell.'

'Already?' said Valerie, teasingly.

'I feel I've been there a long time. Some members have only been in since last October, I'm an old hand to them.'

'But why don't you younger members shake the place up and make both front benches realise what a state the country is in?'

'You will never understand politics Valerie. It is a game of patience and waiting for position. Anyone who shows his hand too early is dismissed as lacking judgement or being too emotional. He wouldn't even make it to be a parliamentary private secretary to a minister.'

'Do you mean to say the only politicians who get on are the ones who learn never to reveal their true feelings?'

'It's a question of control, Valerie. Politicians have to take the broad view and put contemporary events into the context of history. They mustn't get over-excited about day to day happenings. They would soon wear themselves out with emotional fatigue if they did. Do you realise that the value of our Parliamentary system is that it defuses emotions and doesn't heighten them. We force controversy into the rituals of Westminster – like this Queen's Speech week for instance – and the process squeezes out the aggression.'

'What about those politically-inspired strikes? You politicians haven't succeeded yet in pushing trade union aggro into the context of history. They require decision,' said Valerie, knowingly.

'That's another story,' said Commin. 'Ted nearly succeeded, and would have won against the miners if he hadn't hesitated and if he'd had the courage to call the election a month earlier.'

'It seems to me,' said Valerie, 'as if you people in Parliament are removed from the realities of the world outside. You go on playing your political games while the country goes down. Do you know we have the worst inflation in Western Europe, over twenty-five per cent. Have you been in the shops lately?'

'It's a question of the money supply. Once we curb public expenditure and stop printing money so recklessly, then inflation will come down to acceptable levels.' Commin was becoming a little impatient with his wife. It was bad enough having to cope with the onslaught in the bar of the Conservative Club in his constituency, without having it at home for breakfast as well. Like everyone else he had his doubts about the state of the country and the situation in the City had not given him much to be cheerful about. His own firm of stockbrokers, which he had joined after coming down from Cambridge nine years before, had not had an easy time of it. They had shed a third of the staff in the last eighteen months which was better than some partnerships which had gone under or been merged. He was thankful they had the GEC Pension Fund account and the Prudential, which he had handled, he thought immodestly, with a certain amount of skill.

Valerie had taken her cue and was settled in to the *Daily Telegraph*. She was alright really. Bit too pushy with her opinions but a lot of women were like that nowadays. Germaine Greer and Cosmopolitan had all contributed to this sad decline of the female role in life. But he should not complain, Valerie was damned good in the constituency: they all liked her and she did not push her opinions there. She had the sense not to do that. They were glad he had acquired a wife, and a decorative one at that. When he was adopted there were some misgivings that he was still a batchelor: some ugly rumblings about too many unmarried Tory MPs and some they said were reputed to have strange sexual predelictions. As though he could be one of them. To be honest, he knew of three practising homosexuals on the Tory side in the House, and was glad when his marriage proved his normality. Yes, Valerie would be a distinct advantage to him and although only three months old, the marriage looked like a success.

He looked around the large drawing room, feeling comfortable. The furniture, acquired over the years, was eminently suitable for this flat; highly polished and not too modern. Indeed the Georgian sideboard, which he picked up in a sale in Huntingdon, looked elegant and probably worth something by now. One day he must have a dinner party for some front benchers, although he would not dare to ask Margaret Thatcher yet. That would be too presumptuous. He thought a moment about Valerie at such a dinner party. Could she hold her tongue as at the constituency functions. The only parties they had had at home so far were for friends and it did not matter what they thought. He would have to tell Valerie, ever so cautiously, how she should behave when some of the party leaders came. He would have to handle that carefully: she could be so brittle sometimes, but it would certainly have to be done. There was no point in having such a good flat near to Westminster unless they did some political entertaining, and no point in entertaining unless they gave the right impression. At least Valerie would have no trouble with the cooking, but he would have to explain to her that it is not like having friends in; they are people to impress not to relax with. And she would probably go on about political gamesmanship and the dishonesty of it all. There was no winning with some women. They wanted their man to succeed in politics but could not stomach them paying the penalty of pretence that goes with it.

Commin picked through the *Times* Business pages. There was hardly any good news for shares, but he was glad he had advised the Pru to stay in GKN; despite the doldrums of the car industry that company was showing some resilience.

Valerie looked up from her paper. 'The PM said in his speech yesterday that there have been a thousand civilian deaths in Northern Ireland since the troubles began four years ago. Is that right?'

'The troubles in Ireland have always been with us,' said Commin pompously, 'and the troubles in Ireland always will be with us. It's a cross we have to bear. The actual deaths are even greater if you add in the soldiers and policemen killed.'

'It's very brutal,' said Valerie. 'There are killings every day, do you think it can go on?'

'We have to learn to live with it,' answered Commin, finishing the last piece of toast. 'It will die down again soon when the IRA realise they are getting absolutely nowhere.'

'What about the bomb at Waltons the other night?' asked Valerie, 'We could have been there. If you ask me the IRA have decided to bring the killings to London because they are, as you say, getting nowhere in Belfast.'

'These isolated events will hit the headlines one day,' said Commin complacently, 'and be forgotten the next. The British people are very phlegmatic and are never easily moved. It's our chemistry if you like: cold, indifferent and insensitive. It takes a lot to wake up the British. Ireland's just a nuisance and they simply wish it would go away. But they won't demonstrate in the streets about it.'

Valerie was even more perplexed. It seemed to her that if people were losing members of their own families in the bombings, they would want something done about it. She had read somewhere that the level of terrorism and political killings was greater in the United Kingdom than in any other country in Western Europe, and could not understand how the British could stand for it when such

killings would not be tolerated in France, Sweden or even
Germany. How could Portugal or Greece be regarded as
violent countries when all the political turmoil there had
resulted in far fewer killings than in her own country.

. Valerie was twenty-seven and prided herself on being
perceptive. Roedean and a finishing school in Switzerland
had given her somewhat more than grace and good table
manners. She had always read a lot, fiction mostly;
Hammond Innes, Morris West and Arthur Hailey, but she
had once ploughed through Bernard Shaw's 'The
Intelligent Woman's Guide to Socialism' and found it.
rather quaint. Kafka, which a boyfriend had once lent her,
she thought complex and not a little frightening.

After Switzerland she had tried to take up photographic
modelling, and had an ambition to appear on the front page
of *Vogue*, but her willowish figure did not seem suitable and
she was put off by the few professional photographers she
met. They always treated their models like hat stands or
trellises or objects for visual carnal knowledge, and even
when they were sleeping with them they showed no respect.
She had never heard of women photographers of male
models. The photographer's relationship with his subject
was definitely one-sided, she had concluded, and women's
lib should look at it.

When one of her old friends from Roedean suggested she
join her in a Cordon Bleu cookery course she jumped at the
chance and adored it, not only the sheer professionalism
and the delight of all that creative work, but the
opportunities it opened up. She had hardly spent six
months in Britain since the course was completed. The
Riviera and Majorca had been home for nearly three years,
moving from one luxurious house to another, but she had
not liked the month on the yacht: two cramped for comfort,
but then the two years in Greece and the Greek Islands
were fabulous. She had counted seven employers in five
years before the Barbados assignment.

Men had been no problem and were always available.
Fortunately, she had never had the nasty experiences some
girls suffered. One of her school friends had gone to a

French estate as an au pair to improve her French, and
been raped on the first night by both the owner and his
eighteen year old son. The French police would do nothing
and the British Consul was useless. After that Valerie had
made it a golden rule never to work for Frenchmen.

Graham had come to a house party in Corfu in 1972 and
stayed ten days. They had a rip roaring affair, making love
on the beaches at two o'clock in the morning, with the
water lapping their feet, and once even on the kitchen floor.
She shuddered at the thought. The disgrace and
embarrassment if she had been found. Old man Tompkins
would not have liked it at all. He ran his house parties to
win favours from up-and-coming people in the City, but
providing sex with the cook was not something he
bargained for. Graham had been a fabulous lover then. At
one time she had thought she was in love with him, but
apart from two or three meetings over the following
Christmas after returning home to Shrewsbury, she had not
seen much of him. He had seemed so absorbed in politics
and the City, that she thought the affair with her had
simply been a Greek fling. There had been many other
men. The American she had met at Jack Straws in
Barbados had had the most profound effect of all. Like so
many Americans, he had a deep set inferiority complex but
had been especially overawed by her. She could never recall
trying to dominate him, but it had seemed he had an urge
to be dominated. He was a sensitive man with more depth
than she could plumb in the few weeks she knew him. But it
was not a satisfactory love affair, and after it collapsed she
had firmly decided it was time to get married to an
Englishman, one who did not have an inferiority complex.
Hence Graham, whom she had met again soon after her
return from Barbados. Now she was glad to be comfortably,
and successfully, married after seeing a bit of the world,
unlike some of her old Roedean friends who had already
gone through their first divorce, after rushing into hasty
marriages. Hers was carefully calculated.

She looked across the breakfast table at her husband. He
was such a dear, wrapped up in his world of politics and

City games. She promised herself to back him up and not take the situation in Britain too seriously. 'If others can ignore it, I suppose I can too,' she mused.

Commin was preparing to leave. 'Don't worry about these Irish incidents, darling. When we go out to restaurants we'll choose places with basements or first floors which the bombers can't reach. And we won't go back to Lockets. Alright?'

'Yes, of course you're right. I suppose it's just what the IRA want: to get us worried,' said Valerie.

'They don't realise that the English have quiet stamina which sees them through any crisis. The present level of violence is quite tolerable. Goodbye darling, see you late tonight after the House.'

'Goodbye darling, have a good day,' said Valerie.

When he had gone she sank into an easy chair feeling suddenly tired. Suppose Graham had got it wrong? What if the level of violence became intolerable?

Chapter Six

Appointment at the Plaza

Rick Collins had slept better and as he did not need to go into the office he took his time over the yoga. Breakfast with Kathy, after the children had gone to school, was usually peaceful. It gave him an opportunity to talk to her, a chance which eluded them at most other times in the week.

'It's going well with the Venezuelan project,' said Rick. 'We've sold another big batch of Tube Stack and I'm following up the order with a trip in December.'

'When are you going to take me on a trip,' asked Kathy, 'you know Mother will take the children any time.'

'You know how difficult it is, Kathy. The Company like me to be flexible and I can't be if you're trailing along. It wouldn't be much fun for you in Venezuela, it's not a vacation resort.'

'You could have taken me to Barbados. You went there three times,' said Kathy.

Rick twinged with annoyance that the conversation had gone this way. Why did she have to raise Barbados, did she suspect something? He decided to counter attack.

'My mission to Barbados was very important. I probably averted a coup against Errol Barrow. Black power people from Jamaica had already smuggled in arms and as there's a lot of latent unrest on the island, it could have gone up like a powder keg.'

'But Rick, I do wish we could spend some more time together. You're away so much and the children hardly see you. Couldn't we all have a holiday together at Christmas. Perhaps we could fly down to Florida and get some sun.'

Rick felt he had to make some concession.

'Okay, Kathy, I'll see what I can do with the schedule after Caracas.'

By midday he was ready to leave for New York. It would take him two and a half hours to drive there if he kept to the speed limits, and just under two if he ignored them. He wanted to book into the *Pierre* by five and have time to stop for a snack at a Howard Johnson on the way. Rick preferred to be well organised and methodical in everything he did; proper organisation of time was all important. He could not abide lackadaisical people who never turned up on time or could not complete their projects because they were too loose with themselves. The success of America, he had always argued, was in the capacity of Americans to discipline themselves, and he made a fetish of allowing extra time to get to his appointments so that he, at any rate, was a reliable slot in the national construction of a vital and efficient society.

'See you tomorrow night, Kathy, and I promise we'll have the whole weekend together with the children.' Rick could never bear parting from Kathy if there was any remaining friction between them.

This time he headed the car north through Lafayette Hill and Plymouth Meeting towards the Pennsylvania Turnpike. The highway was relatively free of traffic and he enjoyed driving in these conditions. The car carried him along without effort and his greatest difficulty was keeping it within the speed limit. Sometimes he took the northern route, but today he decided to stick to the Turnpike all the way, crossing the Delaware river into New Jersey just after Florence Roebling. The countryside sped by monotonously and although the Turnpike skirted the towns, there was too much evidence of urban sprawl for Rick's liking. He ignored the scenery and allowed the journey to free his thoughts.

There was little doubt that America was going through a crisis; his nightmare two nights ago had shown his own deepest concern. He could play the situation a number of ways. Number one, he could do nothing and just let events take their course. Ford might be replaced by a President

with the authority of actual votes behind him and such a
President could start banging some sense into the heads of
those soft-brained Senators. Reagan might be just the man
and Rick was glad he had announced his candidature.
Number two, he could go to Virginia and talk directly with
the Deputy Director of Intelligence and ask for a transfer to
an Executive post where he could wield more influence in
the Company. Number three, he could get a posting abroad
and hope he could find a nice niche where he could coast
along for a few years biding his time. As the car sped North
Eastwards towards New York, Rick mulled over the
prospects. None of these alternatives really appealed to
him; he felt the energy within him was not properly used
and that the Company had never fully appreciated his
ability. What was the use of his years at the Harvard
Business School and the specialist course in cybernetics if
he could only perform in a subordinate role. He was willing
to do the chores along with anyone, but after nine years he
was entitled to some recognition. It was not as if the
executive heads of the Company were all that clever. Why
had they allowed documents to remain in existence
showing the Company assassination plots against Castro
and Lumumba? It was recognised policy for any secret
service to engage in such activities, but which country
would be so plum stupid as to reveal its secrets? Only
America apparently. Watergate had made the executives
too scared to keep their tongues quiet in case they went to
prison like the 'plumbers'.

Rick became so heated during the journey he forgot to
stop for lunch and before he realised it was passing Newark
Airport. He would be in Manhattan within twenty minutes
and could get a snack at the *Pierre*. It would certainly be
more elegant there than in a Howard Johnson. He
concluded he had a taste for good living; it was one of the
perks of the job that the expense account, although not
unlimited, was very generous. In truth it was the principle
reason he could not afford to leave the Company, quite
apart from the sheer disloyalty of resignation.

He joined the queue of cars leading to the Lincoln

Tunnel and got his dollar bill ready for the toll – good thinking to charge a fee only one way, must halve collection costs he thought. The congestion soon cleared and Rick completed the rest of the journey without holdups. He could not understand the purists who decried the private automobile. There could never be a more convenient and comfortable door to door transport. Be better when all power is electric and pollution free, but no one should take away a man's right to his own carriage; it was almost as important as his home is his castle.

As Rick checked in to the *Pierre* the hotel clerk said,

'Is it Mr. Richard B. Collins?'

'Yes,' said Rick.

'Message left an hour ago, Sir.'

He read it quickly. 'Please phone Mr. Andrew Pearce when you arrive.' Mr. Andrew Pearce was the Company pseudonym for the Deputy Director of Intelligence. It must be something important, he thought.

When he reached his suite on the third floor Rick checked the lock on the door and then carefully searched the room for surveillance devices. The exercise took ten minutes. It was standard procedure and in whatever circumstances Rick always went through with it. Once in a Mexico City Hotel he had found two bugs in the bedroom and another in the bathroom behind the shower. It had given him a shock because if they had been meant for him it would have shown that his cover had blown. But later he discovered the previous occupant of the room had been a Vice-President of General Dynamics on supposedly secret negotiations with the Mexican Government. He had concluded the bugs were an example of industrial espionage and nothing to do with him. It had been a relief. Rick did not like being spied on.

He dialled the call straight through to the Operations Centre. 'Richard,' said the voice at the other end, 'thanks for calling back so promptly. It's the Venezuelan project. Hal has reported progress so far. That's okay. But we want to send another man out with you to Caracas in December. Will you come here for a conference with him? Saturday at

10.00 hours. He has to come over from Dallas, otherwise we would have proposed a time tomorrow.'

'Certainly,' said Rick.

'Good hunting,' said the voice from Virginia.

Damn, Rick cursed to himself. What is the point of suddenly pushing a greenhorn on him for Venezuela. It sounded as though Headquarters did not have confidence in his ability to handle the project. As Rick dialled room service he felt his hand shaking with annoyance.

After coffee and smoked salmon sandwiches, he felt better but still annoyed and what was more the appointment on Saturday would mess up the weekend for Kathy and the kids. He would have to ring her, but not yet; some way must be found to sugar the shock. Kathy was always complaining he put family last, but in his job he had no alternative. Headquarters would not take kindly to priority being given to the inlaws in Harrisburg.

He had two and a half hours to kill before his dinner date with the Deputy head of the Jamaican mission at the United Nations. Perhaps time to see a movie. He looked at the pay TV programme – 'Jaws' showing on odd days it said. Pity today is the twentieth, I would have enjoyed that, suits my mood, he thought. The programme for even days did not interest him so he decided to stroll down to Tiffanys to buy Kathy her Christmas present, it was one way to fill in the time and he might not be in New York again before Christmas, especially if he had to spend half of December in Venezuela with a greenhorn.

The bar of the Plaza was filling up when Nick arrived at five to seven to meet the Jamaican. The shopping expedition had not been very successful and Rick's mood had not been improved by his long walk through Manhattan. The concrete sidewalks and the tall menacing buildings shutting off the light and the air gave him a feeling of claustrophobia. Central Park with its green would have been better.

Rick ordered a double Jamesons on the rocks and took a seat in a strategic corner to watch for the arrival of the Jamaican. This contact, which Rick had made only in the previous three months, was in the nature of an insurance policy. He had not needed him seriously yet, but if the Company ever needed to apply pressure on the Jamaican Government, the information this contact was providing could be very useful. Rick had been collecting chapter and verse on Ministers' girlfriends and secret bank accounts and hoped to add to the dossier tonight.

Annoyingly, the contact was late, and Rick started a second double whiskey. He looked around the bar and speculated on the significance of the customers, wondering if they could be as interesting as the F. Scott Fitzgerald characters who had made the hotel immortal. His reverie was distracted by a guffaw of boorish laughter from the next table. Two English businessmen, also on their second drinks had just exchanged a joke. Rick was forced to listen, although what he wanted was tranquillity to solve his own dilemmas.

'But seriously, though,' one of them said, 'it's about time we told America to stop the flow of arms to the IRA; most of the terrorists' supplies come from over here.'

'The US Government will do nothing about it,' said the other. 'It couldn't afford to upset the Irish vote. There are many more Irish in the USA than in the whole of Ireland, North and South.'

'Can't we ship the rest of them over here and get rid of the problem that way?' said the first with a laugh.

'We wouldn't have any navvies or street sweepers left except for the wogs, and we should shift them back to Africa too,' said the second.

Both men had obviously had more to drink than they could handle. Their tongues had been loosened, probably by a good business lunch. Rick looked at them with disgust, but they did not notice him or care who heard them.

'Did you hear about that bomb in Chelsea?'

'Yes. I read about it in yesterday's papers. On the front page too. They only print bad news from Britain.'

'There is only bad news from Britain. But do you honestly think these isolated bombings make any difference? Those Irish dolts will get nowhere.'

'They only play at violence. Not like the Stern Gang in Palestine, they meant business, and now half the Israeli Cabinet is made up of supporters of the Stern Gang.'

'Financed by New York.'

'That's right. Have another drink?'

'Probably it explains why New York is bankrupt. All the money has gone to pay for Israel.'

'And the IRA.'

Most of the bar's customers were so absorbed in their own conversations that they did not notice the two Englishmen. Rick, however, was transfixed and his temper was slowly rising.

'Did you hear that one about the Irish Air Force?' he heard one of the obnoxious Englishmen say, already almost bursting with some silly joke.

'It's like the Swiss Navy, only fantasy,' said the other.

'No, it exists and they invented a new special parachute. It opens on impact.'

They both laughed again but Rick was grim: the whiskey had been useless in freeing his tensions in the atmosphere generated by the two foreigners. One was telling yet another Irish story.

'There were these two Irishmen in a car. Paddy said to Seamus, "What happens if the bomb on your lap goes off?" "Don't worry, Paddy, I've got another in the boot." '

Rick could stand it no longer. He walked from the bar in utter disgust. It was as much as he could do to avoid hitting the two jokers. The Jamaican had not arrived; he was already an hour late and he was not waiting any longer. 'To hell with Jamaica,' he said to himself, 'why should I waste my time waiting any longer.' He returned to the *Pierre* still boiling over the incident and brooding over his own impotence. He was angry that Ireland could be the butt of Englishmen and that the Irish could allow it; he was exasperated that every race from the Burmese to the Nigerians had won freedom from the English except the Irish, who alone still suffered colonial occupation. There must be some way to end the indignity, thought Rick.

For an hour, alone in his hotel bedroom, he suffered

unremitting anguish as the fears and frustrations, which had been welling up inside of him for weeks, sought to find expression and relief. Several times he went to dial Kathy to talk the problem over with her, but always he held back knowing instinctively that the real answer could only be found within himself. By nine o'clock he had found the solution; by then he felt strangely and unusually calm for it had become so obvious. He could not understand the reason for his spiritual malaise, the very existence of which he had not been prepared to admit. He realised that for many, many years he had denied to himself his own destiny. He had been living a partial fraud, surviving in a career which, for all its lustre and patriotic loyalty, could never give him the satisfaction and achievement which his very blood demanded he should have. He felt the tensions evaporating; at last he could appreciate the unique power and strength granted to dedicated men. The doubts and uncertainties were gone. It would not be wise to tell Kathy everything, at least not yet. He dialled his home number purposefully and this time his hand did not shake.

'Kathy' he said, 'we're going to Ireland for Christmas.'

Chapter Seven

Battles of the Mind on
Bunker's Hill and Belfast

The next call Rick made was to Boston. Michael
O'Halloran was at home which, for him, at this time of the
evening, was unusual.

'Michael. I must see you very urgently. Something's
developed which I can't discuss on the 'phone,' Rick said.

'Are you in trouble?' asked Michael.

'No, not at all. It's about our mutual interest.'

They arranged that Rick would fly up to Boston by the
late night shuttle and stay with the O'Hallorans. Michael
had insisted that he do so, although the family home was
already overcrowded with five children. 'Kevin can bunk up
with the younger boys,' Michael had said. 'He'll be
delighted for you to have his room; you're his favourite
uncle.'

After Rick's plane arrived and they had driven down to
the O'Halloran home in Mount Bowdoin, it was after
midnight and all the children were in bed. Maggie,
Michael's wife, was still up and welcomed Rick with a
friendly kiss on the cheek.

'My, you are a stranger. It must be all of a year since you
were here. How is it down there in the deep South?'

'Now Maggie, I'm only in Pennsylvania, you know,
which is still the right side of the Mason-Dixon line', said
Rick.

'What was Mason-Dixon anyway?' asked Maggie,
playfully.

'Two people actually' said Michael. 'Let me show you
Kevin's room, Rick. It's a bit of a holy hole but the bed is
comfortable. Maggie, why don't you put on some coffee.
We've got lots of talking to do'.

They dumped Rick's overnight bag in the small bedroom which had all the signs of having been being cleared up hastily. Kevin's books were stacked in one corner and showed the catholic tastes of a twelve year old – the history of aeroplanes, Kojak, Jules Verne's 'Journey to the Center of the Earth' and 'Baseball for Boys'.

Maggie soon had the coffee ready. Old fashioned, she believed in grinding it freshly from the roasted coffee beans and the infusion set up a rich aroma.

'That sure smells good,' said Rick. 'Better than Maxwell House.'

'I'll leave you two boys to it,' said Maggie, and take myself upstairs. But, firstly, tell me about Mason-Dixon, I've always wanted to know.'

Maggie was asserting her rights, but ever so gently. She understood that Michael had private things to discuss with his friends and she never interfered. Actually she fully approved of his work for Irish freedom, coming from Irish stock herself. It never seemed to clash with Michael's job as a life insurance salesman, and sometimes she wondered if in fact it did not help. Most of his business came from the Irish community and many of his customers knew of his high standing with the IRA. It made him a popular figure, and often he collected donations to the cause as well as policy applications and checks for his employers, Massachusetts Mutual.

'In the middle of the eighteenth century,' said Rick, 'there was a dispute between Pennsylvania and Maryland over boundaries, and an English astronomer called Charles Mason was called in to fix it. He chose the latitude number which still marks the dividing line between north and south.'

'He worked with Jeremiah Dixon,' added Michael, not to be outshone.

'But please remember, Maggie, the slave states were South of the line' said Rick, 'and I'm still well and truly to the north of it.'

'Well, now I've had my geography lesson I'll say goodnight. Don't talk too long.'

'Goodnight Maggie,' said Rick.

'She's not too happy on the South these days' said Michael when she had left. 'She thinks too many of the Southern problems are coming North. Bussing, for instance. She considers it crazy to hoist kids from neighbourhood schools to take them miles away simply to try to get integration. She thinks compulsory bussing only creates racial resentment, not harmony. The issue has made Edward Kennedy very unpopular in Boston, even among the community.'

'Mike,' said Rick, 'I want to talk to you about Ireland. The problem has been bugging me for days and you are the only friend I can talk to who will understand.'

'When you phoned up you sounded desperate. I thought something had gone seriously wrong.'

'My career is okay and I don't intend to jeopardise it, but I feel I must make a bigger and more practical contribution to a United Ireland. And, frankly, I must tell you Mike, I feel the present High Command are messing up their chances. I'm a professional, as you know, and the amateurism of the movement appals me,' said Rick with passion.

'Our boys have made a big impact. British public opinion is very worked up,' said Michael. 'Soon the British Government will have to make a decision to pull out the troops. Then the Orangemen have to agree to negotiate.'

'Don't jump to conclusions. Englishmen are very complacement,' said Mick, remembering the two jokers in the Plaza bar earlier that evening. 'They find the present level of protest acceptable. Something more dramatic will have to be done.'

'What, hijack a plane?' asked Michael.

'Maybe, maybe,' Rick pursed his lips in thought. 'It would have to be some action which would shake the English to their bones. They regard the Irish as a joke, never to be taken seriously. Somehow we have to knock it into them that we mean business.'

'I've been to Ireland twice in the last year – my contacts you know are the Provos – and I've never known morale to be so high. There is no shortage of volunteers to take the war right into the Englishman's backyard.'

'That's what worries me,' said Rick, 'a lot of enthusiasm which is mostly wasted because there is no overall strategy, no proper planning and no specific targets. What is needed is more discipline and some clear objectives.'

'I must agree,' said Michael, 'the Movement is too divided. I can never understand why the Provos and the Officials can't get together. The split makes us weaker.'

'The English know our weaknesses and how to exploit them. They always try to give the impression of implacable firmness. But they had to take Mau Mau seriously in Kenya and its leader who was condemned by the British Governor as the apostle of darkness and death, is now the President. The English will always climb down in the end after a lot of innocent lives have been lost,' Rick said bitterly.

'There are lessons to be drawn from nearer home,' said Michael. 'What about Bunker's Hill?'

'We might forgive the English their arrogance in the old colonial days, but dammit, they still can't face issues in this day and age, until the facts are rammed down their throats, and that's unforgiveable,' said Rick. 'Look at Cyprus, a British Minister actually said once that Britain would never ever pull out, but they did after they lost the fight against Grivas. Now the Turks have taken half the island and the whole of Western security is undermined. Americans are now unpopular with both Turkey and Greece, both of them supposed to be in NATO, thanks to the mess the English made of it.'

The two men talked on until Michael, who had initially been surprised about Rick's extraordinary animation, became convinced that his old schoolfriend was indeed determined to play a big part in the struggle. Although he had always maintained a reasonable level of donations to funds, Rick had never appeared to Michael as a militant.

Rick woke up when Kevin came in with a short, 'Mornin' Uncle.' His mother had told him on no account to hang about, although it was his own room; she knew it took

Michael, her husband, a long time to wake up after a late night session and she assumed all men were the same. Not so Rick, his training and experience had taught him to be alert within minutes.

When he arrived downstairs, soon after, the small house looked even smaller as there were children everywhere. The baby was in a high chair wielding a spoon on some cereal with grim determination. The two girls Patricia and Bridget were eating breakfast at the large rectangular dining table; Brian – the eight year old – was reading comics on the floor, and Kevin was cleaning his father's shoes.

'Can I do yours, Uncle?' he asked.

'Yes, please,' said Rick slipping off his casuals.

Rick felt at home in this family, although he doubted if he could stand the atmosphere of chaos it generated for long periods. He respected and admired his life-long friend whom he knew and understood better than a brother. Michael O'Halloran was the essence of a family man; he had never been gripped by great personal ambitions, although Rick could remember Michael was very clever at school, always making the top grades. He could easily have gone on to higher education, like Rick had done, but at about sixteen Michael had become so involved in the Irish community in Boston that he had no time for pursuing his own studies. After a four year stint as a clerk in a freight shipping office, Michael had taken up a job in which his immense range of Irish contacts was a distinct advantage: he became a life insurance salesman. Within three years, as a self-employed agent on his own account, he obtained the flexibility which he needed for his community work.

When the IRA supporters committees were set up, Michael was a natural activist and soon became one of the leaders. There were several factions – which did not always correspond with the divisions in Ireland itself – but everyone respected Michael for his energy and enthusiasm.

He was phenomenally successful at raising money. Dances, jumble sales, door to door collections and mail order selling by supporters – with the commission going into the funds – were just some of the techniques he used. Michael was never satisfied and often complained to his wife about the indiscipline of the community. Better organised, he had said, the collection rate could be doubled. His ambition had been to recruit the Church as an agent of the Fund but the Archbishop had come down firmly against any such idea; only a couple of priests gave him real support. Michael thought this was a great pity as the power of religion was so persuasive. He always had in mind the success of the Latter Day Saints who levied, and actually collected, a ten per cent impost on the net incomes of all Mormons. Once he had calculated how much such a levy would produce if paid by all Irish Americans: six million dollars a year. With sums like that the IRA could practically match the total defence budget of the British. And once having expelled the occupying Army, if money on that scale were invested wisely, Ireland could become prosperous, a model land.

Michael had often discussed these hopes with Rick who shared them with fervour. They both felt deeply that most Irishmen were blithely unaware of their own future destiny and even their own past. Few realised that the Celts had been the original residents of the country which became known as England and that they had been subjugated or forced to flee by barbarians from the Continent and Scandinavia. Even so the Monasteries in Ireland had become centres of learning and culture and had, despite handicaps, carried the lessons of the gospels back into pagan Britain.

The Governments of England had nonetheless gone on to occupy Ireland and for centuries had abused its people, using them as cheap cannon fodder in their senseless wars in Europe and even in the armies which attempted, vainly, to prevent the American colonists from achieving their independence. Over hundreds of years, commerce and industry had been suppressed in Ireland in the interests of maintaining the economic hegemony of England. In that period, Ireland was a colony in every sense of the word: exploited, neglected and culturally dominated. Both Rick and Michael were profoundly rankled not only by the undisputed facts of the oppression but even more by the ignorance or indifference of the Irish people who had been robbed of their birthright.

As part of his studies, Rick had read British and European history and had been horrified by the chronicle of events which confirmed the denial of the rights of generations of Irishmen: Of how the House of Commons of Britain and Ireland emerged as the fountain of British democracy, and Catholics were disenfranchised by law for a crucial thirty years, of how the Protestant Orangemen, mostly brought in as immigrants from Scotland, were given privileges denied to the native born Irish. Most of the books he obtained were written by Englishmen and slanted in favour of the English viewpoint. Rick had been greatly annoyed by this and once told Michael that he wished Irish writers, like Jóyce and Shaw, had concentrated on presenting the deep Irish case instead of being seduced by the English literary establishment.

Rick felt at home in the bosom of this family, not only because they were genuinely friendly but also because Michael had been a life-long influence in developing his political philosophy. Rick realised that without Michael's warm reception of his ideas, they might have been stillborn and he, as an individual, might have been totally absorbed into the wider and suffocating American culture which had crushed the Irish enthusiasm out of so many immigrants and their children.

Maggie asked, 'Rick, would you like eggs, bacon and fritters for breakfast?'

'Now you mustn't tempt me into such habits,' replied Rick. 'You know black coffee and toast will do me.'

'You men must keep up your strength with all that talking halfway through the night. If talking solved the world's problems, you two would make as good a contribution as the whole United Nations,' she added playfully. 'Anyway, I'll cook some for Michael, he'll be down soon.'

After the children had gone off to school and kindergarten and the baby put outside on the verandah in her carriage, Rick and Michael resumed their conversation, refreshed by sleep, although there had only been four hours of it.

'What you are saying Rick, is that unless we ensure that the Republican Army acts decisively, all the efforts of the last few years will be wasted,' said Michael.

'Our Irish problem – like that of so many people – is that we have been locked into an attitude of thinking that does not enable us to see the situation in its entirety. Edward de Bono says nearly everybody thinks vertically, that is they are working with existing facts and using them in a logical way. This, he argues, limits severely the solutions which they can arrive at – sometimes the best solutions are reached not by logic but by creative thought,' Rick explained.

'You mean the IRA have been bogged down just doing the same things over and over again?' asked Michael.

'Exactly,' said Rick. 'It has become a regular pattern. A few bombs here, some sniping there, coupled with occasional civil rights agitation. It's predictable, so logical. The English have got their responses worked out already. The pattern becomes boring with the repetition, so the latest bomb or killing has less and less impact, and they can take it as regular.'

'What should we be doing then?' asked Michael.

'Edward de Bono may have the answer. He say lateral thinking must be used in conjunction with vertical thinking,' answered Rick. 'Thought must move sideways as well as logically up and down'.

'You mean, you take yourself out of the problem and look at it from the outside?' said Michael.

'No, not quite. I'm not suggesting looking at it like a Tibetan Buddhist from an astral plane. What one must do in lateral thinking is to generate new ideas and sometimes that means choosing them arbitrarily,' explained Rick.

'How can that be applied to Ireland?' asked Michael, who was not becoming a little confused by Rick's references to vertical and lateral thinking, concepts which were quite foreign to him.

'Well, it's like this,' said Rick. 'For years we have

assumed the battle for a free Ireland should be fought in the occupied area of Ulster. Once, we imagined that the Protestants could be persuaded by reasonable argument to accept freedom – after all Eire doesn't discriminate against Protestants, they have Trinity College in Dublin, many of the best jobs and even the Presidency. But the Orangemen in Ulster are not really Irish, they are too wedded to Britain. They've even elected Enoch Powell, a leading English politician, to represent a Northern Irish seat in the House of Commons. That, more than any other single act showed how hostile the Orangemen really are to a united Ireland. Because persuasion failed, we tried agitation and demonstrations which the English put down with brute force. Then the IRA turned to force – bombs, guns, most of which came from here. Don't you see, it's the logical development of the same ideas and it hasn't worked, so we've got to break out of it?'

'Do you mean the solution may be found somewhere else, some surprising place?' asked Michael.

'Yes, but I'm suggesting more than that,' emphasised Rick. 'If we don't soon find the answer somewhere else, the present situation will drag on, the IRA itself will become so dispirited through lack of real results that the steam will run out of the movement perhaps for another fifty years. Frankly, Mike, I want freedom for Ireland now while I'm alive, not in some following future.'

'Where is the answer?' asked Michael bringing the conversation to a head; much as he enjoyed these philosophical exchanges he was essentially a man of action and wanted the argument to be related to practicalities, not fanciful theories.

'The answer, Mike, is not in Belfast, it's in London. That is the seat of power and that is where the English power must be attacked and crippled. The English must be taught once and for all that no longer will the Irish be treated as ignorant peasants who can be humiliated, suppressed or, at worst, ignored. That's why I was glad to hear about that bomb in Chelsea. At last the war is being carried into the enemy's camp. But the war mustn't be fought at half cock.'

'What do you want to do personally Rick, how can you help?'

'Mike, I want to work on the plan, and if needs be, to execute it, the plan which I believe is needed if we are to win this war. As I see it we need something which will destroy completely the capacity of the English to destroy us, instead of the campaign of attrition which the IRA has been waging for so long, we need one decisive action which can knock out the English will to resist our demands.'

'What is your plan then?' asked Michael, now understanding more clearly what Rick had been driving at and becoming excited by the prospects it opened out.

'The Ultimate,' replied Rick.

Chapter Eight

From Boston, dedicated

Rick knew he could rely on Michael. He was the most reliable man he had ever met. Perhaps it was growing up together and both coming from Irish families which had given them such bonds of understanding. There were in fact few men to whom Rick could entrust the secret of the ultimate. He certainly would tell no one in the Company, the State interests of the United States did not always correspond with the aspirations of Ireland, and the Company, although it often operated without the specific approval of the Government, had America to protect. He expected no direct help from that direction. On the contrary he would have to work deviously to ensure that his employers did not discover his abiding interest in and commitment to Ireland. If someone in the CIA suspected him, of what they would regard as fanaticism, his days in the Company would be numbered.

In explaining his dilemma to Michael, he found it was a tremendous help to get the burden off his chest to someone who knew him as a basic friend and not just as a professional colleague. The close contacts established in the course of business were very suspect to Rick: so called friendships would disappear like water in a hot desert if the heat went on. In his experience people only served their own interests and those of their blood relations, and they invariably used everyone else. Other people were like figures in a pinball machine, their function was to pass the ball on and throw it into the right slot. Friendship, as usually practised, was simply oil to the works, something with which to lubricate human relationships and reduce the jarring and clashing of all the individual self-interests.

Michael understood this as well and kept a disk which particularly amused him as an insurance man; he had played it to Rick.

'There's no one with endurance like the man who sells insurance' went the refrain, 'he's everybody's best friend.'

'It's like that in our business,' Michael had said, 'we have to use the friendship and concern line, the customers love it. With insurance we're not selling a product; it's just a concept, merely an idea, unlike practically every other merchandise it doesn't satisfy an immediate material need of the purchaser. It has to be wrapped up as a friendship package otherwise there's no sale.'

Rick was glad Michael understood and was frank about the cynical side of so-called friendship, because it helped to differentiate their own relationship from the falsity of most of human society. He had been able, over the years, to tell Michael a great deal about his work for the CIA, knowing it would go no further. And on that fateful day as they sat and talked and gave substance to Rick's concept of the ultimate, the eternal value of the kinship – as powerful as any based on blood – became ever more real for them. As they communicated Rick felt that his batteries of emotion were gradually being recharged.

Both men agreed that the utmost secrecy was essential if the plan was to have any hope of success. Rick would try to remain within the Company as it would provide, ironically, the ideal cover for the operation on which he was to be engaged. He would henceforth be living on three levels: the executant of the ultimate, which he had now realised was his real purpose in life, the CIA operative at the next level and the Tube Stack salesman below. It would be psychologically testing to maintain three parallel personalities for any length of time but, he felt, he had the greatest of ideals to inspire him and two people, Kathy, his wife, and Michael, who would be able to deal with him as a whole person. That would be vitally important if he were not to relapse into an uncontrolled schizophrenia. In the Company they had a special psychiatric unit in Florida for such cases, and he did not want to end up there.

It was important to keep the secret away from the Company's ears because it was established CIA policy not to engage in secret activity against principal allies, including the United Kingdom, and if it appeared that CIA personnel were actually engaged in the war against Britain, the embarrassment to the CIA would be devastating. It was one thing for the CIA to plot against Allende or to produce detailed plans for the assassination of Fidel Castro, but to become interested in an armed conspiracy against the British Government was beyond the pale. He was in no doubts that if he were discovered the Company would either liquidate him or lock him up in the top security wing of the psychiatric unit. He knew of a few inmates who had never come out again; there were also several candidates for the treatment who had, wisely, removed themselves from Statesside – like Philip Agee who had written indiscrete revelations in 'CIA Diary' and had accepted self-imposed exile in Britain.

In extreme circumstances, Rick agreed with Michael, it could be wise to work from abroad. Finance from IRA funds – with Michael as Treasurer – would be no problem. But, for as long as possible, the Company cover must be maintained. A transfer to the European Theater of Operations would have to be requested without rousing suspicions. Rick made a mental note to do just that in the course of his meeting next day in Virginia. The appointment of another operative for Venezuela would in fact be a help not a hindrance.

Michael readily accepted the proposal that Rick should go to Ireland with Kathy and the children for Christmas.

'It would be ideal,' he said, 'how natural for you to make such a trip. In fact I can get you all on a package tour going from here in Boston. You'll have ten days there and during that time the people who matter in the organisation will be alerted to contact you. No one – not even your CIA who must keep you under surveillance sometimes – would suspect a thing.'

Before they left the O'Halloran home to put Rick on the

shuttle back to New York, Rick made some telephone calls to ascertain what had happened to his Jamaican of the night before. He was only concerned in case the office should ask him for an up-to-date report or if they had collected intelligence from another quarter. It would be unwise – particularly in present circumstances – for him to appear out of touch with his sphere of responsibility. Fortunately, he struck oil, another acquintance in the Jamaican delegation, who he had also financed, was full of gossip. His contact had been found by the Jamaican Government to have been accepting bribes from the KGB working in conjunction with the Cubans. Through the despatch of a hoax "Western Union" from Kingston saying his Mother was dangerously ill, he had been tricked into flying quickly back home to be arrested as soon as he walked off the plane.

Rick thought he would not like to be in the Jamaican's shoes and made another mental note, 'always check the source of all family cables before acting on them', it was too easy a ruse but one so often effective because the emotional shock of sudden bad family news put a person off balance. Further, he thought – his mind now working rapidly, and vertically, on the new information – the dossiers on Jamaican Ministers would now have to be re-written: much of the previously supplied material must be suspect and probably planted, for some ulterior purpose, by the Cubans. 'Back to the drawing board' he mused. It had happened before and would no doubt happen again. Intelligence was the most incredible flower to gather; it often had the most beautiful petals and lovely fragrance, but it was just as likely to turn to a weed in one's hand.

Rick was glad he had time enough to play a game of table tennis with Kevin, who had returned in high spirits from school. The table was set up in the garage which, predictably for the O'Halloran's, was otherwise full up with household clutter. The family car, which Michael also used for business, had to live under a tarpaulin outside on the drive. Kevin was allowed to win – actually he played a good game – and Rick said to the boy's delight, 'My my, Kevin with that performance we'll have to make you America's ambassador to Peking; ping pong is more important than anything else there and you'll be a hero.'

Rick said his goodbyes to Maggie and the family, genuinely regretting he had to leave already, promising to be back soon and thinking that probably the next time would be with Kathy on their way to Ireland for Christmas.

As Michael drove to the Logan Lawrence International Airport along Warren and Washington Streets, Rick said, 'Pity you and Maggie and Kevin can't come with us to Ireland. It would be a great trip.'

'That would not be wise anyway,' said Michael, still keeping his eyes carefully on the traffic in front and the rear mirror. 'The CIA would soon smell a rat if I went on that trip with you; they must know of my connexion with the movement and it's now doubly important to keep your contact with me distant. I hope you didn't reveal you were coming to Boston.'

'No I didn't. In fact I still have my hotel room key. I didn't check out and I'm booked in tonight. As far as anyone is concerned, I've been in New York carrying out a successful investigation on the life and times of a certain Jamaican gentleman whose life isn't worth much now and whose times are very much numbered.'

'Poor fellow,' said Michael.

'Poor fellow,' said Rick. 'It's the age of the gambler but he who gambles with too many dice is lost.'

'You are a gambler, friend; you take risks and don't ever forget it or you might trip up.'

Michael was driving especially cautiously through the centre of Boston on the approach to the tunnel and spoke slowly and deliberately; clearly he held Rick in deep affection.

'I gamble only on the periphery; the core of my decision, I try to make a cert.'

'Let's hope you've got the "ultimate" right. If you have we'll wipe out the aggression against Ireland as quickly as Harry Truman stopped the Second Great War, when he dropped the Atomic Bomb on Hiroshima. Instead of a messy job, we'll be doing it cleanly and surgically. I will pray it will succeed. If it does you will become the second Collins to be a saint for the Irish cause.'

'I am no saint but succeed it will,' said Rick as he waved Michael off at the Terminal building. He stood for a moment watching his friend disappear into the swirling convey of cars. As he turned to go through the security check he felt, to his acute embarrassment, a tear in his eye.

Normally on a trip from Boston to Washington he would have caught a plane and hired a Hertz or Avis car at the other end, but this time he had, for appearances sake, to check out of the *Pierre* and collect his car. As he had caught an early shuttle he was in his room by twenty-two hundred hours and asleep within fifteen minutes. He was up at three thirty to leave at four, but what he had lost in sleep he made up with adrenalin. The 'ultimate' gave a zest and a dimension to his persona which he had never known before. The early start was essential if he was to reach the Virginia appointment on schedule and, this time, he not only had his reputation for punctuality to protect but some other fish to fry.

As he drove in the dusk of the dying night along the almost empty highways leading out of New York, he felt supremely confident. Strangely, only a short time before, he had felt apprehensive about his meeting with the new man the usurper – for Venezuela as though that appointment was a slight on his own achievements in the territory. Now all that was behind him like an ugly storm cloud which had moved away to show a clear blue sky. What has changed, he thought, is that I have acquired a dedication which puts the other more mundane events into their proper prospective. The moral in this experience is to look for a more inspiring purpose in life whenever the stones on the ordinary road are rough.

By five forty-five, he was skirting Philadelphia, by seven thirty, approaching Baltimore, where the morning traffic was already building up; he avoided the worst, had a quick run to the outskirts of Washington, reaching them by eight thirty and soon after nine crossed into Virginia.

Surprisingly he found he had time for a coffee and a wash and smarten-up in a service station and with quiet satisfaction he arrived at the CIA office with minutes to spare. 'Good job I didn't have a blow out,' he thought.

Before many minutes he was in for some more surprises.

'This is Art Gruber,' said the *DDI, introducing Rick to a bespectacled and scholarly looking thirty year old. 'We want him to take over from you in the Caribbean and Venezuela at the end of the year to release you for a most important project. Art is with IBM as a computer expert, which of course he is,' added the DDI with a knowing twinkle in his eye. 'He will go with you in December to take over Fernandos and the other contacts. We are pleased with all you have done there; Fernandos sounds a good catch. Art is arranging his cover through IBM; that's no problem. I think we shall arrange for you to meet for the first time on the plane and as this is Art's maiden visit, you, Rick, will kindly take him on a drinking session in the true American frontier fashion. That should establish his credentials with the Venezuelans. Now Art you will meet up with Rick at eleven in the annex, for you both to exchange your erudite thoughts; meanwhile will you kindly excuse us?'

The DDI was a man who believed in the economy of words and who considered conversation to be time wasting; even off duty social chit chat was a great bore for him. But the men respected him for he always read their reports meticulously and gave credit generously when credit was due.

'Rick,' he was saying as soon as the door closed behind Art, 'you are due for both recognition and promotion. Your academic business training makes you an ideal choice for a crucial research job in Europe.'

Rick was lapping it up; the news could hardly be better: he did not even need to request a transfer.

'You will go to Italy for a minimum of six months and a maximum of twelve with as many trips back to the States as you want, within reason of course, and your wife's expenses

* Deputy Director, Intelligence

to visit are covered by the Agency at least three times. Your
task will be to research the trading operations of the
Communist Party of Italy. We have definite evidence that
they are using subsidised imports from Iron Curtain
countries into concerns they control to build up assets for
Party work. The Communists are becoming a major
strength now the Vatican is no longer ex-communicating
Catholics who work for it. We want to know everything you
can get on the Commie big business; we do not want Italy
to go the way of Portugal and become the soft underbelly of
NATO. After your Christmas furlough, you will come down
here for a two weeks intensive course in the language
laboratory, when you will speak and read nothing but
Italian. At the end of that you will even think in Italian. Hal
Warren is arranging for you to take over the Italy parish for
Tube Stack so your cover will be no problem. And, Rick, you
will be on your own responsibility – the local station will
know nothing – but the research boys here, and the
computer, will be available to you. And you will be free, of
course, to follow up the business leads in the rest of Europe
with the usual proviso that you file your schedule of
movements as far as possible in advance. In New York you
will get a thorough briefing; in the meantime please
concentrate on Venezuela and the handover to Art Gruber;
he hasn't had as much experience as you.'

Odd, thought Rick, this man is never breathless.

'We are proud to have you in the Agency, Rick. Good.
luck with your new assignment.'

Rick left the plush office with its tufted fitted carpet,
antique mahogany desk and matching leather chairs,
slightly reeling from the onslaught of words. He reflected on
the extraordinary irony of life, in that often a run of good
fortune kept running on through its own momentum. He
would soon deal with Art Gruber and be on his way home
to Kathy, tired but with joy in his heart and lots of news to
tell.

Art Gruber was waiting in the annex library when Rick
walked in. He was not quite as raw as first impressions had
indicated. Rick was pleased to discover that they shared

concern about the Senate Committee investigations. Art had been reading the papers.

'Did you see that the Select Committee has now reported publicly that the Agency instigated assassination plots against Castro and Lumumba and was involved in plotting the deaths of Diem, Trujillo and Schneider?' he said.

'It's been worrying me for days that the revelations are going too far. It makes our work extra hazardous when our own leaders do this to us,' said Rick.

'They all died except Castro,' commented Art, cynically, 'if we had got rid of him too there wouldn't be such a rumpus now. The Senators have got a guilt complex because Commies are still as large as life on our Miami doorstep and they want to find a scapegoat. And it has to be us.'

'It's about time someone started printing stories about the valuable job we do. Two-thirds of South America would have gone Communist by now if it hadn't been for the Agency,' said Rick.

'Senator Church is reported this morning as saying he expects legislation in the Senate by Easter to provide for even more oversight of our operations,' said Art, still cynical. 'We wont be able to go to the john soon without asking Congressional permission.'

As they turned to discuss Venezuela, Rick reflected on what Art had been saying; misanthropic, Art might be, but there is a germ of truth in his words, he thought. The Agency is being tripped up by its own partial failures, success would have obliterated all criticism. And, on his own project in the service of Ireland, fulfillment would itself suffocate all doubts about the manner of its execution.

Chapter Nine

A Death in Suburbia

Just five days after the meeting in Boston between Richard Collins and Michael O'Halloran, Chief Superintendent Bosworth was attending a conference in a rather prosaic office on the third floor of a relatively new building in St. James's, London. The subject had been painfully dominant during recent months; it had absorbed the attention of many senior officers in Scotland Yard; it had involved complex inter-departmental discussions in the Home Office; both MI5 and MI6 were deeply entangled in the problems of identifying suspects and negotiating about them with foreign agencies; even Ministers had been forced to divert their attention from the ever pressing domestic problems of massive unemployment and inflation, to attend to the issues of policy it threw up. Bombs on the streets, and in the pubs of Britain, had not been known on this scale since the second world war.

The counter-terrorist operation mounted by the authorities had been more successful than many of those directly involved had dared to hope when the full extent of the horror first began to make itself felt. The enemy was difficult to locate, it had powerful support within a substantial minority community resident in Britain and the supplies of explosives which it could obtain seemed to be unlimited.

A paper circulated in Whitehall some weeks before had analysed the situation with typical British omniscience. Terrorism, used as a political weapon, had been growing for a decade in Western industrialised countries it has said. Argentina, Uruguay, the United States, the Federal

Republic of Germany and Italy had all suffered from the virus. So had some Iron Curtain countries, though there it was dealt with severely and absolutely no publicity was allowed. It was not a completely new phenomenon in Britain as it had been experienced during the inter-war years when the IRA had previously been active. The novel aspect of the current wave of violence, was the complex involvement of international gangs and the undue attention given to it by the media, particularly television.

The writers of the official memorandum argued that the well publicised incidents of plan hi-jackings by supporters of the Palestine Liberation Organisation, the fanatical assassinations by the Japanese Red Army and the kidnappings of prominent businessmen in Argentina, had all lent an exciting colour and even a certain respectability to terrorism as such. If the motives were political, or pretended to be, the perpetrators of violence absolved themselves from ordinary guilt and became associated, in a romantic way, with the overseas terrorists who were often seen as courageous freedom fighters. It was this new dimension to the problem which made it so difficult to grasp.

Any concession to the political demands of the terrorists was universally condemned in and around Whitehall and would be unthinkable within the well-determined overall policies of successive British Governments. The conclusion of the paper was that all the forces of authority must stand firm, identify the guilty and bring them to justice before the Courts. It was also agreed that the death penalty should not be re-introduced, whatever public opinion might demand, as it would only have the effect of turning murderers into martyrs and making matters worse.

Bosworth fully agreed with all aspects of the policy and, in a small way, had contributed to its formulation. At one time he held severe reservations about the wisdom of rejecting capital punishment as a deterrent, mostly because he doubted whether the prospect of prison terms worried the bombers. Indeed, some of them thought that as political prisoners, they would be released once the IRA had won.

After a series of intensive seminars held at the Civil Service College at Sunningdale, he had been persuaded otherwise by the experts in psychological techniques who always seemed to know what they were talking about.

George Bosworth was very pleased with himself that afternoon. His intensive researches into the origin of explosives used in the bombs had borne fruit. A network had been uncovered leading from the Irish Republic through to the south coast port of Southampton. Some more arrests were in the offing. It was yet another notch in the continuing campaign which, in the end, would result in the termination of these loathsome activities.

As the meeting went on, his mind was drawn to another reason for his feelings of pleasure. Mary had agreed to come back to London. It was the best news that year. She had told him almost as soon as he got through on the 'phone that morning. 'George, I've finally decided to do what you want. This will be my last year in Brighton; I'm selling up.' He could still relish the words and the suppressed excitement with which she said them.

It had not been an easy relationship to maintain over all those years. Fifteen, he thought to himself, it is hardly believable. The time has gone like a flash. One of the inspectors was droning on, and as the Commander was in the chair, Bosworth felt he could switch off a bit. He had already read the report and it was superfluous for the Inspector to go over it all again; he was one of those dreary people who insist on addressing meetings as though he was still in a witness box at a Magistrates Court. Fifteen years, and Mary as lovely as when he first met her.

She had been twenty-seven then and fresh as an English rose. He remembered their early encounters and how he had suspected her of being a fence for stolen goods; shows how wrong one can be, even with evidence staring you in the face, he thought to himself a little ruefully.

In those years in the early nineteen sixties, Detective Sergeant Bosworth of the Criminal Investigation Department was following up leads on a complicated swindle involving insurance claims on stolen antiques. The stall he visited in the Chelsea Antiques Market on the Kings Road in the course of his inquiries, was run by a devastatingly beautiful and talented girl. Some of the missing treasures were on sale there, but Bosworth had hesitated before bringing the inevitable charges of receiving stolen goods. He now recognised that his hesitation was dictated more by his sexual attraction to the girl than the facts of the case. In truth he had fallen head over heels in love, an experience he had never had before. His marriage had not been a failure, but completely devoid of the passion which dominated his feelings for Mary.

Angela had also been pretty in her time but her feelings about sex were quite unlike Mary's. It became painfully clear to him that Angela had used her body as a bribe to get his interest and commitment, and she had then skilfully manoeuvred him into a position where he could be practically blackmailed into marrying her. He was only twenty-three then and still on the police course at Hendon. Apart from some crude Army girls his sexual encounters had been limited, and Angela, in contrast, was wholesome and satisfying to his lust. But, in his immaturity, he had not understood that Angela was purely passive and potentially frustrating for a fully sexed man like him. After their marriage Angela made it clear she regarded intercourse as a wifely duty in which the woman could expect neither pleasure nor satisfaction. She was bored with sex. Bosworth had tried once discussing the problem with her, but she had promptly shut up like a clam.

Mary was so, so different. She was a wistful, yet lively girl, combining a natural beauty with an intelligent understanding of people. Bosworth had found this most unusual. In his experience beautiful women were dumb, and intelligent women dowdy. He could visualise her now, stroking back her auburn hair with those elegantly long fingers. At each meeting he felt beautifully calm as though her very presence could banish all the tensions which afflicted him; he felt earthed with her, particularly when they made love. Mary enjoyed sex with the vigour of a healthy and lithe animal. He became a real man with her and adored her enjoyment of him. Of course his love affair produced difficulties but he prefered coping with them than going back to the dismal succession of prostitutes from whom he had been forced to seek solace before Mary. He was not promiscuous by nature and could not understand the men in the Force who picked up new women every month. They had plenty of opportunities, especially on the vice squad in Soho. He had seen it all after his transfer there from the CID.

The promotion to Inspector had helped. Angela was proud; they had moved to Tooting Bec to buy their own house – it was good to be out of the police flats – and the children did well at the new school. Helping Mary finance the new antique shop in Brighton was a burden but he accepted it willingly. At that time he wanted her out of the Chelsea/Fulham set; there were too many old boyfriends in the area and he did not want their affair blazoned about. It might have ruined his career, particularly if some vicious person suggested he had dropped charges because of his sexual association with Mary.

The cash he received on the side made all the difference. It bridged the gap between the miserable take-home pay he received as a policeman and the cost of two homes. Mary made her contribution for sure, but it would be kidding himself to imagine she could have managed the shop in Brighton on her own. It did good business in the season but the rest of the year was dead.

Bosworth had never had any qualms about accepting bribes from porn dealers in Soho. Many officers on the squad accepted them and if he had not, they still would. They all felt that the dealers were not genuine criminals. The stuff they were selling at that time, which was siezed from time to time for appearances sake, was no worse than the lurid full frontals now displayed in *Mayfair* and *Penthouse* in all the little newsagents shops up and down the country.

Fortunately, during those years they had been able to put some money aside in a Building Society. It had been his guarantee to Mary, who otherwise would have felt very vulnerable. Many times she had asked him to divorce

Angela and marry her. In normal circumstances he would have done so, but the career had to take priority and the children also had to be considered.

Bosworth brought his thoughts fully back to the meeting, for the Commander was talking now in that rather pompous voice of his. Bosworth thought he could do the Commander's job much better. For one thing he had more style – the Commander was too much of a rough diamond to disguise his working-class origins and his attempts to change his accent to something more socially acceptable were pathetic, making him sound more pompous than ever.

The meeting was agreeing to allocate more plain clothes men to mount around-the-clock surveillance on Irish families who were known IRA sympathisers, in the hope of uncovering more bomb factories. The Commander finished the discussion by paying a tribute to Bosworth and all those in his team for their recent breakthrough. Bosworth was pleased to be recognised although he knew the Commander was just doing it for the form.

He returned to his own office, almost facing the underground station, and looked pensively out of the double glazed windows. Across the road were the now disused parking places where the terrorists had once left a vehicle loaded with explosives. He thought about the close shave it had been; the whole side of New Scotland Yard would probably have been blasted if the bomb had not been found and defused minutes before it was due to go off. Eternal vigilance is essential in this business; with it we can get them licked; they're no more than common thugs and gangsters, he reflected, letting his disgust well up, leaving a distinctly bitter taste in his mouth.

He crushed the stub of a Players No. 1 into the ashtray and picked up the direct line telephone to dial a Brighton number.

'Mary darling, I'm simply delighted by your news. It's bucked me up all day. It will be so much better when you live permanently in London again. I can't stand those endless railway journeys and with all this Irish trouble, I've been finding it more difficult to get away. What made you change your mind?'

'I still want to marry you,' said Mary firmly.

Bosworth gulped and mumbled something about being busy and seeing her at the weekend, said goodbye and put the 'phone down.

He considered it most unfair of Mary to raise that issue again, the last time must have been all of five years before and they had more or less agreed that his career should not be prejudiced. The children were now grown up and two of them married with children of their own, and he could not use that excuse again. At fifty-two George Bosworth had learned to live his life with two separate, and quite different, women and the truth of the matter was he did not relish change. He would leave it until he saw Mary over the weekend and discuss it fully then.

Later that evening an event took place which disrupted all the weekend plans of the Chief Superintendent. Ross McWhirter, the editor of the Guinness Book of Records and a famous campaigner against both the IRA and Left causes was shot dead on his own doorstep in the suburbs of North London. He had long feared he was marked by the IRA for assassination; only three weeks before he had said, 'I live in constant fear of my life – I know I am on the IRA death list.' The Scotland Yard bomb squad, including Bosworth, would now have to work extra time to track down the assassins, as this killing, more than any other, demonstrated both the determination and the effectiveness of the IRA gangs. The public, too, would become apprehensive because a known figure had been struck down standing next to his wife. The previous attempts on Members of Parliament, all of which had failed, had been brushed aside as of no lasting consequence but this death sounded an ominous knell which could be heard throughout the country.

When the news reached Valerie Commin, she wept openly. McWhirter was a man whom she had much admired for his stand against anarchy. Nor could she ignore the threat the escalation of violence posed for Graham. But at breakfast the next morning, with the terrible news spread over the front pages of the newspapers, he was less visibly moved.

'Of course, darling, it is a terrible tragedy but, if you ask me he did rather ask for it,' he said.

'How can you say that, Graham. If he asked for it what about you and everyone else in politics?'

'Well we don't all have to fly the anti-IRA flag at the top of our pole and make such a fetish of it,' Graham replied. Actually he had felt quite queasy since hearing the news and did not want to admit to his wife that he was scared about what was happening. In his way he was trying to protect her from a fuller realisation of the acute danger people in public life were in, and at the same time to bolster up his own flagging morale.

'Oh! Graham, sometimes you disgust me,' she said, forcing back her tears.

Now he realised the strength of her feelings, Commin tried to retrieve the position; he could not stand rows with Valerie.

'Darling, I just didn't want you to get upset. Eventually we shall get on top of this IRA horror and in the meantime we mustn't let it get us down. Ross was a jolly good chap and a good Tory too.'

'Graham, something is wrong somewhere. It's not like England to have all this killing and frankly I don't think enough is being done to stop it.'

'Next week I'm going to vote for capital punishment, there's a debate in the House, and if we can bring back hanging it would stop most of the killers in their tracks. They're not very brave really,' said Commin.

'But you can only hang them if you catch them first; look at that Margaret McKearney business: the police make a big fuss about her being the most wanted terrorist and they can't even get her extradited from Eire,' replied Valerie, in no way placated by Graham's remarks.

'Yes there is something curious about that case,' he said

and quickly changed the subject. Valerie was so obviously distraught.

In Dublin, in Cork, in Boston, in Philadelphia and in other places where the militant supporters of the IRA gather, there were toasts that day to the success of the killing and to the escape of the officers who had executed it. Richard Collins drank his toast alone, although he knew in his heart that the assassination of one man would not, in itself, achieve too much result.

Chapter Ten

To Christmas in Ireland

The next few weeks for Rick were feverish. The impending transfer of his responsibilities to Art Gruber meant he had a lot of work tying up loose ends, as well as devining ways in which his contacts could be handed over to Art. The visit to Venezuela went very well and, fortunately, Fernandos was favourably impressed by the computer man from Dallas. The prospect of sharing some extra commission on the installation of an IBM computer for the Venezuelan Navy, was an important factor in attracting him to the other American.

Rick was sorry in many ways to lose contact with Carlos Fernandos, with whom he had developed a close rapport. He found the Venezuelan easy to talk to and, in some areas, extremely erudite. His period at the Sorbonne had not been wasted.

Santiago de Leon de Caracas, to give the capital its full name, was a pleasant place to visit in December in the dry season. The night life was exotic and the two Americans could enjoy it with the virtue of men who were actually engaged in the serious task of perfecting an espionage network. Twice they also took themselves off to the beaches, driving a Mercedes borrowed from Fernandos. The long road tunnels through the mountains got them there quickly.

Fernandos, Rick discovered, was not really a negro but a mestizo or mixed blood, and this group comprised two-thirds of the population of Venezuela. Only a fifth were white and less than a tenth were negro. The Indians, a tribe of which had been called Caracas, giving their name to the town when it was founded in the mid-sixteenth century, had been virtually eliminated and now comprised only two per cent of the population.

Rick was also most pleased that both Art and Fernandos shared his dislike of the English and both were very disdainful of the waning British influence in the world. Fernandos turned out to be bitter about the English past, referring the two Americans to the fact that fifty years before the achievement of North American Independence, Britain had signed the Asiento Treaty with Spain under which for over a century the Spanish empire in South America had been supplied with slaves from Africa. It was that cruel exploitation of human beings, he argued, which had given England the trading profits on which to base both its Industrial Revolution and its development of a Colonial Empire. The English, he said, boasted about their liberal philosophy but the true ideas of freedom and democracy came from France which had, in turn, inspired the American colonists to fight for independence. The English are perfidious, Fernandos had emphasised, and their class divisions were more pronounced than anywhere in the world because they had not woken up to the twentieth century and lived firmly in a past that had long since gone.

In their discussions Rick was careful not to raise the subject of Ireland Gruber knew his interest, he might be indiscreet or inform the Company.

Returning home to Conshohocken County in mid-December, Rick found the cold of the Pennsylvanian winter a sharp contrast to the heat and the lush tropical vegetation of the Caracan mountains. To Kathy's envy when he undressed that night, he displayed a golden tan, all except the white patch of the swimming trunks.

'I thought you said Venezuela was not a tourist resort?' said Kathy, teasingly.

'I caught the tan sitting round the pool at the hotel, we were still working,' he replied not daring to admit to the beach visits.

Kathy was not really jealous and was in high spirits

anticipating the coming Christmas and New Year in Ireland. Her parents in Harrisburg were sorry not to be having their grandhildren with them as usual, but as an Irish family themselves they were glad their eldest daughter was seeing the mother country.

Early in the morning on the Sunday before Christmas they piled everything into the car and drove to Boston. It was a six and a half hour journey but Rick and Kathy preferred it to the drag of taking planes with the children in hand. Door to door the journey was not that much longer and as they wanted to call on the O'Halloran's it was so much simpler in their own car. They arrived in Mount Bowdoin without mishap around three in the afternoon; put the Collins' youngsters, who were exhausted and excited, to bed in one of the children's rooms whilst the parents sat and talked.

'What time is your plane leaving?,' asked Michael.

'At eleven fifteen tonight,' said Kathy. 'It's a TWA charter and we'll have to report an hour before departure.'

'Good' said Michael, 'we'll be able to have dinner together to launch you on your way.'

'What about the children?' asked Kathy.

'We'll take yours, of course, but ours can stay here with Grandma who can sit in for us,' answered Michael.

'We should include Kevin,' said Rick.

'Sure we will, Uncle Rick,' said Michael.

They wondered whether to eat the German specialities at *Jake Wirth's*, Italian at *Boraschi's*, finally deciding on good old-fashioned New England food at *Patten's*. The restaurant turned out to be an excellent choice. Before they left the O'Halloran house the two families exchanged Christmas presents which added to the children's excitement. As the two wives were helping the children to face the cold night air, Michael took Rick on one side and said, 'It's all fixed. I've spoken to the Provisionals and they will be contacting you soon after you arrive. Have no doubt they'll know you. On no account try to contact them, you might end up with the wrong group or, worse still, a police informer.'

The plane left on time with a full load factor of charter

groups of tourists, mostly Irish-Americans, and arrived on the next day before noon at Shannon International Airport. Kathy and Rick managed to snatch only three hours sleep as the aircraft was flying into the dawn across the North Atlantic, and the night was correspondingly short. The hostesses insisted on serving a miserable boxed breakfast at three a.m. Boston time. The children slept most of the way waking up just before Shannon to see the beautiful bays and rugged mountains of County Clare stretched out beneath them. The green of the valleys and fields was quite stunning. Rick turned to Kathy, smiling. 'We now know why they call her the Emerald Isle.'

The tourists, apart from the old hands, were struck by the leisurely pace of the airport personnel who received them with a typically friendly Irish welcome. The bustle and haste of Boston seemed a million miles away. 'This airport is so quiet,' remarked Kathy to Rick. 'Where has everyone gone?'

'I suppose it was built for transatlantic travel in the days of the short range aeroplanes and the traffic just didn't materialise,' he said. 'You can fly now non-stop by Jumbo from Miami or Los Angeles to London, Copenhagen or Frankfurt, so why bother to stop off here anymore?' said Rick. 'It's been by-passed by the march of technology.'

When they had gone through passport checks and baggage collection, the courier showed their party to a coach and Rick was able to get a good look at the fellow-tourists they would be with for two weeks. Mostly they were middle-aged people but some were families and there were several children in Deidre's and Mark's age group, which was good. Several older women, apparently unattached, stood out with their blue rinsed hair. They were the same type as he had seen on many other holiday routes: widows of the successful businessmen who had died in their prime through coronaries brought on by overwork, leaving it all to the wife to spend on twenty-five years of world travel.

Just after they left the airport the tourists were surprised to see an industrial complex as modern as any in the USA. The vision did not tally with their image of a backward, neglected West of Ireland, and in the coach there was much admiring comment. Rick too was surprised and swelled a little with pride at what the mother country was doing.

The Collins' family were accommodated at a smart and comfortable hotel called the *Shannon Shamrock* and were soon settled in. After a light buffet lunch they all went to bed to recover from the long journey. Rick was wondering when the Provos would contact him. He had warned Kathy he was expecting to be approached, but had avoided telling her the full story for fear of alarming her.

After four hours they woke refreshed, ready to do battle with the programme organised by the package tour operators. The first item in the itinerary was a medieval banquet at nearby Bunratty Castle.

'They waste no time do they?' Rick said to Kathy. 'The next two weeks will be hard work.'

The children were bright and lively at eight o'clock; they were tuned in to Eastern Standard Time and for them it was still only afternoon, which was just as well as they had a strenuous night in front of them.

Bunratty Castle at the mouth of the Bunratty River was the answer to a tourist's prayer. It had everything an American would want to imbibe: history, atmosphere and romantic culture. They were given a quick description of its lurid past: the first stone castle was built on land formerly owned by the Irish King in the thirteenth century by a Sir Thomas de Clare who, among other deeds had the King of Thomond, a certain Brian O'Brien, arrested at a banquet in the castle and dragged to his death by horses. Later the O'Brien family obtained the castle and in the fifteenth century, restored it to its former glory, after which it was continuously occupied for four hundred years.

As Rick, Kathy and the children arrived in the great hall, Irish colleens, dressed in low cut velvet gowns, handed the guests mugs of mulled wine. They were then shown downstairs to the banqueting hall to their places on benches at long tables. The meal was served on pewter plates and although they each had a knife, they were expected to eat with fingers. The children were delighted at this concession to naughtiness. During the banquet, singers and players passed around the hall singing old Irish airs and playing the catchy tunes on replicas of ancient instruments. Plenty of the potent medieval drink of mead was flowing for the adults, children had to settle for soft drinks.

The guests, by now thoroughly relaxed, were themselves singing with the abandon of happy people far from the restraints of home, and banging their mugs on the tables. The hall reverberated to the raucous noise. Suddenly Rick was aware of a young man who had slipped on to the bench to sit next to him. He did not look like a tourist and what he said to Rick, capping his ear with his two hands, confirmed that he was not with the party.

'Mister Collins,' he said, with a rich brogue, 'welcome to Ireland, the land of your people. We shall come for you tomorrow mornin' at eight terty; please wait outside your hotel for us.' He was gone as quickly as he had arrived, gliding unnoticed, through the revellers.

Neither Rick nor Kathy could get to sleep for some hours, despite the mead, and they assumed it was due to the time change which had affected their metabolism. In Rick's case his inability to sleep was also affected by the strange encounter in the Bunratty Hall. He had not expected the Provos to contact him in this way and he could hardly wait for the meeting tomorrow. The blood was coursing through his veins at the prospect of at last joining the IRA successors of the legendary Michael Collins who, he was proud to remember, came of the same stock as his own forbears.

He had set the alarm on his watch for eight o'clock and put it under his pillow to save waking Kathy at that hour, when she would still be in her middle-of-the-night sleep. As soon as it sounded he crept noiselessly from the bed. He shaved quickly, skipped the shower and then dressed by the chink of light coming through the bedroom curtains. By eight twenty-five he was outside the hotel. There was no mistaking the men, three of them, waiting in a little Ford car from Dagenham.

They opened the passenger door and without saying a word one of them lifted the seat to allow him to double up and climb on to the cramped back compartment. It was only after they were on the road outside the hotel that they spoke.

'To be sure it's a real pleasure to meet, Mr. Collins,' said the man who had lifted the seat. He was about forty and had a healthy ruddy complexion from years in the open air. His suit was ill-fitting, with all three buttons of the coat done up, presumably because of the cold morning. His hands which he held apologetically on his lap were large and fleshy, and the nails, although quite clean, were rough. He seemed to be the leader as the others did not speak at first. One concentrated on driving and the other – in the back compartment, looked at Rick with a welcoming smile. He was younger than the others, about twenty-five, Rick guessed.

'I'm glad to be with you,' said Rick. 'It's been a long journey.'

'All the way from Philadelphia in Pennsylvania,' said the man in the front.

'I didn't only mean distances,' said Rick, 'I also meant the years.'

'What would you be meaning by that?' the man asked.

'I am descended from the stock of Michael Collins and it's a half century since he walked in this land,' said Rick, with feeling.

'Yes, we know,' said the man sounding very gentle, 'and we all revere his memory to this day.'

It transpired that they were taking the road into Limerick and as they drove through the town, already busy with early morning Christmas shoppers, the gentle man said, 'This is Limerick, it has known much suffering. For centuries we have fought for our freedom here. Ten centuries in fact. First against the Danes and then against the Anglo-Normans. We've had many heroes; Brian Boru who fought the Danes; Patrick Sarsfield who fought the English King William. The King defeated us but he respected us. He allowed the garrison to go free and, what

is more, he had the decency to allow all Catholics their
religious freedom.'

'Were the Irish people then allowed peace?' asked Rick.

'No,' said the man. 'The English Parliament were sitting
in London and they repudiated the Treaty of Limerick,
which the King William had signed.'

'And who did they represent?' said Rick.

'Only the English ruling class. They withdrew all our
rights. Even today Limerick is still known as "the City of
the Violated Treaty." '

'Did we fight back?' asked Rick, already identifying with
the countless oppressed Irishmen of centuries before.

'Indeed we did, Mr. Collins,' said the man. 'Indeed we
did. In the years that followed, over half a million Irishmen
left Ireland to fight for the Catholic Kings of Spain and
France. Many of them never returned from the wars in
Europe against the English. Look there at that main
crossing off O'Connell, that's Sarsfield Street named after
Patrick himself.'

They drove on out of the city into the narrow country
roads. Rick was struck with the strangeness of it. The high
hedgerows, the untidiness of the fields as though not yet
tamed from nature. At this stage they had only passed a
couple of automobiles but had seen three ponies pulling
traps. Two of them were apparently carrying milk in
churns towards the city. Rick felt he had moved back at
least fifty years in time. It was a sensation which for all its
primitiveness, he had not even felt in rural Mexico. Mexico,
perhaps because he had seen so much of it on movies, had
seemed contemporary compared to this.

Their destination was a village, nearly ten miles out of
Limerick, called Shehan's Cross. It did not seem to have
much of a center, just one or two general shops and a Bar
and to Rick, accustomed to the milling crowds of
Philadelphia, Boston and Caracas, it was a ghost village,
devoid of people.

They turned up a rough unmade road for a few hundred
yards and stopped by a single storey stone cottage with a
slate roof and thatch on the out-houses. The garden was

well maintained and still had some vegetables which Rick could not immediately recognise. In the near distance he could distinguish the sounds of animals, otherwise, now the car had stopped, the whole area was dominated by a penetrating silence. In no other place had he ever experienced such calm. In his well-cut brown suit and suede shoes, he was obviously an intruder on this scene, a stranger still with the dull echo of aeroengines in his ears.

The gentle man, now wreathed in smiles of welcome, motioned Rick through the low front door. He bent down to enter thinking as he did so, that in those days they built for small people. The door opened directly into a surprising big room with large, slightly uneven, flagstones for a floor covered in the centre by a worn square carpet. There was only a half-light, provided by the two narrow windows, and Rick's eyes took some time to adjust, but his nose could sense a smoking fire, which he assumed was burning peat. He had to continue standing slightly stooped as the white-washed ceiling was so low.

A man, about fifty and rather more smartly dressed than the three who had brought him to the cottage, stood up from a wicker chair by the fire, and shook Rick by the hand. The grip, strong but firmly controlled, relaxed as he said, 'We are all very glad you have come.'

Chapter Eleven

Confrontation at Shehan's Cross

It transpired that the reception was not quite as Rick had anticipated. He was left alone with two officers of the Provisional IRA, while the other men who had been in the car, remained outside; their questions were blunt to the point of roughness. After Rick had taken the chair he was offered, he was asked firmly, 'We know of the fine work done in the United States to raise funds for our cause, Mr. Collins, and you come to us with excellent references, but what can you possibly do for us which we can't do for ourselves?'

'I'm a professional organiser and my experience could be invaluable. I am an Irishman in my blood and I feel I can make a useful contribution,' replied Rick modestly, rather shaken by the tone of hostility in his questioner's voice.

'From the earliest days of the struggle we've had good help from America. We recognise that with gratitude. The example given fifty years ago by John Devoy and Judge Cohalan will never be forgotten. But, frankly, Americans – even Irish-Americans – sitting in their armchairs watching our Irish struggle on television, cannot understand what we are going through here today. Our men are still dying every day and we are nearly sixty years on from the Easter Rising.'

'I know that,' said Rick. 'I know that. I feel deeply about it too. I owe it to my family links to do something to avenge these deaths.'

'Mr. Collins, America is full of Irishmen who have an emotional attachment to the old country, but if we tried to accommodate you all, we'd do nothing else. Don't you see

that, as an intelligent man, Mr. Collins?' The officer was
bending forward looking intently at Rick with piercing
brown eyes. Rick, who had become accustomed to the light,
could see the officer's features more clearly now. He was
clean shaven apart from long sideburns and his dark brown
hair, although long, was neatly combed. He was wearing an
old fashioned double breasted suit and Rick's trained eye
recognised a telling bulge just beneath the left armpit. His
respect for this man was growing.

'Look, I am not here as a tourist and I am certainly not
advocating that you waste your time organising sightseeing
tours for sympathetic Americans. I repeat, I want to work
for the cause and I will make every personal sacrifice to do
so. I owe it to my forbears,' said Rick, earnestly anxious to
communicate his sincerity to this iron-willed man.

'We know about your forbears, we know about your
family background, but you've all been cut off from the soil
of Ireland. Your grandfather left when he was a young
man; he never came back; your father never came here in
his lifetime either and this is your first visit. What can you
possibly know of Ireland?'

'Well, I admit, I don't know much personally, but my
commitment is absolute for all that. If he had lived,
Michael Collins would be eighty-five this year and he
wouldn't have spurned help from his American cousins; de
Valera didn't spurn that help,' said Rick remembering what
he had read about the campaigns of 1919.

'Your understanding of Irish history is not the same as
mine, said the officer, 'the American money was good, but
the political help was dismal. Fifty years ago the American
Irish tried to make us compromise on the issue of
Independence, they wanted us just to take Home Rule. De
Valera broke with them on that. If the American Irish had
wielded any influence on the American Government at that
time, they could have made Britain concede a free United
Ireland at the Versailles Peace Conference after the First
World War. But their influence was useless, Woodrow
Wilson ignored the American Irish and said nothing to the
British; and we had to fight all over again for our own

freedom.' The officer was becoming more bitter. 'If we had been Jewish the American Jews would have been much more effective in their support for us than American Irish ever were. See how the Israelis were given American backing to extend their territory right down to the Suez Canal, yet we can't even keep the Bogside in Londonderry.'

'I think part of the trouble is that in America we don't know enough about events here. The goodwill is strong but it needs to be organised. And we don't have that much influence over American newspapers and television,' Rick said, rather lamely, and now more than a little disconcerted by the attack. At Camp Peary during his training days, he had experienced many tough mock interrogations but the technique he was now suffering had not been demonstrated in the Company curriculum. The man questioning him was supposed to be an ally, who should be grateful for any offer of help. He had, of course, never seen such personal commitment by an American. Rick decided to re-iterate his family connexions to temper the onslaught. And he made his remark to the second man who had not said a word in the cottage, but who had spoken warmly of Michael Collins in the car.

'As our friend here knows, it's my blood link with Michael Collins which inspired me to come here and to commit myself to the cause which he died for,' added Rick, playing on the emotion. It was all to no avail.

'Mr. Collins, I respect your motives, in fact I believe you, but what you say reveals your ignorance of our history. I know some people regard Michael Collins as an Irish hero, but he was killed by the IRA because he had become a lackey of the English. He signed the agreement which allowed the six counties to remain in the United Kingdom, then he recruited men who had been in the British Army to fight the IRA. That was a terrible period. My own dear father was in the IRA fighting against the Irish State Army, which Collins commanded. After the passage of time we can now respect Michael Collins as a leader of the early struggle, but we can't forget the error of the Treaty. If Collins and the others had held firm in December '21,

Lloyd-George and Winston Churchill would have been forced to concede a United Ireland,' the officer said firmly, 'and Irishmen wouldn't be dying today on the streets of Belfast and in the cottages of South Armagh. And, did you know, Mr. Collins, that your Michael Collins was elected to Dáil Eireann as the member for South Armagh in the elections of June '21? And did you know that he fought the election saying he was against partition, and yet within six months he had signed the Treaty which brought partition about. And he sacrificed South Armagh to the British.'

Rick was flabbergasted by the vehemence of this attack. The bitterness of it was enveloping him. What could he say to withstand its effect and yet he felt suffocated by it. His knowledge of Irish history could never match the officer's but at least he felt he should make some effort to justify the name of Collins.

'But didn't the Dáil Eireann ratify the Treaty?' he asked.

'Yes, but only by a majority of sixty-four to fifty-seven. The decision was condemned by de Valera, who broke down and wept and then resigned as President of the Dáil.'

'Weren't Michael Collins and de Valera close friends?' asked Rick.

'They had been, but de Valera attacked the Treaty Collins signed and encouraged my father and others to oppose it,' he answered.

'Although Michael Collins had arranged de Valera's escape from Lincoln Prison only three years before?' asked Rick clutching at incidents which might confirm the Collins honour.

'Some of us are very suspicious about that supposed escape. It was too fishy for words. Both Collins outside and de Valera inside had keys to the main gate. How could that have been possible? Collins must have had the agreement of the English to that escape. It must have been part of the deal which lead up to the Treaty.'

Rick felt dispirited. He had never realised how deep were the divisions in Irish ranks and how strongly opinions were held. This man in front of him, calm and controlled and yet vehement, had a power and an intensity which could move

mountains. Rick was gripped by a fascination, almost as
though the passion of the man had hypnotised him. For one
second he wondered if his role for Ireland had been
extinguished and, if he would have no part to play in this
intense Irish saga. But the thought was quickly banished,
because only a coward would turn his back on an Ireland
which needed him. Only a skunk would flee from a
situation simply because it was dangerous and involved.

The conversation, or rather interrogation, had opened
Rick's eyes to the profundities of Irish feeling as well as to
the depths of the divisions which had divided, and still
divided, Irishmen. And the answer came to him like a flash:
the divisions exist because the English oppression still
exists, but once that oppression was removed, then
Irishmen could achieve their essential historic unity. But
the problem still remained, how could he convince this
strong man of his own sincerity?

'I appreciate what you are saying,' said Rick, 'and I
accept that we Irish Americans have been protected from
the full understanding of Ireland's turmoil, but please,
please let me help. I can't believe what you say about
Michael Collins' treachery, but if I can do my bit to bring
the English tyranny to an end, and help to achieve a United
Ireland, then I can, with my effort, redress the bitterness
against another Collins and assist in redeeming his name.'

'There's something else we must discuss before we can
get there,' said the officer, darkly.

'What's that?' asked Rick.

'How do we know that you are not a spy for the English
or a spy for the Americans?' asked the officer, his lip curling
up in distaste. 'We know that the English have been in close
touch with the CIA and the FBI about arms supplies from
the United States. Perhaps, you are acting for them?'

Rick felt sick in the pit of his stomach. He had come as a
friend and now he was being viewed as a possible enemy.
Supposing these people eliminated him because of their
suspicions. They had not been seen at his hotel and no one
knew where he had gone. He was in a defenceless position
with two armed officers with him in the room and probably

two armed men outside as well. Rick had left his guns at home; suddenly Philadelphia seemed a long, long, way away.

'My loyalty to Ireland is complete,' said Rick, not knowing what else to say, 'didn't O'Halloran and the Boston committees report on me?'

'Yes, we've had full reports on you, and we know too that you are a member of the CIA.'

Rick's mind reeled from the blow. Where could they have found out; his CIA connexion was a closely guarded secret and even the local Stations had no knowledge of it; how could an officer of the Provisional IRA, in a remote Irish farmhouse, be so informed. He went pale.

'Mr. Collins, we have a better secret service than you give us credit for. The one thing we did learn from Michael Collins was to keep our lines of intelligence well organised. We have friends in surprising places.'

'Did O'Halloran tell you?' asked Rick.

'Yes, he did,' said the officer, 'Normally we wouldn't have told you our sources but it is important for you to know that loyalty to the Movement is greater than any personal friendship. O'Halloran would have been demoted if he hadn't informed us fully. He wasn't our only informant, however,' he added, showing by his tone he was going no further.

Rick was shaken by the revelation of his friend's infidelity and the officer added, 'If you join our ranks we would expect you to give us all information about O'Halloran and any other contacts you have. In a state of war our officers can have no such secrets from each other.'

The atmosphere in the cottage seemed to go cold and the silence, now the officer had stopped speaking, felt oppressive. The three men sat without moving. Rick was dazed and confused. The gentle man was as silent as ever and continued to observe the scene with the imperturbability of a sentry. The officer looked grim with his arms crossed over his chest. Rick could just distinguish the muffled noise of a pony trap on the road outside. It was a comfort to know that simple life was still going on somewhere.

Whatever the outcome of this extraordinary interview, Rick knew that his life would never be the same again and there could be no going back. What they had discussed was, in a sense, superficial to the stirring of emotion inside him. Ireland he felt, had been the catalyst to opening his soul and it was truly to Ireland that his life must be dedicated, however long his life might be and however these men might treat him.

The silence was broken by the officer. 'We have decided you will be recruited into this unit under my command. We expect you to be entirely committed to the IRA; your work for the CIA will be completely subordinate, although for appearances sake, it will be allowed to continue. We do not bother about the activities you engage in on behalf of the CIA except that when they impinge on our work you will inform us fully. I may add that two points have influenced our decision: firstly the reports on you from Captain O'Halloran, who was unstinting in his praise of your abilities and enthusiastic in his admiration of your loyalty to Ireland; secondly you have impressed us today by your demeanour.'

'Thank you,' said Rick with relief.

'My name is Padraig O'Connell,' said the officer, 'let me introduce you to my comrades. This is Sean Devlin,' he motioned to the gentle man who now unclasped his hands to grip Rick's firmly. At this point a tall man in his early thirties strode in through the open door from the scullery, stooping as he walked towards Rick. 'I am Peadar MacSwiney,' he said. 'I could hardly restrain myself sitting out there all this time. You came through your interrogation with flying colours.'

For the next hour, fortified by sweet thick tea served from a large brown earthenware pot into enamel mugs, they discussed Rick's immediate program whilst in Ireland on the package tour. It was agreed that the cover would be maintained throughout and that no one, outside O'Connell's command, would be told of Rick's recruitment. The officers would contact Rick within a day or so on the route to be followed by the tour, and meanwhile he should conduct himself as any other normal

American father in Ireland for the first time. Remember, he was warned, informers and spies are everywhere, reporting not only to the English but also to the Irish Government. And if his interest in the IRA became known, the British or Irish Intelligence Agencies would report the fact to the CIA 'just as sure as the Liffey flows into Dublin Bay,' added Peadar MacSwiney.

Rick had the tour programme on him and two of the officers sat at the table making notes from it. As they were writing, they looked at each other with a knowing look. 'Mr. Collins,' one of them said, 'in six days time you will be passing through Rosscarbery and going on to Kinsale. Just out of Rosscarbery you will be passing Sam's Cross where Michael Collins lived as a boy. In '21 the Black and Tans destroyed Woodfield, his family home.'

'I'd heard about that from my father,' Rick said. 'Didn't they throw all the children's clothes and souvenirs into the flames?'

'They always did that. The Black and Tans were made up of soldiers recruited from the criminal classes of England. They loved destruction for destruction's sake,' O'Connell said.

'Are the Collins family still around there?' asked Rick.

'There is a tavern at Sam's Cross and it was kept by a cousin of Michael Collins. I think he had his last drink there before his assassination,' said O'Connell. 'I don't know who is left of the Collins but,' he added, 'I should not advise you to contact any of them. You have to be very careful, don't trust anyone; they may inform on you.'

'I will be careful,' said Rick.

'We shall see you again soon to discuss the ideas you have. Give our greetings to your wife, she's a colleen, we hear,' said MacSwiney.

When Rick returned to the hotel only the driver accompanied him, the officers and men had other subjects to discuss. He sat in the front passenger seat and, with the window open, allowed the clean cold fresh air to wash over his face and head. The strain of the morning was beginning to lift and he felt a subdued elation, one he had experienced before but could not quite identify. After Limerick, and on the road back to Bunratty, he realised what it was: he had returned home.

Chapter Twelve

The Road to Sam's Cross

Kathy was angry. 'I've been out of my mind here. Where on earth did you get to?'

'I left a note to tell you I was going out,' said Rick apologetically.

'I didn't see it,' said Kathy.

'I'm sorry,' said Rick.

'I thought we came on holiday,' said Kathy. 'Have you been kidding me, are you really here on Company business?'

'No, I'm going to do some work to help Ireland, that's all. I thought you understood that,' he replied.

'Oh! Rick, don't let it be too dangerous,' said Kathy.

They took the children to have lunch and spent the afternoon looking at the Folk Park, behind Bunratty Castle, with its cottages reproduced as the typical dwellings of hundreds of years before. The children were pleased to have met up with a family from North Boston with twin boys of eight and a girl of nine. They played games with them around the Park and in the Castle itself. Rick and Kathy had so much on their hands that they did not return to their conversation until late that night.

'Kathy,' Rick said, 'for months I have been feeling upset about the situation in the Company. A lot of operatives have left and they are making money writing books and spreading mud about us. Now Congress is making hay with all the revelations and we don't have any secrets left. Director Colby spends a lot of his time answering criticisms rather than being able to get on with the job of running the agency. As a result America will lose out against Russia and Cuba in countries like Angola.'

'Do you want to leave?' asked Kathy, hopefully.

'No, of course not. I'm not a rat leaving a sinking ship. I can do a great deal for the Agency – and for America – with all the experience I've had. I've got this new job it Italy, which is very important, and that could give me even more promotion. But, Kathy, you know how I feel about Ireland: I can do something valuable for Ireland at the same time as I do the Italy job,' he said emphatically.

'Are you sure you're not taking on too much?' asked Kathy, with a troubled frown.

'No, I think Ireland will help me to take my mind off the problems of the Company and all the troubles in America.'

'Perhaps you should think now of leaving the CIA,' she said, cautiously.

'We couldn't afford for me to do that, not with the recession on at the moment. In a year or so things will get back to normal in the Company – and in the country – and I won't be so uptight. Just give it time.'

'How long will you be involved with Ireland?' she asked.

'About a year to complete the project, no more.' he answered.

That night, worn out by the tourist exertions and the new sights and sounds travellers see, the Collins family slept soundly.

The next day all was great excitement. It was Christmas Eve and the party left early by coach towards the South West and to Killarney, where they were to spend Christmas. Their destination was the *Europa*, a German-owned hotel which they found was run with typical Germanic efficiency. There were a lot of German guests and the notice signs were in German as well as in English. They looked through large plate glass windows at the fir-covered mountains. As Rick said to Kathy, 'We could easily be in Bavaria.' A voice from another and older member of the Boston party said, 'You sure could, I was there after the war and this is just like it. The Germans and the Japs have moved into Southern Ireland in force; with all the tax concessions it's worth their while.'

'Are there many German factories here then?' asked Rick.

'Dozens,' said the man. 'Of course, there never was the antagonism here against the Germans that the English had. At one time, you know, the British thought the Irish would form an alliance with the Germans; the Limeys were terrified the German navy would get a submarine base on the West Coast of Ireland where they have all those deep harbours.'

'Really?' said Rick.

'Yep,' the man went on with relish. 'The Germans gave encouragement to the Irish to get their independence during the first world war and they thought the Irish would repay them in the second. There was a fellow called Sir Roger something, that's it, um ... Casement, who organised a shipment of arms from Germany. They captured him and hanged him as a traitor. Actually, I think, some Americans were behind Casement. There was a secret body of Irishmen in New York – called the Clan na Gael – ran by a cantankerous old man named Devoy. They arranged for Casement to go to Germany to form an Irish brigade from Irish prisoners-of-war so as to fight the British.'

'Really?' said Rick.

'Yep, those secret Irish societies were something really great then. Probably Ireland would never have gotten out of Britain's grip without American help. D'you know, de Valera was an American. Born in New York, he was. Father wasn't Irish at all. Spanish or Cuban or something,'

'Interesting,' said Rick.

'Yep. I've been in Ireland before. The Irish connexion with America is so interesting. The British hate it. They always get tough on any Irish-Americans they can lay their hands on. Look what they did to William Joyce.'

'Who was he?' asked Rick, genuinely not knowing.

'Sorry I forgot, you're younger than me – by twenty-five years? – you certainly wouldn't remember the war. Joyce was a broadcaster from Nazi Germany they called 'Lord Haw Haw.' They captured him, tried him for treason and he was hanged. They had absolutely no right to do it. He was an American citizen all the time. We Americans should have tried him, if anybody, but we never did. Actually the poor fellow never killed anyone himself, he just got under the British skin with his jibes and they didn't like it. When the British get it in for someone, they make sure they get him. Anyway, what are you in, friend?'

'In stacking for warehouses,' Rick said, 'it sounds dull but it's very interesting really, because it makes up like a toy game.'

'I was in engineering after I left the Army, retired now; gave it up when I was sixty so I could see the world and enjoy myself. What's the point of carrying on and having a heart attack. You must excuse me, there's my little lady. Glad to meet you.' He disappeared into a milling crowd of hotel guests who were collecting around a massive Christmas tree lit up with lights and surrounded with brightly packaged presents. Rick sighed with relief and turned to find Kathy who had, conveniently, slipped away.

Christmas was great fun. It started with a crowded Midnight Mass at St. Mary's Cathedral, which was very moving and went through to parties, dances and trips. The hotel guest list was an equal mixture of Irish, Germans and Americans and they all got on famously. The heavy German food did not particularly appeal to Rick but the children loved the enormous plum puddings with the holly on top, brought in blazing with Stock brandy. They spent the day time exploring the countryside around the fabulously pretty Lough Leane, giving the children pony rides on the rough tracks, and visiting the ruins of the fifteenth century Muckross Abbey. Evenings were times for party games which the Irish played boisterously, the Germans deliberately and methodically, except when they were drunk, with the Americans in between. Both Rick and Kathy were very happy; neither of them could remember a better Christmas.

After they had left Killarney and were on the winding roads to Kenmare and Bantry, Rick, to his annoyance, saw the old ex-engineer heading down the coach to take a spare seat across the aisle from Rick.

'Hullo, there, thought I'd come to see you. Are you enjoying the trip, lovely country isn't it, nothing like it in the States except Oregon and that's wilder. Say wasn't that bad about that CIA man being shot dead in Athens?'

'What did you say?' asked Rick, now pricking up his ears.

'Didn't you hear about it? He was some CIA chief – ran the whole organisation in Greece. The Government must be worried about it. Just think if gunmen went around killing off all our spies,' the man was pleased that his information was appreciated.

'What was the man's name?' asked Rick.

'Walsh or Welch, something like that,' said the man. Rick was horrified, realising the dead man must be Dick Welch, the head of the local station who had previously headed up the CIA station in Lima, Peru.

'How did you hear the news?' he asked, to check its authenticity.

'I carry a powerful transistor wherever I go,' he said. 'I picked it up on AFN – you know the Army programme out of Frankfurt.'

'It must be true then.'

'No doubt, they're blaming the boys who've blown all the secret info about the CIA in the last few months. Any CIA man is now going to be marked out for killing. It's not a job I'd like to have,' he said, grinning from ear to ear. 'Give me the straight Army every time, much safer. See you folks when we get off at Bantry. Nice talking to you.' He found his way back to the front of the coach gripping the seats to stop himself falling as the vehicle lurched round the sharp corners of the Irish roads. Kathy took Rick's left hand and squeezed it hard. They didn't say a word, but each knew the other was numbed by the news.

They completed the forty-five mile journey in a daze and hardly noticed the fabulous scenery as the coach climbed up the steep roads to the pass between Turners Rock and Baurearagh Mountain. Then the road dropped quickly down to Glengarriff and spread in front of them was a magnificent view of a bay. The guide was speaking into the amplifier system. 'Now ladies and gentlemen, we are

reaching the famous Bantry Bay which has been the scene
of much Irish industry and where today the biggest oil
tankers in the world can berth. Truly this remote place has
been the meeting place of nations. The French fleets sailed
into this bay in 1689 and again a hundred years later. In the
bay itself you can see Whiddy Island where are the ruins of
Reenabanny Castle built by the O'Sullivans, and on the
south side there is now a huge oil terminal.'

The guide went on talking but Rick and Kathy closed
their minds to him. They might physically be in the remote
South West of Ireland, but at that time their thoughts were
on the fatal shots fired on the other side of Europe, which
had finished a man's life. The event was not, for them, an
isolated one to be reeled off as an item of interesting news
and then quickly forgotten. It was the culmination of the
fatal procession of incidents, each one of which showed the
steady decay of America, and put at risk all those who tried
to serve her interests. Dick Welch was among the first to
suffer the consequences of the exposure of CIA secrets, who
would be next and where would it end? They hardly
noticed that the coach had arrived in Bantry.

After lunch they both felt better and enjoyed the more
leisurely drive to Ballydehob and past Roaringwater Bay to
the town of Skibbereen where they would be spending the
night. At dinner Kathy knew Rick's thoughts and did not
raise the subject for fear of upsetting him. On occasions like
this they were glad the children were with them – so
innocent and happy and still unaware of the terrors of
grown-up life. Maybe there are people who retain their
childhood innocence all their lives, thought Rick.

He looked at Mark and Deidre and wondered at what
point they would begin to suffer the tension and fears of the
adult world. They were sentenced, like all other children, to
inherit not only the good things of the world but, as a price
of that legacy, an accumulation of hates from past
generations. Rick tried to think of instances where the
hatreds had been stopped or abated. There were few. Jew
against Arab, Moslem against Hindu, white man against
Negro, Walloon against Fleming, Protestant against
Catholic: the antagonisms went on, without ceasing,

through the centuries.

The thoughts haunted him after Kathy had put the children to bed. They were sitting in deep armchairs around a large blackened fireplace with the peat burning briskly. There were times, he thought, when the terrible cycle had been broken, but like a chemical change it needed an explosion or some traumatic event to do it. The last great war was terrible, but it had resulted in the end of Nazism and in the end of the implacable hatred between the French and the Germans. The price paid had brought some lasting reward. The Atom Bomb had finished the war against Japan. Harry Truman had justified the mass murder of hundreds of thousands of people in Hiroshima and Nagasaki, on the grounds that more lives were saved by the war ending sooner. So the traumatic event had its effect. If worked, like electric shock treatment for brain disorders.

The processes of Rick's mind were bringing him to complete self-justification of his plan. As a sensitive person he had to be convinced of its moral purpose. He was not, like the Black and Tans, interested in destruction for destruction's sake. Far from it. His action would have the great merit of being selective and producing the traumatic shock necessary without involving unnecessary people.

The Easter Rising in 1916 had produced the shock which secured partial independence for Ireland within seven years. Without that shock England would still be in occupation today of Dublin, Skibbereen and the whole of Ireland. No doubt there had been faint hearts in 1916 who had argued against Michael Collins and the others who mounted that offensive. They would have said, 'Leave it to constitutional means,' but 'constitutional means' can only work when the offending party has been forced to accept the inevitability of defeat.

His plan had the value of Harry Truman's. It would produce an atom bomb effect but without widespread murder and destruction. Kathy went to bed leaving Rick on his own by the dying fire, now thinking about his next meeting with O'Connell and his group. Would they understand the significance of his plan? Suddenly he became conscious of a man standing behind him. It was

Peadar MacSwiney, the younger of the Provo officers.

'I'm staying with my sister at the moment, thought I would call on you. How is the trip?' he said.

'Going well,' said Rick, very pleased to see him.

'We are arranging a conference for you the day after next in Cork. Please say you are ill and miss that day's touring. We will wait for you by the back door of the *Metropole* ten thirty in the morning, after the rest have left, to take you to the meeting. You won't be back until late. We have a lot to discuss. Goodnight,' he said without much ceremony.

'Goodnight,' said Rick, accepting the absence of a handshake as a recognition of his belonging.

He crept silently to bed. Kathy was fast asleep and he soon joined her. It had been an exhausting day and he had found his peace of mind before its end.

The next morning the coach collected the party from the three hotels in the small town and set off for Rosscarbery, a charming jewel of a town set on a tiny bay. After Rosscarbery the guide announced a diversion from the main road to Clonakilty.

'We are going through the by-roads to pass the home of one of the founders of our Republic. All Irish leaders came from modest beginnings, our people only make money when they go to America,' he added daringly, but confidently, having established a rapport with his party over the past few days. After about two miles he said, 'This is Woodfield and it was from this tiny hamlet that the man known as the Big Fellow left to go to London. There was no work for him here so he had to go to England like so many of our people even today. Michael Collins came back from being a Post Office clerk to lead our country to freedom. It was a tragedy of the highest order when that great man was struck down by gunmen's bullets not twenty miles from here. He was only thirty-two when he died, and was acting as Chief Minister and Commander-in-Chief. All Irishmen mourn his loss.'

Rick looked out at the untidy fields and the simple cottages and felt proud. Out of such acorns grow great oaks, he thought.

Chapter Thirteen

Conference in Cork

The next place they visited was Kinsale, the picturesque seaport which received its Charter from King Edward III in 1333. Rick was amazed to hear from the guide that no Irish and no Catholics had been allowed to settle within the walls of the town, until the end of the eighteenth century, as for five centuries it had been kept as an exclusive preserve of the English.

The constant reminder at every stage of the tour of English injustice and English brutality strengthened his resolve to end the domination, finally. His solution was tough, but force could only be combatted with force. There was not an example in history of man's domination of others being broken without violence: death and some suffering to the oppressors was necessary, but out of that could be produced a greater good.

They passed through Belgooly, Ballymartle, Ballinhassig and Fivemilebridge, marvelling still at the age-old quality of the countryside as though it had hardly been touched for a thousand years; and on past the airport which, looking out of place in its modernity, was like the outpost or foothold of an alien and distant technological culture. Then into the city itself straddling the river and inspiring Spenser to write of it as standing on 'The Spreading Lee that, like an island Fayre, Encloseth Cork with his divided flood' as the guide quoted.

Cork, the second largest city in the Republic was tiny by any American standards, and its population would have been easily accommodated in one suburb of Philadelphia, but to Rick and Kathy, deprived for a week of contact with any town, it seemed a thriving metropolis. Rick had special reasons for his interest in Cork. It had been the spring for the gushing of protest against English rule, for it was here that the early Fenian Brotherhood had gained its first strength. Not for nothing had the city earlier gained the name 'Rebel Cork'.

They were accommodated in the *Metropole*, a large gloomy hotel which failed to convey much charm. However, it did have television and the children were pleased about that, although they had hardly missed it, such had been the excitement to their young senses of the new environment. It also had newspapers – in the South West Rick discovered that his pre-Christmas *Monitor* was more up to date than the local, late-delivered papers. Here, in Cork, he could read the *Irish Times*, at least, on day of publication.

He looked for old copies of the papers and found the three that had been published in Christmas week. He was anxious to check up on the story of Dick Welch's murder in Athens, but there was no report of it. Perhaps the old man had got it wrong, he wondered, but, no, he could hardly have concocted the story himself. Rick's eyes caught a report on the front page of the December 22 issue. BOMBING THWARTED AT BELFAST AIRPORT. The account described the hi-jacking of a lorry, the loading of a bomb and the explosion in a specially built pit. The attack had been frustrated and Rick felt a twinge of annoyance that the effort should have been so amateurish.

The report contained a statement by the Provisional IRA. 'We still honour the truce, fragile though it may be, but if it becomes apparent that our basic demands are to be rejected, then we have no alternative but to renew the armed struggle with an even greater intensity and ferocity than ever before.'

Rick reflected on the words 'greater', 'intensity', 'ferocity'; but what was the point, he thought, of doing more of the same isolated acts which had not worked before. They were just serving up more of the same medicine and the patient would get used to it. The demands made in the statement were clear enough – the withdrawal of British troops, 'the right of the Irish people to determine their own destiny', and amnesty for political prisoners, but it seemed to him that they lacked leadership. My plan, he though, will make that leadership superfluous as the demands on the English will be conceded without question.

Kathy was upset that Rick would miss the day's tour to Blarney Castle. Over the last few days she had seen her husband develop a new intensity in his manner and she was relieved that he now had some interests outside the Company. Not so secretly she had hoped for a long time that he would resign his appointment with the CIA and get a more settled job. Perhaps, she wondered, the new interest in Ireland would prove to be a stepping stone to his fulfilling her hopes.

At the appointed time Rick met Peader MacSwiney behind the *Metropole*. The young Irishman was driving a small van without any tradesman's markings and asked Rick to take the passenger seat. 'This is one of our delivery vans,' he said, 'we have a garage where we can paint them up in an hour or so with any name you choose for a butcher, baker or candlestick maker. And it's more comfortable to drive than a hearse.'

They crossed over St. Patrick's Bridge to the north side of the Lee and turned eastwards along the Lower Glanmire Road, passing a rather run down railway station on the right.

'Just over there,' said MacSwiney, pointing towards the north with his left hand, 'is the big Collins Barracks named after your forbears. We don't welcome attention from them. A lot of the soldiers are with us in spirit but they know their pay packets come from Dublin and they're scared to upset the powers that be.'

Now the road was skirting the River and Rick noticed with some surprise that it looked as filthy as the Delaware. They then passed through a depressing housing estate, which had the unlikely name of Tivoli, and Rick, remembering the attractive cottages of the village, wondered whether the Irish were not better off in the countryside.

After two miles they turned left at a roundabout: the signpost ahead said 'Cobh'. 'That was the road taken by thousands of people on their way to America,' said MacSwiney. 'They went on the emigrants' boats from Cobh; it was called Queenstown then. It was the ebbing away of our life-blood. Over two million went to America in a hundred years, imagine that: two million people. If we'd had work for them here, Ireland would have prospered. It wouldn't be the backwater it is today. The English left the industrial development – and the jobs – in England, that's why the Irish had to leave Ireland. They were forced out by the potato famine – and more than a million died of starvation. Imagine that: a million out of an eight million population dying of famine. It wasn't the fifteenth or sixteenth centuries, Mr. Collins, it was only in the last century. Imagine that: England at the height of her power, with a great Empire and very very rich, allowing a million people to die just across the Irish Sea. The English were more interested in India than in Ireland,' he said. 'A million deaths in India really did worry them, but there it was one million out of two or three hundred millions, not one out of eight as it was here.'

The view had become prettier now as the road had the Glashaboy River on one side and a wood on the other. 'Mr. Collins, imagine that: the population of Ireland down from eight million in 1850 to four and a half today in the whole of Ireland. We're the only country in the world to have fewer people than a hundred and twenty-five years ago. And birth control banned by both the Church and the Law! It doesn't make sense does it?'

Rick nodded in agreement.

They reached a Post Office, pulled into an alley way and stopped. 'We'll walk from here,' said MacSwiney, 'we won't leave the van outside the rendezvous, just in case.'

Rick glanced around. This was another of those quiet, Irish villages and yet only a few miles from the centre of the second largest city in Eire. It was clear to any observer that the country had been denuded of people. They passed the gates leading to the Irish College, crossed the road to walk up a slight hill and turned into a small family house facing a Church.

The front room was tiny, but just big enough for the five men. Rick noticed the Christmas cards on the mantelpiece and on the small roll-top desk, and the dozens of books in the two glass fronted bookcases. The home was obviously that of a studious man. There were present, in addition to Rick and MacSwiney, O'Connell and two others, who were introduced as Patrick Maloney and Joseph McKeon.

O'Connell opened the conference.

'I've asked Maloney and McKeon, two senior officers in my unit, to come down from Dublin to join us. Their association with any plan could be invaluable because of their international contacts; both have been on the continent and in Arab countries to get aid and supplies. They are completely trustworthy.' The two men, both in their early thirties, flushed at the compliment. O'Connell clearly held their respect.

'We have this report from Captain O'Halloran in Boston,' O'Connell went on. 'He says that our comrade here Richard Collins is a man of great experience in the American secret services, and has conceived a plan to help our cause. He is confident, that if successful, the plan will secure for us complete victory. And for this reason the plan has been called 'the Ultimate'. Is that correct, Mr. Collins?'

'Yes,' said Rick. 'I called it 'the Ultimate' because it will be the final point in the struggle.'

'Please explain,' said O'Connell.

'At every stage in the struggle against the English the Irish have always fallen short of success. The English do not take us seriously and they always think that any action we take can be controlled. If the campaign goes on as it is, there will be more deaths of Irishmen and little to show for it, except more English intransigence. What is happening in the six counties with Irish Catholics killing Irish Protestants and vice versa, is foolish and the English are laughing at us,' said Rick.

'Collins is right,' O'Connell intervened. 'The sectarian murders do no good and simply give the impression to the English public that this is a religious war, which it certainly is not. The political side of the struggle has not got across to the public over there. They don't understand that some of the foremost leaders for Irish freedom in the eighteenth century were Protestants – men like Henry Grattan and Wolfe Tone.'

'Wasn't Wolfe Tone killed?' asked Rick.

'He committed suicide after the English condemned him to death. They were frightened of him because he'd organised help from France after the French Revolution of 1789,' said O'Connell and added, 'Robert Emmett was another Protestant; the English hanged him. Considering the Protestants are just a small proportion of our population, their contribution to our cause has been outstanding.'

'It seems to me,' Rick went on, 'that the attack should be directed to where it really hurts and where it will be effective – not against other Irishmen. Once the enemy is defeated, those Irish who toady up to the enemy today will be one hundred per cent on our side tomorrow. And if any Scots or non-Irish want to leave Northern Ireland after the victory, they can do so. There should be no reprisals because my plan does not envisage building up the antagonism within Northern Ireland: it directs the hatreds to where they should go: England and London, in particular.

'But our boys are already active in London,' said MacSwiney. 'They've also let off bombs in Birmingham, Manchester and Glasgow.'

'And what good did it do?' asked Rick. 'It simply made the English public mad. We surely want the English man-in-the-street on our side, but he won't be if his favourite pub is being blown up. The bombs and assassinations are too sporadic to have the right effect: it's a case of two steps forward and three back.'

'I thought that about the Herrema kidnapping,' said O'Connell. 'He was a pleasant enough Dutchman and a popular man giving employment to Irishmen, and his experience, blown-up in the papers and on RTE,* didn't do us any good with public opinion here. Sure it was a bit of private enterprise by Gallagher and Coyle – we didn't give it any official blessing – but its failure means we can't now use the kidnapping weapon ourselves.'

'I am not suggesting kidnapping or propagandist moves to get strength in negotiations,' said Rick. 'The English have shown that they don't want negotiations.'

'What are you proposing then?' asked Maloney, who had begun with doubts about the clever American but was impressed by the good sense he was propounding.

'My plan,' said Rick, with quiet deliberation, is to eliminate the entire British Cabinet.'

'Wow,' said Maloney.

'Holy Mother of God,' said McKeon.

'It could be done,' said MacSwiney, intrigued.

'It was proposed before, y'know,' said O'Connell to everyone's disbelief.

'Not recently?' said Maloney.

'It was a long time ago,' said O'Connell, 'and if the plan had been put into effect then we would not have had to swallow an imposed and disreputable Treaty.'

'When was it put forward?' asked Rick.

'It was the plan of Cathal Brugha, the first Irish Minister of Defence; he put it forward in 1921,' said O'Connell.

Rick had never heard of Cathal Brugha and silently wondered if O'Connell had invented the unlikely name.

'Brugha was the strong man of the first Irish Cabinet, and he had the same ideas of dealing with the English as you have,' said O'Connell, turning towards Rick, 'but he was opposed and sabotaged by your Michael Collins.'

Rick was shaken. 'What?' he said weakly, 'is that really true?'

'Yes', said O'Connell. 'The Minister of Defence personally recruited the assassin; he was called Sean MacEoin, and was under Army orders. When Michael

* Radio Telefis Eireann

Collins, who was the Minister of Finance, heard about it, he arranged for the order to be countermanded by the Chief of Staff. It was a terrible thing to do. The Minister of Defence was simply following a policy which other Governments have often endorsed – including, I may add, the United States Government, Mr. Collins; I read the other day, it had planned the assassination of Castro,' he looked at Rick with a powerful stare.

'What happened to Sean MacEoin?' asked Rick, now fascinated.

'He was arrested by the English, in curious circumstances, without ever leaving Ireland. Michael Collins was conscience-stricken by the news and tried to help MacEoin to escape, but failed. MacEoin was a brave man; at his trial he said he was no murderer but an officer of the Irish Republican Army who had taken up arms in defence of his country. He said it was a privilege of all people to defend their native land and he craved neither mercy nor favour, just his rights as a soldier. It was to no avail, the English hanged him in Mountjoy Jail.'

Rick, alarmed at the renewed criticisms of Michael Collins, was very anxious to prove his own credentials.

'In view of what you say it is even more important to make the Brugha plan work now. If Michael Collins did sabotage it in 1921 – and I don't accept that – then the fact that I am proposing it now – fifty-five years later – should help to restore his name.'

O'Connell looked intently at Rick, and said:

'Mr. Collins, if you can implement the Brugha plan, you will not only add glory to the Collins name, you will be saving us from another half-century of anguish in Ireland.'

Chapter Fourteen

The up-dating of the Brugha Plan

For the rest of the day the five men sat in that tiny room working on the details of the plan. It was at this stage that Rick's training as a CIA officer proved to be of great value. The others, although extremely keen and well-experienced in matters of arms and explosives, were unable to strip away the inessentials of their thinking without guidance. Again and again the IRA officers came back to the concept of a propaganda move, limiting the operation to the killing of one Minister, perhaps the Secretary of State for Northern Ireland, or the Minister of Defence. Rick had to pull them away from such ideas by explaining that one or two deaths simply would not be effective enough. It would only be the Ross McWhirter assassination writ large, and no one man is indispensable, he argued. The elimination of all the Government Ministers at one time would, however, have a decisive effect as, in the circumstances of British party politics, they were irreplaceable – at least for a long time.

Even the killing of the Prime Minister, on his own, would not achieve the required objective. He would be speedily replaced by the Foreign Secretary, the Chancellor of the Exchequer, or some other senior Minister after a quick poll among Labour MPs. England would have a national mourning, there would be a grand funeral service in St. Paul's Cathedral, attended by many other Heads of State or Prime Ministers, probably matching that of Winston Churchill or John F. Kennedy, security would clamp down, but it would be business as usual before long and the charade would continue: the assassination of Lincoln did not destroy Lincolnism, nor did that of Kennedy destroy

Kennedyism – the change of direction was very gradual after their deaths.

But in Britain if the entire British Cabinet went in such circumstances, there would be a national constitutional crisis. No senior Minister would be alive to take over the reins of Government. Nor could twenty by-elections be held in a situation where the whole Party leadership had disappeared. It would be against all British ideas of fair play for the Opposition to take over the Government. Even if the Queen was ill advised enough to send for Mrs. Thatcher, as the leader of the largest party in the Commons, she could not accept the commission to form a Government, as the country would not stand for it, let alone the Labour Party or the Liberal Party. There would be a constitutional impasse.

Coalition might be proposed as a solution but would soon be rejected as impracticable, as no one could be found to lead it who would be acceptable to all sides. The Labour Party would, in any case, be leaderless and unable, for that reason, to enter into a coalition.

The five agreed that the British would have to sort out their own constitutional problems after the cleansing, but that immediately, when morale was lowest in England, an ultimatum should be issued by the IRA. It would state quite bluntly:-

1) All British troops must be withdrawn from Northern Ireland within seven days.

2) All United Kingdom citizens who had no wish to be considered as Irish, should have assisted passages to Great Britain and leave Northern Ireland within one month.

The ultimatum would make it clear that if England did not agree to these conditions the successor Government, however made up, would also sooner or later be eliminated. Powerful elements in Scotland and Wales would certainly agree to the terms because the breaking of English power would bring home rule, or independence, much nearer for the two Celtic nations.

Effective power in England would move from Parliament

back to the Crown, because Parliament would be impotent. The Queen would be able to act freely, untrammelled by the narrow considerations which had usually dictated British policy in the past.

It would be her duty to ensure the continuation of her Government and she would realize that this would only be possible if the IRA conditions were accepted. There would be no quarrel with England, in England, if England removed the occupying forces from Ireland. The English people would also be able to see the truth of this simple proposition once the clouds of mystery, confusion and propaganda had been blown away.

The Queen, as Commander-in-Chief of the Armed Forces, would have full constitutional authority to order the withdrawal and the British Chief of Staff would be foolish to advise her differently. The interests of the army were not served by fighting a war against guerrillas in Northern Ireland and the Army would be glad to get out.

With the demise of the Home Secretary, the Queen would be advised to welcome the proposed withdrawal from Northern Ireland. Everyone would be relieved at the removal of the cause of the terrorism within Great Britain and the task of the police in dealing with the increasing scale of ordinary crime would be that much easier.

The Lord Chief Justice, who would temporarily take over as head of the Judiciary on the death of the Lord Chancellor, would have to advise withdrawal because of the large number of men being brought before the Court for terrorism and murder, which would congest the Old Bailey.

The Governor of the Bank of England, in the absence of the Chancellor of the Exchequer, would re-assume his precedence over the Treasury, and would have to advise Her Majesty that if the crisis went on, the collapse of the value of the pound sterling from its previous $1.76 to the £ to a value approximately equal to one dollar to the £ could not be ruled out.

The Chairman of the Stock Exchange, following the announcement of the immediate suspension of all share dealings until further notice, would submit a respectful petition to Her Majesty pointing out that a failure to agree the IRA demands would lead to a catastrophic collapse of share values when dealings were allowed to recommence and a panic flight of capital from the country.

Pressure would come from industry and commerce, and also from the trade unions, for peace and stability and they would advise acceptance of the demands. The shock would affect the whole British people and the Committee of Ministers of the European Economic Community would also advise acceptance as economic and social collapse would have repercussions among all member states and weaken their military security as well.

The President of the United States would of course send a sincere message of condolence to Her Majesty and to the whole British people in their hour of grief and put the American armed forces on full alert, but he would be pleased to see peace at last in Ireland.

The General Assembly of the United Nations would probably be called in special session and might propose the setting up of a U.N. Peace-Keeping Force to patrol the troubled areas of Northern Ireland. But reunification would swiftly follow.

As Rick and the four IRA officers analysed the inevitable results of the implementation of the Brugha plan, it became clear to each of them that the pressures on the Queen to accept the ultimatum would be irresistible, and their resolve to ensure its successful implementation hardened.

They then discussed possible lines of attack and now Rick outlined what methods were relatively simple and, if possible, infallible. Failure, or discovery of the plan, must be prevented as it would bring the whole of the IRA and the campaign for a United Ireland into lasting disrepute. No one can quarrel with success, Rick had argued, but failure is devastating. He raised the analogy of Harry Truman. If the dropping of the two atomic bombs on Japan had not worked, and if Japan had gone on to win the war, or even if there had been stalemate or much later victory, Truman could have been tried as a war criminal.

McKeon had seen a film about a gang who stole an H-Bomb and primed it to go off in Whitehall, and he suggested seizing an H-Bomb as another possibility, but the others rejected it as a stupid idea. It could only be used as a threat to destroy millions of innocent people, including thousands of Irishmen, in London. The discussion, however, gave Rick an opportunity to establish the principles of simplicity as he saw them. Seizure of an H-Bomb was a major operation in itself that would require at least hundreds of men and would endanger security. Informers would certainly hear of the plan.

'We must exclude all fanciful ideas and get down to practical opportunities,' he said. Stealing an H-Bomb was not a practical proposition and they could waste all their energies on pursuing such ambitious plans without getting anywhere. It was impractical to think of using more than ten men, and this ruled out an armed attack on Whitehall or Chequers, the Prime Minister's country home, where Ministers sometimes met in Cabinet session. The use of aircraft was also ruled out as that operation was hazardous and would probably warn the enemy to take precautions.

McKeon suggested approaches to a friendly country, possibly one of the Arab states, to provide sophisticated equipment, but Rick knocked the idea. Governments were very leaky, as he knew from his experience, and the prospects of the CIA or the KGB or the French Secret Service *not* obtaining the information, were very remote. As soon as any Government discovered the plot they would pass it on to the British authorities. The Russians would not keep it to themselves. It would be no advantage to them if the Irish problem were solved. They preferred it to continue as a running sore in Britain's side.

The group broke off for tea and sandwiches. These were produced by Maloney and McKeon, as the couple who were tenants of the house had been sent away for the day. During this late lunch break – Rick noticed that the time had already reached three o'clock – O'Connell started to chide Rick on the lack of effectiveness of the CIA. We must learn from CIA mistakes he kept saying, somewhat to Rick's annoyance. He felt like saying they should also learn from IRA mistakes but curbed his tongue in time. O'Connell had a sharp intellect and he did not want to engage in more verbal battles.

O'Connell was well informed on the subject of CIA operations and no doubt had done his research when he knew Rick was coming under his command. He spoke of the amateurish attempts by CIA officers in Leopoldville to assassinate Lumumba, the former Congo leader, of how CIA technician Joseph Scheider had equipped himself with rubber gloves, mask and syringe, to inject poison into Lumumba's food; but the plan failed because no one could get near Lumumba. 'According to your Senate investigating committee,' O'Connell said – Rick cringed at this point – 'the instructions to kill Lumumba came directly from Allen Dulles.' But even the head of the CIA could not achieve the assassination and it was left to Moise Tshombe to do the dirty work.

'You help to prove my point,' Rick argued. 'The CIA plan was too complicated. Tshombe's was simple.'

O'Connell raised the case of Castro, where the CIA had completely failed. The Kennedy Administration wanted Castro killed and apparently, said O'Connell, quoting something he had obviously read very recently, both John and Robert Kennedy 'chewed up' Richard Helms, the CIA chief, for 'sitting on his ass and not doing anything about getting rid of Castro'. Then the CIA sent Castro a box of cigars which had been made lethal with botulinum toxin, but they went to the wrong person. 'How stupid can you get,' remarked O'Connell, 'delivering cigars to Castro – it would be as stupid for the Americans to send poisoned Guinness to Dublin.'

O'Connell was equally scathing about the CIA recruitment of the Mafia to do a gangland 'contract' on Castro, a plan which failed because the gangsters lost their nerve. And as for the plot to have an exotic seashell placed on the seabed, designed to explode when Castro went skin-diving, and the attempt to donate a contaminated diving suit to the Cuban leader, O'Connell had the group laughing their heads off at the improbability of the bizarre schemes.

Rick felt chastened, but O'Connell did not stop and

made a telling observation: because the CIA had mishandled the early assassination attempts, President Kennedy had felt compelled to authorise the Bay of Pigs invasion of Cuba in 1961, nearly bringing about a world war. 'But,' claimed O'Connell, 'the action we are planning against the British Cabinet will not bring war, but stop the civil war in the North.

During the afternoon and early evening, the group turned its attention to logistics. It was agreed that Mac-Swiney and Maloney would be released from their gun and explosive importing duties and allocated to work full-time with Rick on the project. MacSwiney had close links with the Germans anarchists and Maloney had useful contacts in certain Arab countries. They would not reveal any crucial details, but help from those sympathetic quarters could be obtained within the general context of the war. Aid to the IRA had already been given willingly, and O'Connell was confident that relevant assistance would be forthcoming again.

As to the blueprint for the action, the group accepted that initial sketches should be produced by Rick, using all the information and resources which MacSwiney and Maloney could gather for him. Rick cautioned them on the need to be patient, explaining that in the CIA the effective projects were those which had sufficient time devoted to them. Rome was not built in a day and the whole British Cabinet could not be eliminated within a week or a month. Hasty action would invite detection and danger.

Asked to estimate the time required, Rick said gestation should be between nine and eleven months and execution between seven and ten days. They looked in their diaries and marked off the critical dates between September 29 and November 29, 1976.

As Rick would be based in Italy from February, Maloney and MacSwiney would visit him as required, but arrangements would also be made for Rick to travel to Eire. For this purpose an Irish passport would be obtained in an assumed name and Rick would always travel on the direct flights, avoiding changing planes at London Heathrow. We

give strict instructions to all our people when going to and
from the continent, never to go through British airports,
explained O'Connell. The British police have no
compunction about arresting travellers who remain in the
international transit area and who never cross the passport
desks. To give them this opportunity Scotland Yard had
taken over the control of Heathrow from the British Airport
Authority police.

O'Connell added that there were ten direct flights to
Paris from Dublin each week and direct flights to Rome on
Tuesdays and Saturdays. The Irish passport, he said as an
afterthought, could be obtained not in an assumed name,
but in the Gaelic for Richard Collins – namely Ristéard
O'Coiléain.

'Now, Mr. Collins,' he said with a twinkle, 'you will have
to learn some Irish to justify that.'

Rick returned to the *Metropole* to meet Kathy and the
children in time for dinner.

'You missed a good day,' she said, 'Blarney Castle was
very interesting – and it's only three or four miles from
Cork.'

'Did you kiss the stone?' asked Rick.

'No, but Mark did,' she replied, 'he had to do it hanging
upside down to make it for real. Now, beware, he will have
the "gift of the gab".'

Rick smiled, he could think of one man who certainly had
kissed the Blarney stone: O'Connell.

Chapter Fifteen

An Irishman from Germany

Peadar MacSwiney, as a man of Cork, was keen to show Richard Collins more of his home city; the Irishman was also anxious to establish the closest possible understanding with the American. Ristéard O'Coiléain, as he now preferred to think of him, had burst into his life with amazing effect. In all the four years of his active involvement with the Irish Republican Army, MacSwiney had not encountered anyone with such strength of character, determination and brilliance of thinking. O'Connell was very good in his way and the Commander of his unit obviously had a good brain, but MacSwiney was acutely aware that O'Connell lacked a sense of direction. O'Connell, and the others he had met in the High Command, never seemed able to provide the younger man with a coherent glimpse of the final objective. But the stranger from Philadelphia had done it at one meeting.

MacSwiney could not at first understand what it was about the make-up of the American that had caught his imagination. What O'Coiléain had said and the manner in which he had approached the problems of the struggle, reminded him of his own attitude five years before, when he had first returned from Germany. At that time MacSwiney had been very upset by the experience of his reunion with his native Ireland. As a boy in the early nineteen-sixties, he had been taken to live in Hamburg; his father, an engineer, had obtained a well-paid job in the Blomm and Voss Shipyards. The German economic revival at that time was sucking millions of foreign workers into the Republic to service the growing demands of industry.

MacSwiney Senior and a few other Irishmen joined the throng of Yugoslavs, Turks, Algerians and nationals of similarly backward countries seeking work in the most dynamic industrial country of Europe.

Peadar and his younger sisters were sent to the local schools. He soon learned to speak excellent German and made many German friends. After two years in hostels they lived in a pleasant brick house in Buxtehude, on the outskirts of Hamburg, rented from a German engineer on a five year contract on an irrigation project in Tehran. MacSwiney, on overtime almost every week, was earning a good income of which he managed to save about a third. After the first three years, Mrs MacSwiney went to work in a bakery and her wages added to the family resources.

As the MacSwineys could not both save and afford frequent journeys back to Ireland, the young Peadar saw little of his native land during his most formative years. He could only recall two Christmasses back in Cork, one when he was eleven and again when he was sixteen. In his teenage years he began to suspect that his father's sudden departure from Cork was not entirely motivated by job considerations. He found out on one of his later trips that MacSwiney, Senior, had fathered an illigitimate baby by his son's own schoolmistress, whom Peadar could vaguely recall as a happy, vivacious teacher. The scandal had been too great and the move to somewhere like Hamburg was inevitable if they were to escape the constant reminder of it.

MacSwiney, Senior, had been determined not to emigrate to England to work as many other Cork men had done. He had a deep emotional resentment against the English, caused by the traumas suffered by branches of the family during the troubles of 1916 and 1922; he could not stomach the prospect of working in an English firm under Englishmen for the benefit of the English economy.

There were thus two cultural influences on Peadar as a young man. The romantic attachment to Ireland, which was encouraged by his father's constant descriptions of Irish glories and aspirations, and the heavier philosophy of North Germany.

Soon after his sixteenth birthday, Peadar took on work in a Hamburg shipping office, where his knowledge of languages and his lively interest in geography and aspects of trade, were valuable assets. Through this office Peadar formed a close association with a group of young Germans who combined a hectic, and sometimes exotic, social life with long discussions on political philosophy. They most enjoyed stripping the cant from the shibboleths of contemporary society. As their parents by their own efforts had built a comfortable environment from the ashes of war, the offspring could afford to indulge in the luxury of analysing that society's fundamental faults. And night after night they did so with relish, questioning the materialist standards which could only be measured in Deutsch Mark terms, and probing the conscience of the German race which could produce both Beethoven and Schiller and the Commandants of the Nazi concentration camps.

Many of the group were deeply antagonistic to their parents who had been caught, as almost all Germans were, in the fatal sway of Hitlerism. They could not understand how their parents could have served in the Army or the S.S. Some of them flirted with the Young Communist Movement as it seemed to them that Communism, being the antithesis of Nazism, would help salve the guilt bequeathed by Nazi fathers.

Peadar went to some of these meetings but was not impressed by the concentration on jejune dialectics. He thought Communism failed because it did not concern itself with practical problems and he also felt that most of the Communist members were not facing up to the issues of human freedom raised, for instance, by the Soviet occupation of Czechoslovakia. He could see too many parallels between Russian aggrandisement and the English cultural and economic domination of Ireland over the centuries.

For a year or two he was an active member of the SPD youth movement, preferring the more positive and practical philosophy of the pragmatic socialist party, to the dictatorship of the intellect which went with Communism. It was in the SPD, when he was supporting the campaign for the return of an SPD majority to the Hamburg Senate, that he met Ingrid. She was just seventeen, slim, but with a well proportioned body which she carried with the grace of a model. Her flaxen hair was pleated in the old fashioned way and hung down to her waist. Her cheeks were round and soft, her eyes a deep aquamarine with a sparkle even when she was angry, and her wide lips, on which she put no visible makeup, were lush.

Ingrid's father, a successful lawyer in Hamburg, was one of the candidates and Peadar had been allocated to work in his district of Barmbeck. On election night when Peadar and Ingrid were both invigilating the counting of votes in a room at one of the beerhalls, they suddenly discovered they were holding hands. It had happened involuntarily. Ingrid was attracted to the tall, handsome Irishman. He had a courtesy and a charm which had eluded the rough, brash Germans of her acquaintance. She liked his wavy and long russet hair, his bushy sideburns and deep voice with its accent tinged with a trace of Irish brogue in spite of perfectly accurate and well spoken German. Besides, she loved his genorosity of spirit and his gentleness.

He did not demand instant sex, which so many of the other boys expected. After the election he was seeing her for three weeks before she allowed his hand to wander over her breasts, and he was always patient. Other men would have dropped her flat for being a tease, but not so Peadar who once told her, flatteringly, that true Irishmen were prepared to spend years wooing the maiden of their choice and would then make the union last.

One hot summer when Ingrid was nearly eighteen, she went, with Peadar, to a socialist youth camp on the Baltic coast near Kiel. Most of the girls were sleeping with the boys and the atmosphere of unforced permissiveness encouraged Ingrid to lose her inhibitions. As only a very few of the girls had decided to go into single sex tents, it was easier for Ingrid to slip into Peadar's small tent.

On the first night they were together, they remained

naked, under a single blanket touching and fondling but neither wishing to destroy the magical quality of the encounter by going any further. Next day, when they were swimming in the cold water of the Baltic, Peadar took Ingrid's hand firmly and gasped that he loved her and would be faithful for ever. Ingrid clutched at the young Irishman to return his expressions of love with kisses on his neck, cheeks and mouth. It was a gorgeously hot day, tempered by a cool breeze coming over the water from Sweden and they sat for hours on Schönberger Strand, arms entwined, in a windbreak with its back to the sea.

Peadar remembered reading about the Celtic customs of courtship, of how the boy and the girl are put together in a straw hut for a night with the girl's virginity protected by a belt, and this test of endurance was supposed to separate the genuine love from the carnal lust. He had never believed the fable but now after the experience of the night before, he understood the relevance of it. He now knew that he respected Ingrid and treasured her and she would be loved forever.

That night they made love. At first it was painful for Ingrid, who was still a virgin but Peadar, who had lost his virginity at fifteen in circumstances he wished to forget, was understanding and gentle. They reached a glorious fulfillment in the union of their bodies, each of them experiencing a new rich dimension to their lives. From that time Ingrid vowed never to flirt with another boy, for in Peadar she had found her ideal. Some of the young Germans, wishing to penetrate the nubile young woman, resented the foreigner for what they considered, wrongly, to be his successful conquest. Peadar avoided quarrelling with them openly as they could never be expected to understand the sincerity of his relationship with the girl.

Eighteen months later tragedy struck the family. MacSwiney Senior was crushed by a falling crane in the shipyard. After a tense three weeks in hospital, when several times he came close to death, he was discharged as a permanent cripple. The family could not stay in Germany as they were migrant workers and, as Ireland was not yet a member of the EEC, the full State social security benefits were not available. With a lump sum in compensation for the accident, the family returned to Cork. Peadar had wanted to remain in Hamburg to be near his beloved Ingrid, but could not allow his mother, now distraught with grief, to return without the only male able-bodied member of the family.

They returned to Cork just as violence was flaring up seriously in Northern Ireland. The talk was all about the civil rights movements in Londonderry and Belfast and equal opportunities for Catholics: the Protestants had always obtained the best houses and the best jobs. A twenty-one year old firebrand called Bernadette Devlin had won an election to the Westminster Parliament and was speaking fervently about the injustice. The leader of a little known Protestant religious sect, Ian Paisley, was haranguing the non-Catholic crowds on the evils of Popery and the dangers of any concession to Catholic Eire. The situation was rapidly developing from the relative quiescence of the previous thirty years to one which looked explosive. Passions were running high.

Peadar searched for a job in Cork to suit his talents. An insurance office offered him a position as a clerk and a hotel a job as a porter, with prospects to become a receptionist, but he rejected both. Then he was approached by the local command of the Provisional IRA who needed him to supervise the import of arms from Germany and other countries. It was a risky appointment as the Irish Government, under pressure from the British, were maintaining vigilant coastguard patrols to detect such smuggling. But the Republican cause had many friends among the fishermen and sailors, who used the harbours of Cork, Kinsale, Glandore, Crookhaven and Bantry, and usually they found a way to avoid the coastguards and the Irish navy.

Peadar was enthused by the cause as all his reading of Irish history had convinced him that Ireland's grievance was deep and must be remedied. The opportunity to travel also encouraged him to join the command, as it could include journeys to Hamburg where he could see Ingrid. Before he left there had been a tearful farewell with Ingrid pledging herself to Peadar whatever happened.

The romantic impression that Peadar had acquired of the Irish rebellion against the English, was rudely shaken within months of his return. Most Irish people he found, languid and disinterested; for them the Northern squabble was a long way removed and should not be allowed to impinge on the tranquillity of Eire. 'Why get mixed up in it,' he heard people say. 'If the Catholics want to live in a free Catholic society, let them move south,' adding that too many Catholics in Northern Ireland protested vigorously against the English but took their handouts in the form of social security payments without hesitation.

And in the Movement itself he found many lethargic people, eminently good at propping up Dolan's Bar until two o'clock in the morning, lambasting the British but hopeless at undertaking practical work for the cause. He suspected many of them were secret informers. As for the activists, few of them were outstandingly able. Too often they waited for another to give a lead, rather than taking the initiative themselves.

Peadar was struck by the number of senior leaders who were born in England with only one Irish parent, and some he suspected had no Irish parents at all. They were always the most pressing and bitter as though they had to compensate for their English connection. Several of them had adopted Gaelic names and attempted to learn Irish. Many of the leaders and strategists were not able to project their minds properly to the future and Peadar wondered if, in fact, they regarded the campaign as a permanent fixture of Irish-English relations without any possible solution.

Because of this he found Ristéard O'Coiléain refreshing. It was because they were both expatriate Irishmen, drawn to the cause for objective and idealistic motives, and able to see through the humbug of those who had never been stirred from their complacency, that he had a rapport with the American. He was glad that action to bring results was now proposed. In the past four years Peadar and his group had brought considerable quantities of guns and ammunition into the country, and had successfully transferred them to the guerrillas in the north. But he had strong doubts as to whether the tools he had sweated to obtain had been used to the best advantage.

On the day after the conference, Peadar called early at Rick's hotel to suggest that he took the family for a day's outing. He had managed, overnight, to borrow a friend's car, a respectable looking Vauxhall which could take everyone quite comfortably. Rick thought a moment and then agreed but he cautioned Peadar, 'On no account talk about the project in front of my wife or the children.'

Kathy was pleased to meet Peadar. He was the first Irishman she had met as a friend in Ireland, and she was especially glad to meet one of Rick's contacts. When Peadar talked about his importing from Europe, Kathy thought Rick must have been advising them about foreign trade, on which he was something of an expert.

Peadar took them to a huge stone circle at Dromberg, mainly because he was fascinated by Irish pre-history and assumed the Americans would be also. They were amazed by its size and symmetry, not as big as Stonehenge appeared in photographs they had seen, but nevertheless impressive as evidence of the astronomical understanding of the early Irish. 'These stones were erected just around the time of the Lord Jesus' birth,' explained Peadar, 'but the pottery discovered near here dates back to 2,000 BC.'

At a simple meal in a nearby tavern, Peadar described some of the history of his city of Cork. It had been a centre of medieval literature and culture but even before that the monasteries had been influential. The place was raided by the Vikings at least five times, and then by the English who made it a dependancy of the Crown. Over the centuries the Irish tried to recapture their city and sometimes succeeded only to be fought back, on one occasion by Cromwell and on another by the Duke of Marlborough.

'It was a valuable prize for the conquerors then,' said Rick, and went on to ask Peadar about his own family connections with Cork.

'We've always been in Cork. MacSwiney is a famous name.'

'Why?' asked Rick.

'In 1920 the English assassinated the Lord Mayor, a man called MacCurtain, and one of my old relatives was elected in his place. His name was Terence MacSwiney. The English, however, flung him into Brixton Prison in London and in protest the Lord Mayor went on a hunger strike. He kept it on for seventy-four days but the English did nothing to save him and he died. Today Terence MacSwiney is looked upon as a martyr.'

'My God,' said Kathy, 'you mean the British actually let a Lord Mayor starve to death without doing anything about it?'

'It's only too true,' said Rick, shaking his head.

When they arrived back at the *Metropole*, Kathy took the children upstairs for supper in their bedroom and Rick asked Peadar into the bar for a drink. He felt drawn to this young man, for he had both an engaging manner and considerable intelligence and even sophistication, quite unlike the others he had met, whose qualities were considerable but different.

Over several whiskeys Peadar told Rick about his German background and his experience in negotiating for arms on the Continent. Now Rick could understand the reasons for the young man's flair; his value to the project would be very great.

'When I get back to Europe in February,' Rick said, 'we will meet up in Paris and go to Germany together. I want to locate some special equipment and you can help me a lot.'

Chapter Sixteen

A New Year in Dublin

Rick was pleased with the progress he had made with the Provisionals, and the abrasive effect of the confrontation at Shehan's Cross had worn off by this time. He was satisfied that Peadar would be a first rate member of the organising team and Patrick Maloney also had good potential.

On the coach from Cork to Waterford, Rick let his eyes take in the green panorama of South East Ireland, but his mind was on other thoughts. There were still a number of hurdles to overcome. Finance was one. O'Connell had agreed to release his two best men, but Rick had no guarantee that all their expenses would be paid. Although O'Connell had not admitted it, he had the distinct impression that the organisation lived from hand to mouth. It had always been the case with freedom movements, he supposed, but what they missed in money they made up with dedication.

To fulfill the project meant using sophisticated equipment and that would be expensive. As the coach trundled on he tried to work out a budget. It was not easy as there were still too many unknowns, but he could not see it costing less than two hundred thousand, and possibly much more. It was possible he could 'borrow' some of what he needed from the Company, but this thought he soon discarded. The CIA has vast funds at its disposal. Its total expenditure was enormous – no one knew how much as so much of its work was shrouded in operational secrecy, but it ran to hundreds, maybe, thousands of millions. To siphon off some of the funds would be possible, particularly in the new context of the Italy job, but to use Company money on this scale on an unapproved project, could be found out. Since the Church Committee had started its Congressional probing, an element of parsimony had crept into the Company and the Treasurers were more careful how they doled out the funds. Rick considered it would be stupid to be vulnerable to suspicion on the money question when there were so many other areas with a danger of detection.

He was still wrestling with the problem when they arrived at the Waterford glass works. This was the part of the package tour he could well do without: the tourists were a captive audience, sentenced to be bombarded by the expert guides who thought everyone should be as interested in the techniques of glass production as they were. It was not fair to include the commercials when the tourists had all paid the full cost of the holiday. Rick had seen in the programme a visit scheduled for the Guinness Brewery – that was different, at least they would get to sample the product.

After Waterford it was on to Kilkenny to see its castle and to buy souvenirs. Rick was by now looking forward to Dublin and there, on the last stage of the holiday, he felt he could have some respite from being a packaged tourist for the convenience of the tour guide. Soon they were passing through some fabulous countryside and following a wide, fast-moving and incredibly clean-looking river. Rick, for the first time that day, was distracted from his thoughts for here stretched out before him was the emerald isle of his dreams.

Just as the coach approached the bridge over the River Nore taking them into County Wexford, Rick noticed the old engineer descending on him again. Would he never give up, though Rick.

'Haven't seen much of you; you missed Blarney, pity for you, you should have kissed the stone, help you sell that warehousing stuff,' he said.

The guide, interrupting the interrupter, was now talking into the microphone. 'We are passing through the town of New Ross' – Rick thought it was a dreary place – 'which was the home of the Kennedy clan. The great-grandfather of the American President John F. Kennedy emigrated to the United States from here.'

The old engineer took the cue and turned to Rick.

'Well, what do you know about that? Amazing, isn't it, that a simple farmer from this backward place can come to America and create the rich, powerful dynasty of the Kennedys? Land of opportunity, America, that's what freedom can do, can't beat it.'

Rick grunted, wishing the old man would go away.

'Funny,' the engineer went on, 'so many Presidents came from Ireland. Even more from Northern Ireland than from the South. Did you know that six Presidents had both parents from Ulster, including Jackson, Buchanan, McKinlay and Wilson, and seven other Presidents had one parent from Ulster. Fantastic, isn't it, for such a small place to produce so many Presidents, and yet now they can't find anyone with any ability to run their own affairs. Doesn't make sense does it?'

But one point did make sense to Rick. He remembered what O'Connell had been saying about America's failure to press Britain to allow Ireland her freedom as part of the Versailles Peace Treaty. Woodrow Wilson was President. That explained it. An Ulsterman was simply not in favour of a free Ireland and no wonder the United States did not stir itself at that time. Blood runs deep.

In Dublin Rick willingly went through the rituals of the tour for Kathy's sake; she was taking it all in with the fortitude of a tourist who was determined not to miss a cent's worth. They went to the National Museum to see the Tara brooch and the Feakle treasure and to Trinity College Library to see the Book of Kells.

'Fancy all these wonderful works of art, over a thousand years old,' Kathy said. 'Makes America seem very young doesn't it? But it's comforting to know that our Irish roots go deep.'

Rick was glad his wife was feeling that way; it would help her to understand him later. Then, much to Rick's surprise, O'Connell rang him at the hotel to invite them both to join him to see in the New Year. 'We can celebrate,' he said, 'the birth of the year in which Irish freedom will be achieved at last. Two hundred years after America, but better late than never.'

Rick gave a big tip to a chambermaid to babysit the children, who were exhausted by the traipsing around Dublin and had no energy left to get up to any mischief.

'I'm taking you to the Abbey. It's a special Irish treat,' O'Connell said, after introducing his wife, Maureen.

'Is that the theatre?' asked Kathy.

'Oh! no, its a tavern, but it's not the tavern in the town, it's right out on the peninsula in Dublin Bay,' he replied.

They drove off to Howth along a coast road which overlooked the cold, grey sea, twinkling here and there with the lights of buoys.

'Here we are,' said O'Connell, 'the home of the Irish ballad,' taking them into a festive scene of happy people. 'Be sure to listen, 'tis beautiful music; they play on the spoons here,' as well as the fiddles and the uileann.'

'What's the uileann?' asked Kathy, enjoying herself hugely.

'It's an old Irish pipe,' said Maureen, 'I can play one.'

The place reeked of Sweet Afton and Guinness fumes, but it was far from unpleasant for the two Americans, who adored the atmosphere of Irish joviality. This would be a night to remember.

About an hour before midnight, Rick became aware of a young man watching him and O'Connell intently. No ordinary visitor to the tavern would have noticed him but Rick was not a normal guest; his sixth sense – heightened by his training – told him that the man was not entering into the spirit of the night. He was dressed in a white roll-necked sweater and dark tweed jacket and for most of the evening he had sat on his own in a corner, nursing his drink. Without letting the man notice his interest, Rick stole several glances in his direction.

It was true: the man was watching with the dull, unmoving face of someone who is resenting doing a job when he wants to be somewhere else. Rick cross-checked

his first and second impressions to make certain he was not
becoming slightly paranoic: it was an occupational hazard
as a secret agent. But he was now convinced he had not
made a mistake as the man's interest was more than a
passing curiosity. They were under surveillance. No doubt
about it. Who could it be?

'In Dublin's fair city,

Where girls are so pretty,' the Abbey Singers were on
again.

'I first set my eyes on sweet Molly Malone.'

It was a curious situation, among friends, but being
watched. If the man was from the CIA local Station it was
very dangerous. It could mean the Company itself had
suspicions about his activities. Could he be MI6, he
wondered. It would not be beyond the British to have their
spies at work even on New Year's Eve.

The crowd was now singing lustily,

'Crying, cockles and mussels, alive, alive, oh.'

Rick leaned over to O'Connell and whispered his doubts
about the sinister-looking man.

'She was a fishmonger

But sure 'twas no wonder

For so were her father and mother before.'

O'Connell made his way to the back of the tavern and,
buying more Guinness and whiskey, was talking to one of
the barmen who nodded his head as if acknowledging a
request.

'Crying cockles and mussels, alive, alive, oh.'

O'Connell returned and said loudly, 'Here you are, drink
the best Guinness straight from the brown Liffey river,' and
sotto/voce, 'don't worry we'll soon find out who he is.'

'And that was the end of sweet Molly Malone.

But her ghost wheels her barrow

Through streets broad and narrow,

Crying, cockles and mussels, alive, alive, oh.'

The barman came back after half-an-hour and later
O'Connell said quietly to Rick, 'He's only plain clothes
Garda. He'll be sure to ask who you are, so I've dropped the
word to the barman to say Kathy and Maureen are cousins

and this is a family reunion. It's not you he'd be after, I'm
the object of his eye. Worried we'll be blowing up the Four
Courts again, or something of the like.'

The New Year of 1976 came in with a rousing welcome
from the boisterous crowd, the men kissing every girl within
reach.

'I'll not be seeing you before you leave on Saturday,'
O'Connell said to Rick, after they had driven back to
Dublin and the wives were chatting separately. 'One thing I
want to say. I think Maloney should go to Libya before he
meets you in Italy next month. He can raise some money
there for the project. Gaddafy hates the English. We've
already had lots of help from him.'

'That is a good idea,' said Rick, relieved that O'Connell
had thought of the financial side, 'and thanks for the party,
it was great,' he added as the wives returned. 'Wonder
where we'll all be next New Year's Eve.'

'Maybe at a celebration party in Belfast or Stormont,'
O'Connell said, indiscreetly.

On the TWA Charter plane back to Boston from
Dublin's fair city, Rick felt supremely happy. Kathy and
the children had enjoyed the holiday; they had spent more
time together, despite his diversions, than he could ever
remember before. The children now had a feel for mother
Ireland, which pleased him. Most important, Rick in
himself sensed a greater strength and resilience than he had
ever thought possible. He was a new man, a man reborn.

As the Boeing 707 winged over Ireland towards the
Atlantic, he reflected on this experience. It was
extraordinary that during the five or six weeks since his
nightmare, which he could still remember vividly, he had
been transformed as a person. Just those few weeks before
he had been living in a narrow dimension. He had always
imagined himself a deep person but he had been kidding
himself. He had never penetrated more than an inch
beneath the surface. Ireland had enabled him to dig deep
down and find the real Richard Collins.

He looked down the plane, which seemed so narrow and
small after the 747s and DC10s he was more accustomed to

flying. How many of these hundred or so people had been able to find the truth about themselves as he had done, he wondered. Probably very few. Most of them were skating on the surface of life and fooling themselves that it was the real thing. Fooling themselves and fooling other people. The relationships between people were shallow because so few of them ever came to understand their own individual depths. They could not communicate their full potential to others as it was lying dormant, undiscovered, like a deep gold mine or oil well.

For most of the journey so far a blanket of cloud had obscured his view of Ireland but he felt it was there, below, as a great source of energy, re-charging his batteries. Then the cloud cleared and he could see they were crossing a wild and rocky coast; County Mayo, or maybe Donegal, he thought. Then they were over the sea.

Rick fell asleep to the rythmic drone of the engines. He slept surprisingly well, and sooner than he had expected woke to find they were over Newfoundland and on the final leg over Nova Scotia to Cape Cod.

They had left after breakfast and arrived just after midday, thanks to the time zone change. Logan International airport was very busy. They had to join long lines of travellers waiting to pass the booths where the Immigration Officers were examining passports and checking the names in huge folders.

Eventually Rick reached the officer on his line. The man expertly checked the index and then looked at Rick knowingly.

'You're all through, Mr. Collins, but that man over there is waiting to see you. Would you step this way please.'

For a moment Rick felt a tremor of fear. He was being beckoned into a side room which was obviously used for special interviews.

'Wait for me in the baggage arrival area, Kathy. Here are the tags. I'll be right with you.'

She did not have time to answer.

The tall, youngish and studious-looking man who was standing nearby, shook Rick's hand.

'Richard Collins?'

Rick nodded his head.

'I'm Andrew Bird. I'm with the Company too. I was told this morning to pull you off the plane. They want you in Virginia fast. I've got you booked on the next flight south. It goes out in an hour.'

Chapter Seventeen

If only the
Catholics were Black

The New Year for Graham Commin started well. The Stock Market was buoyant and the Financial Times index soon went through the four hundred barrier. There was a renewed zest in the City, as though the worst of the recession had passed. The pressure for shares had been so great that at times they could not cope with the buying orders. It was just like old times.

Valerie, though, was getting moodier. She did not have enough to occupy her mind and had not even yet adjusted to Britain since her long stay abroad. She became too upset by passing events which did not affect her directly. The Irish business was also none of her concern.

All the same, he reflected, the situation was a bit worrying. Some people had thought the release of all the detainees, who had been kept in prison in Ulster without trial, would improve the chances of a peaceful settlement. The Secretary of State had thought so too. But instead the tide of horror had grown. Almost as soon as the New Year celebrations were over, the bombs went off: in a Protestant pub in County Armagh killing three people. Within forty-eight hours the retaliation came with a vengeance: on the first Sunday evening of the year at Whitecross, also in Armagh, six gunmen broke into the family home of the Catholic Reavey family and shot dead two brothers aged twenty-five and twenty-three, while they were watching television. The remaining brother ran upstairs to hide under a bed. He was pulled out by his legs, shot in the stomach, and left for dead. He survived to crawl two hundred yards to a neighbouring farmhouse for help.

Another group of gunmen called at an isolated farmhouse near Lurgan in the north of the County, pushed past the mother and strode into the living room to shoot dead three members of the Catholic O'Dowd family. A party was in progress to celebrate the return home of Barry O'Dowd who worked on a North Sea oil rig. He was playing the piano at the time for the children present when, in front of their young eyes, he and the two others were killed without warning.

There had been no evidence to link any of these people with earlier crimes. They were innocents, made the victims of a ghastly tit-for-tat assassination game which rivalled the gang killings of the Mafia in their gross brutality.

The reaction to these murders of Catholics had come even quicker than had the Protestant backlash. Within twenty-four hours a mini-bus was ambushed; it was carrying home textile workers who had spent the day making Irish linen. All the occupants were ordered out and the gunmen asked if there were any Catholics in the group. One, the driver, was allowed to go and the remaining eleven were mown down with machine gun fire. Only one survived, the rest dying on the open country road, as if murdered by a Nazi SS squad.

Commin could see no end to it. Where the hell was the solution? He could only be thankful that he personally was not involved. It was a madhouse. Even the Secretary of State was now calling the killers gangsters and psychopaths. The *Daily Mirror* had printed one of its dramatic editorials calling for British troops to be withdrawn. Maybe they were right, but it would be the coward's way out.

The Government, to give them their due, reacted firmly to the renewed killings. Another six hundred troops were going in, bringing the Ulster garrison to over fifteen thousand. Harold Wilson had called a special meeting at Number 10 and then announced that the crack Strategic Air Service unit was also being transferred to South Armagh. It looked and smelt like war.

Commin decided he would attend the debate on

Northern Ireland when the House resumed. It would mean postponing two important meetings on the GEC Pension Fund but that is a price one has to pay, he thought.

Valerie was glad he was going.

'I don't know why you MPs don't get to grips with these problems,' she had declared in her strident tones, 'that's what you're there for.'

She did not understand, never would. Parliament could never control such a situation; it could only act as a safety valve in the – usually vain – hope of stopping more violence. Valerie expected too much. Probably they would have to let the violence wear itself out, like an electrical storm, before the politicians could step in with the constitutional remedies which would then be acceptable.

Anyway it was important for Members to rally round and be seen in the House, taking an interest even if they could not do anything.

Commin felt self-satisfied when he took his seat in his usual place four benches back and above the gangway. On the same bench, below the gangway were Enoch Powell and six or seven other Ulster members. He certainly would expect them to be present, but, considering the extent of the breakdown of law and order, the rest of the House was surprisingly empty. At least he had done his duty.

As soon as Question Time was over, the Prime Minister was at the Despatch Box speaking, with a grim looking Home Secretary sitting immediately behind him on the front bench. He referred to the brutal murders of civilians and the killings of nine regular soldiers in Armagh alone during 1975, and went on to announce new security measures which would be taken. He paid tribute to the Government of the Republic of Ireland which, he said, was equally determined to stamp out cross-border banditry and murder.

He went on, 'Northern Ireland is part of the United Kingdom. The Government have a duty to protect all their citizens there. This duty will be discharged to the full.'

Commin thought it a brave statement; he was glad that Margaret Thatcher, when she asked her question as Leader of the Opposition, did not attempt to make party capital out of the situation. It was not the time for that.

When the Secretary of State got up to open the debate there were even fewer Members present. Commin, forgetting that on many previous occasions he had been absent, felt disgusted at this demonstration of Parliamentary apathy. There were, he counted, only twenty-five Labour Members present and only a few more Conservatives. He looked up at the packed public galleries. What could they think? The Press were also attending in force. He counted them. My God, he thought, sixty reporters up there – as many as the Members on the floor of the House below. Incredible that less than a tenth of the membership of the House was in the Chamber to hear the main speeches in the debate. Maybe Valerie was right about the ineffectiveness of Parliament.

As the debate wore on, the numbers dwindled still further. Only thirty-five backbenchers for Ted Heath, a former Prime Minister, though Margaret had come back to hear him. He is speaking well, though Commin; firmly, sensibly and without any notes. A good performance and good sense. He says there is a considerable sense of unreality in the debate; how very right. He says the military should be strengthened and should use the weapons the terrorists use against them, like rockets; right again thought Commin. And the roads leading across the border should be mined. 'The political situation cannot be separated from the military one,' Heath was saying, appealing to all political sides to work together at least until the crisis was over. Commin was impressed.

The Opposition spokesman, Airey Neave, had also spoken well and with feeling, as befits a courageous man who had escaped from the notorious Colditz Castle during the Nazi war. And he was not afraid to bring out the brutal fact that if British troops withdrew from Northern Ireland the massacre to follow could cost two hundred and forty thousand innocent lives.

One figure from the Secretary of State's speech stuck in Commin's mind. Public expenditure in Northern Ireland,

he had said, would be £1,300 million in the current year
and the province could not sustain its living standards if it
were not part of the United Kingdom. Commin did a quick
mental calculation. One and a half million people: the
figure meant State spending of £850 yearly for every man,
woman and child. They must be the most subsidised people
in the world, thought Commin.

Sir Nigel Fisher, the venerable Tory backbencher, spoke
next, urging the Ulster Protestants to work out a coalition
with the Catholics to avoid the continuation of direct rule
from Westminster. And yet as he developed the logical
argument he undermined it with his next words. Commin
could hardly believe his ears as Fisher went on:

'It has never been possible to apply logic to the realities of
Ireland – or of women. Emotions matter much more. Rex
Harrison in 'My Fair Lady' bewailed 'why can't a woman
be more like a man?' But they are not. It is just as unreal to
demand that the Irish should be treated in the same way as
the more logical English. I know about this on both counts
because I am married to an Ulster woman.'

That man has more courage than me, thought Commin.
I could not make a speech like that about women and then
go home and face Valerie. She would tear me apart.

He wandered from the Chamber to get a cup of tea in the
Members tea room; along the corridor, coming from the
Library, he met one of the nicer Labour Members who was,
he understood, a Catholic descended from Irish stock.

'How's the debate going?' asked the Labour MP.

'Good, thoughtful stuff,' Commin said, 'but I thought the
Ulstermen are being too intransigent. They should agree to
work with the minority, at least for the time being.'

'The trouble goes back too far,' said the Labour man.
'The Ulster Protestants think they are so superior to the
Catholics. They think of Catholics as primitive people. I've
just come back from South Africa. The whites there have
the same attitude as the Ulstermen, 'keep the natives in
their place and never let them have any political power.' It's
very tribal like that in Northern Ireland, too.'

Commin sat in the tea room drinking his tea and eating a

toasted scone reflecting on the conversation. It all seemed so difficult, the problem of having an Africa on Britain's doorstep. Africa was, however, an interesting analogy. The French had once had a large bit of Africa as part of Metropolitan France with the settlers firmly entrenched for generations. They had fought a bloody war against the Algerians to keep it an integral part of France. They had failed and de Gaulle pulled them out.

It had been simple for the French to identify the enemy, as the Algerians were mostly coloured. In all the colonies where, since the war, the British had granted independence, the colonies had been black. Somehow that had made it easier. If only the Catholics were black, the Irish problem would be straightforward and simple to solve, thought Commin desperately.

He went to his room, which he shared with another Tory member, to sign some constituency letters left for him by his secretary. Then he went to the Press bar to meet the lobby correspondent for the newspaper which circulated in south coast towns, including his own constituency. It was a chore he had to do from time to time.

The paper was fairly good to him, reporting his speeches and his questions. He arranged to put down at least one Parliamentary Question every week on local affairs so as to appear to be active. The publicity value was out of all proportion to the little effort involved.

'How are you, Graham?' asked the correspondent affably.

'Bit depressed by this Irish business,' answered Commin, honestly.

'Have a drink.'

'Thanks, I'll have a Scotch and water.'

'Is there any more your side can do?' asked the newspaper man.

'No, I think it is right for us to keep party politics out of it and maintain the bi-partisan approach. The Government must be given all possible backing for its actions.'

'You don't think the *Mirror* is right in saying the public want British troops to be phased out?'

'Not at all. Most people want British lives to be protected and that means the troops must stay. It would be unthinkable for Britain to allow the terrorists to win,' said Commin, speaking more firmly than his actual thoughts should have allowed. It was always necessary to be positive and firm with newspapermen. Doubt was interpreted as weakness and the constituency would not like to read that he could not make up his own mind. It was safer to keep soundly on the Party line. If not, one got the reputation of being a dissident, or, even worse, an eccentric.

They talked about a local hospital cut back and Commin explained he was writing to the Minister about it, thinking as he did so that it would make a good paragraph. 'MP acts on hospital' the headline would read. He knew perfectly well, in present circumstances, no Government could afford the expenditure, least of all a Tory one which would cut back even more. This dishonesty in politics disturbed him from time to time, but he rationalised his doubts by remembering he was but a new boy – only two years in Parliament.

Commin returned to the Chamber to hear the closing speeches. The Reverend Ian Paisley, talking about the fine work of the Ulster Special Constabulary who were replaced by British troops, was saying, 'In all the years when the USC paraded in and controlled the roads of Ulster they did not shoot as many Roman Catholics as the British Army shot in a few hours in the city of Londonderry. I am not criticising the British Army. Facts are facts.'

Commin was tempted to slink off from the Chamber and get back to Valerie in time to see the ten o'clock news on television, but chose to stay for the wind-up speech by the Minister of State. He looked across at the empty green benches behind the Minister. Only fifteen Labour Members were now present. Among them was John Stonehouse, who had disappeared a year earlier and had been called the 'runaway MP'. Perhaps, Commin thought, the others should now be dubbed the 'stayaway MPs'.

The speech of the Minister did not seem to add much to the debate, but something he said shocked Commin: of the arms captured from the Provisional IRA, eighty-five per cent were manufactured in the United States, bought with dollars and transported to Northern Ireland. It was melancholy news.

Commin collected his car from the underground car park, glad to be returning to what passed for normality. Ireland had become a hideous nightmare. He was home within five minutes.

Valerie was waiting for him, eagerly, already in her dressing gown.

'How did it go today, darling?' she asked proudly, oozing sexuality.

'Honestly, darling, it was terrible. I've never felt more depressed in my life,' he replied.

Chapter Eighteen

The Third Level

'Why do they want me in Virginia?' asked Rick as soon as they were alone together in the small room.

'Search me,' said Andrew Bird wreathed in nervous smiles. 'It sounded mighty important though. They got me up at eight this morning. I was going up to New Hampshire for the weekend. My wife is furious.'

'Can I 'phone through from here?'

'Not wise, none of these airport 'phones is secure.'

'Oh! well,' said Rick, trying to put on a brave face, 'if we're in the Company, this is our life. Here, there and everywhere.'

'I'd be so lucky,' Bird said. 'I've been stuck in Boston for near-on two years and my folks are down in Kentucky. Hardly get to see them.'

'What's your job here?'

'Supposed to be watching international arrivals, but I spend more time watching the local politicians.'

'I thought Hoover had reserved that game for the FBI,' said Rick with a grin, thinking of the juicy details of private lives the former Director had acquired before his death.

'I have to double-check the FBI too. But it was Chappaquiddick that triggered off my operation.'

'I see,' said Rick, knowing too well what he meant. It would be best, he thought, not to push it any further. This man Bird is a stupid blabbermouth and Rick could not take the risk of him reporting on his own supposed interest in the dirty side of American domestic politics, particularly if it concerned Edward Kennedy and the Irish connection. In any case if Bird had responsibility for the local parish, it could include watching the Boston Irish. Michael, he thought with a shudder. I must see him before Bird does.

'I'll go and see my wife through with the baggage. Be back in twenty minutes.'

'Anyway I can help?'

'No, thanks. I'll manage.'

'See yeah. Mind you're not late. They'll be mighty mad with me if you're not at Dulles when they expect you,' said Bird, and he settled down to read the back page of the *Monitor*.

Kathy had already got the baggage, though how she managed it in the milling crowd with two kids to handle, Rick could not understand. Resourceful girl. She was pushing the cases down the line towards customs examination, and had a worried frown.

'Rick, what is it all about, is everything alright?'

'They want me in Virginia, Kathy, and I don't know why. That fellow is an idiot and knows nothing. But I want you to get away from the airport as quickly as possible. I don't want him to see Michael.'

'Why not?' Kathy was tired and perplexed.

'Take it from me. There are too many spies about. Just my natural caution, Kathy.'

Michael was outside the barrier. As Rick helped him to load the baggage on a trolley he said under his breath: 'Get the hell out of here. There's a CIA man on the airport. He mustn't see you. If they've rumbled Ireland, we'd be in trouble. Maybe they haven't, so don't lets take any risks.'

'How was it over there?' asked Michael quickly.

'Couldn't be better. You'll have to call me Ristéard now.'

'Goodbye Kathy, drive carefully now, bye Mark, bye Deidre.'

'Bye Daddy.'

Rick turned to go back through the customs hall and walked straight into Bird, who was standing by the barrier watching him.

'I had to come back. They wouldn't let you in again without a special pass.'

'Let's go and have a coffee. I haven't had a decent

American cup this whole year,' he said to take the watching Bird away.

Rick was glad to get on the plane and away from the Company's place man in Boston; Bird was the perfect example of the shallow man. What a deadbeat. The Company should be more discriminating. Rick ordered a Canadian Club, as there was no Jameson's on board, adjusted the seat to recline and stretched his legs. Must try to sort this out, he reflected, and not be so sensitive. Anyone with more sense than Bird might have noticed how jittery he was.

At Dulles they had a car waiting for him, which was unheard of; usually he had to hire his own.

At the Headquarters offices they were waiting for him; only this time the Deputy Director Intelligence had someone with him from DDP – the Deputy Directorate Plans.

'This is Walt Chambers of Western Europe Division. He wants to up-date you on Italy. Things have been moving fast while you've been seeing the New Year in over there, in sleepy old Ireland,' he said with a friendly voice.

Rick was relieved. He wasn't to be grilled about the Irish connection. They were certainly wrong about sleepy Ireland, but he'd let that pass.

'Glad to meet you,' Walt Chambers was saying, 'we're glad you're going into our area. We've heard good reports on your work in Barbados and Venezuela. Now you can cut your teeth on some real hard nuts.'

'Yes,' the DDI was saying, 'the bubble's bursting in Italy. We want you there next week, by the tenth latest.'

Walt Chambers was adding, 'Moro's Government is collapsing. The Socialists are pulling out of the coalition. It's bad news. It could let the Communists get a hold of the reins of power. They're already extremely strong in the industrial towns. There are Communist mayors everywhere and the Party is posed to leap forward. Think of the effect on France if the CP took over in Italy. We would have to do a complete re-think on the Common Market if any of the member countries went Commie.'

Rick was reeling from the effects of the journey and jet lag, only he was still emotionally tuned in to Ireland. All this talk about Italy was washing over him and he did not feel involved. But he could not afford to show disinterest. Company members were expected to walk off Transatlantic flights and be alert immediately; there were no excuses.

'That is really serious,' said Rick. 'What brought on the crisis?' He was playing for a little time to let his emotional metabolism adjust to the situation. He had been fully expecting trouble from the Company over Ireland and his links with the Provisionals. His mind was still a jumble of recent memories: the plain clothes Garda man in the Abbey Tavern; 'Sweet Molly Malone' – the refrain came welling back, incongruously, 'cockles and mussels, alive, alive, oh!'; O'Connell talking; Michael Collins, a traitor to the cause; Brugha the hero; Ristéard, you are now Ristéard. He tried to snap back to the present.

The DDI and Walt Chambers were still describing the issues in Europe, both apparently oblivious to Rick's glazed look of transfixation.

'And we can't ignore the effect on Spain. Juan Carlos is having a job holding the lid down after Franco. A Communist Italy would push Spain over the brink; the CP is even stronger there than in Portugal.'

'The crisis,' the DDI added, 'is the fault of the Company, the Senate and Congress. That's the plain truth and that's why you've got to get out there urgently. We can't rely any longer on the local Station. It's too hot.'

'Well it's like this,' DDI said. 'The Church and the Pike Committees can now subpoena any facts they want from the Company. Unless we're very careful we'll have no secrets left. The Committees are made up of all manner of Senators and Congressmen and some of them, are very hostile. They leak the information to the press and it also gets out to foreign Governments.'

'This is mad,' said Rick.

'Of course it's mad,' said DDI, 'we're tearing ourselves to bits in this country and toppling foreign allies like Moro in the process.'

'What leaked to Italy?' asked Rick, alarmed now.

'The six million dollar donation from the Company to Moro's party, the Christian Democrats. Just that.' The DDI added cynically, 'Just that. Just about the most damaging info possible.'

Walt Chambers came in, 'It's bad, really bad. The Commies can now play up the Christian Democrats as the whores of America. That's all we needed. It just about destroys their chances.'

The DDI said: 'We must counter-attack real soon. To do so we need every scrap of information you can get on CP finances. I want to know which trading companies they control and how they get their imports from Russia and East Germany. I want to know which bank accounts they use and I want copies of all their bank transactions.'

'Won't that be difficult?' asked Rick.

'Yes, that's why we're sending you. The local Station can't handle it,' said DDI.

'The way things are worked in Italy,' said Chambers, 'you can get anything if you bribe the right people; even a private audience with the Pope.'

'You'll have all the money you need,' added DDI. 'And it'll already be in Switzerland ready for transfer to any Swiss numbered account. Five years ago we placed a Company man in Credit Suisse to do a check on an American aircraft company's slush funds. He's still there, providing valuable info.'

Rick made a mental note not to open an account with Credit Suisse, numbered or otherwise.

'How will it be transferred?'

'Simple. Our man will arrange for the account to be opened. It will be necessary only for the Italian concerned to cross the border for a couple of hours; easily done at a branch in Lugano. Having the transfers in Geneva saves your Italian informant the trouble of lugging suitcases of Lira across from Como, which Italians have been doing for years, and there's less risk of him being detected.'

Walt Chambers came in again. 'We've got a good man to help you, name of Luigi Cassoli. He's not in the Company so you'll have to handle him carefully; strictly an agent not an operative.'

'Where's he from?' asked Rick.

'Mafia,' said Chambers.

'But good,' said DDI. 'We used him in Cuba but pulled him out early. If we'd stuck with him we'd have rubbed Castro out ten years ago, instead of messing it up.'

'He must be getting on a bit?' asked Rick.

'He's fifty-five or six, but as hard as nails, as fit as your all-American boy at twenty-five,' said DDI.

'His contracts are good. He's old enough to know some of the key Mafia figures in Italy. You'll need their help,' said Chambers.

'Is it wise?' asked Rick.

'In this battle we use anyone,' said DDI. 'Remember, at all times, out there in Milan, Florence or Rome you are on the frontier defending America. Senator Church may not like it but while we run the show, anything goes.'

'It would be crazy to fight a war with one hand tied behind our backs,' said Chambers.

'Crazy is the word, Walt. Nobody else fights with his balls screwed up, so why should we. Congressmen come and Congressmen go. Presidents come and Presidents go. But the Company will still be in business when they're forgotten. We can't depend on the temporary politicians. They do enough harm as it is.'

Rick could sense the note of bitterness in the remarks of his superiors. It did not sound much like the language used at Camp Peary in training days. The tension is affecting everyone, he thought, and decided to probe deeper.

'I heard about Dick Welch's death while I was away,' he said.

'Tragedy, damned tragedy,' said Chambers, 'he was one of our most reliable men. He was exposed to that assassination by the renegades.'

'Yes,' said DDI, 'his name was published by a body calling itself "the Fifth Estate for Security Education". Have you ever heard such a ridiculous name? It's run by ex-Company people Philip Agee, Victor Marchetti and that mob. But it's dangerous. That's why we want you to go into Italy incognito and have nothing to do with the local Station.'

'The Fifth Estate have arranged to publish the names of all our agents in France in the Paris Communist paper,' added Chambers.

'It's criminal. Now all our men are vulnerable to attack,' said DDI. 'No other Secret Service in the world would allow its servants to be exposed in this way.'

'I think the Fifth Estate is a Communist front organisation,' added Chambers. 'They never publish details about the KGB.'

DDI looked closely at Rick. 'We regard you as one of our most dedicated men, that's why we're frank with you. Your operation will not be revealed to Senate or Congress.'

Rick was gratified but not a little uneasy. The morale in the Company must be disintegrating fast when the top men talk in this way. They must feel vulnerable personally, he thought.

Chambers was speaking now: 'The Helms business finally convinced us to operate some of our activities at the third level.'

'What's happened to Helms?' asked Rick.

'Well you know he's now Ambassador to Iran; there's a story around that he's going to face criminal charges for a minor burglary which the Company undertook just outside Washington a few years ago,' said DDI. 'Can you imagine what it would do to our relations with the Shah to charge our own Ambassador with a common burglary?'

'That's fantastic,' said Rick. 'What's the third level?'

'Well you know,' answered Chambers, 'there's the overt level, which is public, the covert level which was secret, except that now the Senate or Congress release it to the Press, and there's the new third level which is secret, secret.'

'It's revealed to no one and we'll deny it ever happened,' said DDI. 'That means', he continued, 'that you'll send no reports back through Company communications except of the most routine kind.'

'We'd like you here on Monday to immerse you for a few days in the language laboratory. It won't be a perfect job in the time available, but at least you'll be able to ask your way to the Via Veneto like any good American salesman,' said Chambers.

'And Luigi will meet you on Tuesday. On Friday you'll both fly to Rome. But separate planes, of course,' said DDI.

Chapter Nineteen

Italian Imbroglio

Before Rick left for Rome, Michael O'Halloran flew down from Boston to see him. They were both anxious to have the meeting, Rick to thank his friend for the introductions, Michael to ensure there were no hard feelings for the full report he had given the Provisionals. But the success of Rick's journey had forged even greater bonds of friendship and it was not necessary to communicate their feelings in words.

Michael was doubly pleased: the cause had been well served and his friend now had the composure and contentment of a man whose mission in life had been confirmed. The basic ingredient in that composure was faith. It was as simple as that: Rick now had faith. But, Michael recognised that he had one blind spot. His conduct at Boston airport, when that curious CIA man was around, confirmed it. Rick's weakness was clear: he could not confess his faith to the uninitiated and if he thought anyone suspected his commitment, he became paranoid.

Michael had news for Rick.

'Did you see the report of the British Prime Minister's speech attacking Americans who support the IRA?' he asked.

'Heard something, but newspapers weren't easy to come by and I didn't read full reports,' said Rick.

'Well Harold Wilson had the cheek to say we were splashing blood on the much loved shamrock.'

'He doesn't seem to realise the blood he is splashing using his troops in Northern Ireland,' said Rick.

'He named one of our organisations, the Irish Northern

Aid Committee, Noraid, and blamed it for financing arms.'

'I don't suppose he mentioned the British starting the trouble by colonising Northern Ireland with Scotsmen?'

'Oh! no – nothing like it. He talked about fourteen hundred deaths and sixteen thousand injured or maimed as though they were all our responsibility.'

'Did Noraid reply?' asked Rick.

'Yes, old man Higgins, you know, the Chairman, called an immediate press conference. He denounced the speech as a British plot, and do'you know, our subscriptions have all gone up as a result?'

'Wilson should attack us more often,' he added.

Italy was a cultural shock to Rick. Apart from the trip to Ireland, this was his first visit to Europe. In any case, to Rick's mind, Ireland did not count as part of Europe; it was an island suspended on its own in space and time. Italy was different. Vibrant, alive with activity, chaotic but functioning, it seethed with the vitality which had sent the legionaries to conquer the known world two thousand years before and had implanted the indelible marks of civilisation from one end of the continent to the other.

The Italian people, in their own habitat, were more expressive of their true natures than the migrants who had been curbed or warped by the pressures of new lands. He remembered the difference he had once noticed between Mexicans in Los Angeles and those in Mexico City, the former inhibited by the strait-jacket of an alien culture.

It was a shock to him to see the nonchalence with which the Italians regarded the evidence of their history. The whole of Rome is a museum, he thought, but Italians went about their busy daily lives seemingly oblivious of the evidence of greatness all around them. The Colosseum, had become the centre of a big traffic roundabout, or just a prop to the tourist industry. Everywhere he looked there were massive works of art, monuments on street corners, ignored by the Romans who behaved as unseeing extras on a gigantic film set. Little groups of Japanese were to be seen taking turns photographing one another with the sights of centuries as the backdrop.

But Rick had no time for sightseeing as such. He had booked a suite at the Grand Hotel which he would use while he arranged some more permanent accommodation. At such an active establishment it would be easy for Luigi to come to his rooms on the third floor without being noticed. Later he acquired an apartment which served the same purpose as it had been a convenient back entrance on a busy street.

The Government was about to collapse. Rick could not understand why no one seemed concerned.

'Governments are like skittles in this country,' said Luigi, 'if one survives more than twelve months, then that's news.'

Isn't anyone worried about the constitution?' asked Rick, thinking of the threat of the return to Fascism.

'Corruption is the basis for our way of life, not the constitution,' said Luigi. 'Everyone is on the fiddle. They gave up years ago trying to assess taxes on incomes because all incomes were understated. Now they base tax demands on a man's life style. They have neat little files on the businessman's cars, homes, carpets, mistresses – the lot.'

'Don't people object to that?'

'No chance. Wait 'till it's all on computers. Then there'll be no limit to the secrets they could tabulate.'

'It's frightening.'

'It sure is. But try telling these people. Hopeless. They're too busy trying to make a bit more on the side.'

'How does the administration carry on during these crises?'

'The almighty Lira, it oils the wheels at every stage. Swiss francs are even more effective as a lubricating agent,' he added.

With Luigi's help Rick made contact with a number of employees of the Communists' trading companies. To each of them he represented himself as a salesman for warehouse stacking equipment. Good old Tube Stack, he often thought, the perfect cover for negotiating with anyone. It was needed everywhere, like food and water. Art Gruber would have a more difficult cover job with computers.

As far as the contacts were concerned, Rick was doing a survey on requirements and was prepared to pay for information. After several weeks he had amassed a lot of basic facts which, together with the files on the companies, copied – at considerable expense – in Government offices, provided the basis for checking particular transactions.

It was like joining together the pieces of a detective story and Rick enjoyed the exercise immensely. Machine tools from Czechoslovakia were distributed in the whole of Italy by a company calling itself Machina-Corso. The Directors were a lawyer and an accountant in Milan – both leading members of the Communist Party and both obviously nominees. The machine tools were invoiced from Brno at a ridiculously low price – at least half the price similar tools were quoted to German importers. After a mark-up of over a third the machines were sold on to engineering firms as the end-users at prices which undercut the competition. The usual underhand kick-backs and commissions were paid to the buyers and that ensured that sales were hideously easy.

At every stage everyone was happy. The importing company made grossly fat profits, the agents, selling excellent machine tools at a lower price than German or British products, were pleased and the companies using the tools were delighted at the bargain they had obtained. Only the Czech economy was a loser, and the Czech workers at the factory whose wages were kept low in a grotesque game where the Czech trade was manipulated in the interests of political infiltration abroad.

The Machina-Corso handed seventy-five per cent of its profits to the Communist Party of Italy. Rick also discovered that five to ten per cent of the profits were going into two Swiss bank accounts disguised as buyers' commission to Swiss-based agents, who were certainly not necessary to the transactions and almost certainly did not exist. Rick suspected that the money was in fact going to two high-ranking officials of the Communist Party who were embezzling it for their personal use. He could not discover who they were without travelling to Zurich and finding an employee of the bank concerned who could be bribed. It would not be easy as few of the reliable Swiss were bribable.

If, eventually, he could confirm his suspicions, it would be priceless information for the Company and at the right time the two officials could be exposed with devastating consequences for the Party. Its credability with its faithful comrades would be undermined and the resulting internal squabbles would be damaging to the Communist electoral chances.

By February Rick was well pleased with his progress on the CIA project. He calculated that subsidised exports from East Germany of electronic calculators, of handicrafts from Poland as well as of the machine tools from Czechoslovakia, amounted to a total benefit to the Italian Communists of at least eight million dollars over a two year period. There were other subsidies which he had not been able to identify. The total would be considerably more than direct cash payment passed to the Christian Democrats by the CIA. No wonder the CP was making progress. Rick could not discover any subsidised exports from Hungary or Yugoslavia, and assumed this was because of their independence from the Warsaw Pack. The USSR did not subsidise directly, which was surprising to Rick; but at that time he did not know about the gold transfers.

He was sufficiently ahead with his investigations to take time off from Company business to attend to the planning of the Ultimate. He called Peadar MacSwiney to fly to Rome for a meeting. Maloney, who had spent two weeks in Libya, could fly straight up from Tripoli. Rather than bring them into the centre of the city he booked three rooms, under assumed names, at the Enalc Hotel in Ostia. They would be less likely to bump into Luigi or others they wanted to avoid at a seaside resort in February. Ostia, only twenty minutes from Flumiciano Airport, was also easy to get to.

The three men, who had not seen each other for five weeks, had a lot to discuss. Peadar had been to Cologne and Hamburg twice. Patrick Maloney was in high spirits. The Libyans had agreed to advance an extra hundred thousand dollars. Did they need detailed information?

'Oh! no,' replied Maloney, 'they are so pleased with the escalation of violence in England, they make no conditions, and only one request.'

'What was that?' asked Rick.

'To stop indiscriminate bombings in stores like Selfridges and Harrods, where there are a lot of Arab customers. They are terrified that an IRA bomb will one day blow up a leading Arab diplomat. They say such an accident would set back Libyan help for the cause by years.'

'The killing of the Libyan at the Vienna OPEC kidnapping last December did not worry them,' said Rick.

'He was only a lowly official, they weren't concerned about him but they would have been if Sheikh Yamani or one of the other Ministers had been killed,' answered Maloney.

'I had the impression that the whole kidnapping was a put-up job by the Libyans,' said Rick.

'I think it was,' said Maloney, 'they supported the Jackal – that Venezuelan, Sanchez – to sieze all the oil Ministers and take them on a trip under machine guns from Vienna to Algiers, on to Libya and back to Algiers. They wanted to warn them – particularly the Saudis – not to go soft on the Israeli issue.'

'The Libyans are tough when they want something,' said Rick.

'Certainly are, they will do anything. Fanatical,' said Maloney. 'They would like the IRA to use Sanchez in some raids on British politicians who are pro-Israeli.'

'That would be most unwise,' said Rick. 'It could sabotage our own plan. Imagine the security operation the British would set up if a Minister were siezed in that way. We must stop them.'

'I think I have,' said Maloney. 'Sanchez is being assigned to another project for the next three months. I told them the

IRA is winning the war against the English and we only need their help for the final push. They believed me.'

'Can we use them to buy the equipment we need?' said Rick thinking quickly.

'Why should they be used?' asked Peadar MacSwiney, who had been able to buy guns in Germany and France without too much trouble.

'The equipment we need,' explained Rick, 'is sophisticated and it's extremely unlikely even you could buy it direct.'

'But on my last trip to Cologne I met two German arms specialists who have been with I.G. Farben. They are very pro-IRA and will help us all they can.'

'Unless they steal the equipment they couldn't obtain it. And remember at Cork we ruled out theft as being too liable to detection,' said Rick.

'I think in their present mood the Libyans will do what we ask,' said Maloney, 'and provide all the money we need.'

The equipment may have to be made to order,' said Rick, 'and only a Government could place a contract which an arms manufacturer could accept. That's why we need the Libyans.'

'I see,' said Peadar slowly, 'my Germans can devise the specification to our instructions.'

'Exactly,' said Rick.

'And my Libyans place the contract with I.G. Farben or other German firms as if for their own military requirements,' said Maloney.

'Exactly,' said Rick, 'and we obtain what we need without anyone being any the wiser. The English would never suspect until it was too late.'

Chapter Twenty

Ostia in February

The Lido di Ostia on a Wednesday morning in February is like a ghost town. Along the seafront the huge concrete bathing pools are all padlocked. Apart from a narrow passage between them here and there, no access is allowed to the sea, which, as with everything else in Italy, has to be paid for. The souvenir stalls, with their mass produced trash and outsize toy animals, stuffed in the sweat shops of Naples, are shut and bolted. One or two will open tentatively on a weekend at the end of the month. Most of the hotels are closed. The few still open rely for business on the airline crews on overnight stopovers from nearby Fiumicino, and the occasional businessman slipping down from Rome for a night with a pick-up.

Now and then a Fiat 600 would putt-putt along the deserted road but otherwise there was little to disturb the American and his two Irish confederates strolling along the promenade. Within a month or so the town would have to contend with the thousands of Romans who use the concrete coast as a breathing lung, away from the dust and the approaching heat of an Italian summer.

The place was ideal for the three conspirators to meet, mild enough to walk in open neck shirts with the warm breezes from the Tyrrhenian Sea ruffling their hair. Better this than the mists of Ireland or the dank cold of Hamburg, thought Peadar MacSwiney, whilst Rick, comparing it to Coney Island or Atlantic City was thinking that the American resorts could not rival Ostia in off-season squalor. A built-up seaside without its crowds and bikinis is like the faded stage of a grand opera without the artistes.

It suited their purpose to be alone. The Enalc Hotel,

maintained as an official training school for cooks and waiters, had to stay open all the year, the few guests pampered by the trainees who outnumbered them two to one. It was probably quite safe to converse in the bedrooms but, to be absolutely certain they were not overheard, Rick took his two companions for long promenades. One could never be sure about the other people in the hotel. The young Englishman he had noticed sharing a table with a voluptuous Italian teenager might, for instance, be from the British Embassy. Although his thoughts were obviously on other delights than official business, if he should hear a strange chance remark his mind might click back to his duty. In Rick's espionage experience a lot of valuable information had been obtained through someone's pure carelessness and over-confidence, and he did not want to make the same mistakes.

Rick was talking: 'We must, very soon, identify what equipment we need to complete the operation. It must be tested and completely fool-proof. And it must be delivered effectively.'

Maloney agreed that IRA planning usually left a lot to be desired; he had been particularly upset a few weeks before, by the seizing of a two and a half ton truck-load of explosives by the British army at a checkpoint at Newry. It was a year's supply lost.

'I agree,' he said, 'we can't afford a single error. The mistakes of some of our boys could make me weep.'

'Peadar,' added Rick, 'I want you to go to London to do a survey of certain places in Whitehall. Spend at least a week on it. It must be absolutely accurate to the nearest inch and I want the timings of Cabinet Ministers movements to the minute.'

'Won't it be dangerous for me to be seen in London?' asked Peadar. 'The police and the secret service are keeping an eye on all Irishmen known to have Sinn Fein or IRA connections.'

'In your case, we're lucky,' said Rick. 'You've never once been picked up, even in Northern Ireland so you're not on police files.'

'Just as well. It's all on computer now. Apparently the bastards can feed in little scraps of information on a suspect and get out his complete history in seconds.'

'And have you had your photograph taken?' asked Rick.

'Not as far as I know.'

'They send their sneak photographers into every Sinn Fein and Republican meeting,' said Maloney. 'They even have their sneaks posted at IRA funerals – among the gravestones. Some of my pals have had more photos taken than Richard Burton.'

'I think it's safe for Peadar to go to London, but he must stay away from all Irish contacts. He must behave as an ordinary tourist,' said Rick. 'For that reason he should take Ingrid with him.'

'What?' said Peadar. 'Do you want to involve Ingrid in the plan?'

'No,' said Rick, 'Ingrid should know nothing but having her with you will provide the perfect protection against suspicion. You could both fly in from Hamburg on Lufthansa, stay at a small hotel in Bayswater, and behave like a couple on holiday.'

'I think I would like that,' said Peadar, who saw too little of Ingrid. He had wanted her to join him in Ireland but the twin pressures of her father and her need to get her law career established, had persuaded her to stay in Hamburg. She had graduated the year before and was in practice with a small firm specialising in criminal work. Her love for Peadar had not changed but she hoped he would settle in Germany, and allow her to continue her career. Her father was wholly opposed to any marriage to an Irishman, but could not forbid their relationship.

As for Peadar, he felt his responsibilities to his mother in Cork had been honoured, and he would be very happy to live in Germany after the IRA mission had been fulfilled. His enthusiasm for the Ultimate was strongly influenced by this wish. It would solve the Irish problem sooner and provide him with the freedom to marry Ingrid.

So it was agreed that Peadar would return to Hamburg and ask her to go with him to London. She could be told he was inquiring for a job to represent a company dealing in agricultural machinery in Germany, and fitting in a holiday at the same time. The prospective job was not imaginary; Rick had taken the precaution of locating one or two possible firms.

During the Ostia meeting Peadar was given a careful explanation of what he needed to obtain. It included a detailed plan of the Houses of Parliament, showing the location of Ministers' rooms, access points to the Chamber and to the various Committee rooms which the Prime Minister and his colleagues might use. Peadar would be expected to take Ingrid to the Palace of Westminster and walk through as many areas as possible both on sitting days and also on weekends so as to get the feel of the security arrangements.

Rick also needed an extra-large scale map of Whitehall with the principal Ministerial offices all indicated; special attention had to be given to the plan of Number 10, Downing Street, and Peadar was advised to take dozens of photographs of Ingrid standing outside the front entrance and also at the rear of the building on the St. James's Park side. The maps Rick had already studied were too small for this purpose and he wondered if Peadar could photocopy the plans of the area held in the architects department of the Greater London Council, under some pretext or another. That would be for Peadar to fix.

Through detailed observation, Peadar was also asked to check all the security arrangements at Westminster, Departments of State and at Number 10, Downing Street. He was also to tabulate the times when the maximum number of Ministers, including the Prime Minister were together in one place, and where.

It sounded a big assignment for a week's visit, but Peadar knew he could leave Ingrid for a half day, here and there, with the excuse that he was job hunting, and with luck get all the information Rick wanted.

Meanwhile, Maloney was asked to return to Libya and set up further co-operation with the Libyan Army Colonels. Rick explained that he needed a place where the equipment obtained from Germany could be tested. Maloney would tell the Colonels that the IRA were improving their attacks on military installations and telephone exchanges, but needed a practice area. At that stage Rick himself would fly to Libya to check the testing for himself. The exact performance of the equipment would be of critical importance.

After returning to Philadelphia to submit his reports on the complex Italian situation, Rick brought Kathy back to Rome for a week's holiday. He felt incredibly relaxed. Italy was an enormous dilemma for American policy-makers but he did not feel personally involved. It was someone else's problem if the Communists took over power.

When he paused to think about it, he was surprised by his indifference; it was unlike the Richard Collins of a year, or even a few months, before. Kathy could notice the change – she read the papers and knew about the Italian Government crisis.

In the apartment off the Viale A. Manzoni which, Kathy was pleased to see Rick had made into a comfortable home, she settled back with a Punt e Mes and soda and tried to unravel the Italian scene.

'How is it, Rick, that even without a Government this country carries on as before? Unless someone had told me, I would have had no idea there is a crisis here,' she said.

'Italy has been through it before and the people who actually run the administration know it will come back to normal sometime. It's a case of organised chaos. There is no co-ordination but individual departments keep going through a momentum of their own.'

'But doesn't it make it difficult to get decisions?'

'Don't worry, if enough money changes hands the decisions can be made even without a Government.'

'Won't the people get fed up and put the Communists in to clean things up?'

'Yes, they could. Already a third of the electorate votes Communist. It's not considered the evil deed it was to vote anti-Christ. The Pope no longer believes in a head-on collision because he knows it will get him nowhere; he prefers to take on the homosexuals – they're not as popular as the Communists.'

'Wouldn't it harm America if Italy went Communist?'

'Yes, it would be a big blow.'

'Aren't you concerned yourself, Rick? Remember how upset you were about Barbados. That island is nothing compared to Italy in importance.'

'Fortunately, I am now disengaged personally, Kathy. It would be too big a burden for me to carry an emotional commitment here.'

'You seem different.'

'I am, Kathy.' Rick sipped his straight Campari, his concession to Italianisation. 'I'm a changed man since Ireland. I'm glad about it. It has liberated me.'

'In what way?'

'Well, I'm still concerned about America's security, and I will do my job in the Company with the next man, but to be totally involved destroys objectivity.'

'But you're involved in Ireland? Does that destroy objectivity?'

'That's a different sort of commitment. It is a commitment to the integrity of my own family's country. Once that integrity has been achieved, I can afford to withdraw. It will no longer be a burden to me.'

'That was the year you were talking about,' said Kathy, revealing that she had followed more of her husband's thoughts than he had imagined 'Rick, when you've completed the help you are going to give Ireland, will you be able to resign from the Company as you hoped?' Kathy was anxious to remove Rick from the dangers and the tensions of his CIA career; she was not daring enough to pry further into the Ireland project, although she appreciated it was something significant, and she had a woman's intuition that it could be a key to easing him out.

In the last few weeks she had read with concern about the publication in Italy of the names of all the CIA staff there. It was unjust that her Rick could be exposed in this way. He had assured her that only the local station would be named but Kathy thought it was only a matter of time before the enemy came round to his name as well. The memory of the Welch assassination still haunted her.

Rick could sense Kathy's concern and a loving feeling for her came over him. It was wonderful that she had these feelings.

'Yes,' he said with the determination that had eluded him for two years, 'Yes, Kathy, after Ireland, I will complete my remaining projects with the Company and then resign. It will be about time for some peace. We would have earned it.'

Chapter Twenty-One

An Amateur Photographer
in Whitehall

Peadar could not believe his good fortune. Ingrid was enthusiastic about a visit to London and the week's holiday was arranged very quickly. The plan to get Peadar a job in Germany, possibly in Hamburg, excited her. At last she could see a way of defeating her father's objections to the marriage and keeping up her own career.

As Rick had suggested they flew Lufthansa into Heathrow, checking through immigration without any problems. Outside Terminal Two they caught a taxi to a small hotel in West London. Ingrid thought the tall shape of the cab very odd. It was a hangover from the days of the hansom cab, when the gentleman was expected to wear a top hat, Peadar explained, glad to cast himself in the role of guide, although he had never actually been to England before.

As soon as they had checked into the hotel Peadar took Ingrid to Westminster. It had a fatal fascination for him; in this tiny area the dramas of centuries had been played out and here, within just a few months, the blow would be struck which would revenge the injustices of all those years. In another taxi – the strange vehicles seemed to be everywhere – they passed around Marble Arch and down Park Lane to Hyde Park Corner. Ingrid remarked that the size and smartness of the hotels did not confirm the stories in *Der Spiegel* about Britain's economic collapse. Do not be deceived, Peadar warned, the hotels are for tourists who can live cheaply in England because of the decline of the pound sterling. Very few ordinary Englishmen can afford to use them. A meal for two could cost an average week's

wages. Although he had not realised it, Peadar, having
lived in Hamburg so long, had adopted the superior
attitudes of the Germans in his outlook towards the
English.

The cab driver, realising they were tourists, was shouting
out comments through the open glass panel behind his
head.

'On our right,' he was saying, 'Buckingham Palace. The
Queen has a big garden behind that wall. Once it was never
looked over. Now anyone in the top rooms of the Hilton can
look down on the Queen. It's not right, is it? Now this is St.
James's Park – lovely lake in the middle – and ahead is
Whitehall where the civil servants waste all our money.' He
dropped them at the public entrance to Parliament, took a
tip with a 'thank you, Sir' and turned back into the stream
of traffic.

Now Peadar was all eyes and ears. They stepped up a
short flight of stairs to the head of a great hall. Here
Ingrid's bag was given a cursory examination by an
attendant dressed in a blue serge uniform and standing
inside a booth. He was not a policeman and did not seem
particularly efficient at his job. Peadar noticed an electronic
metal detector of the sort used at airports for checking
pockets and armpits for guns, but it remained in its box.
The attendant paid no attention to Peadar's clothing and
Peadar made a mental note that a man of his build wearing
padding and outsize clothes, could conceal several guns and
hand grenades.

Then they followed the other visitors into another smaller
hall which had an ornate appearance with white marble
statues of Parliamentarians from previous centuries. Ingrid
and Peadar were motioned by the attendants to sit on the
benches lining the hall and for a few minutes they were able
to study wall panels illustrating the history of England.
There was one panel including Scotland with England, but
no reference to Ireland. Peadar thought cynically, that this
omission confirmed the English attitude to the Irish as
colonised people, and felt resentful that eight hundred years
of association was looked on in this way.

Soon they passed through a large domed hall, and then along a narrow corridor and up some stairs. Here were more attendants who took Ingrid's bag, and the camera, giving her a numbered tag as a receipt. No one examined Peadar. The frocked attendants beckoned them into the gallery looking straight down to the Chamber of the House of Commons.

Looking at the plan which had been handed to them, he could pick out the Speaker's Chair. A distinguished looking man was sitting in it wearing a full bottomed wig. In front of him were two clerks at a desk and table, also wearing wigs. And on both sides of the Chamber, sitting on green benches, were the Members of Parliament. They did not make an impressive appearance. One or two on the front benches had their feet on the table. Others looked disinterested. One could even have been asleep.

There were several aspects of the scene to which Peadar paid particular attention. Unlike the Dáil Éireann, the public gallery was not screened from the Chamber by wire mesh. Therefore, any visitor could throw a missile into the well below. With a powerful throw it could be possible to reach the Government front bench with a grenade. He had read of a C.S. tear gas canister being thrown into the Chamber some years before, causing the House to adjourn for hours while the fumes and smell were dispersed. If that had been a grenade many members could have been killed. It was surprising that despite that experience, no precautions had been taken to prevent a recurrence. The security check at the entrance by Westminster Hall was a farce and so was this.

Peadar came away from Westminster convinced that the House of Commons could be penetrated; somehow it seemed too easy, but his initial thoughts were later confirmed. Returning on his own next morning, he took a close look at Westminster Hall, where the IRA bomb had exploded a year before, and noticed several tradesmen's vehicles driving into New Palace Yard. They were all waved in by policemen guarding the gate without any examination of credentials or contents. It seemed they were all catering

suppliers carrying wines, vegetables and meat to the
Parliamentary kitchens. He made a note that an entrance
with high explosive could be effected by hi-jacking a vehicle
or – better still – infiltrating a sympathiser on to the staff of
one of the supplying companies as a driver. It would be
possible in this way to drive one ton of explosive through
the front gates past the house where the Speaker lived,
under Big Ben, into the inner courtyards of the building
where it could be parked immediately under the House of
Commons Chamber.

If a vehicle were placed in this position at three thirty on
a Tuesday or a Thursday, Peadar ascertained, it would be
able to cause the Chamber to collapse from the force of the
explosion at a time when the place would be packed with
Members. The Prime Minister would be just finishing
answering Parliamentary questions, and other Ministers
would be present too.

Peadar was very pleased by this discovery. It seemed the
best way to secure the Ultimate. Throwing grenades from
the public gallery might not work if they were not timed to
explode at the precise moment of impact. Brave persons on
the floor might pick them up and throw them into the
lobbies alongside the Chamber, where they could explode
without causing deaths. Furthermore, throwing grenades
was haphazard. They might not get the Prime Minister and
other Ministers who might have the presence of mind to
rush from the Chamber as soon as the grenades fell.
Obviously all Ministers had received briefing on what to do
in the event of an attack, and making themselves scarce
would be the primary anti-terrorist advice.

Although he thought he had hit upon the best plan, he
nevertheless followed through all Rick's instructions and
carefully recorded all the details Rick had asked for. He
took dozens of photographs of Ingrid. She was pleased with
all the attention but Peadar, as Rick had advised, put the
focus on the buildings behind her. He ended up with a good
collection of shots of the Houses of Parliament taken from
the Square and Westminster Bridge, of Number 10,
Downing Street at the front entrance and the rear of the

building taken from St. James's Park and the Horse Guards Parade. It was at this point he noticed a policeman permanently on duty at the rear brick wall of Number 10, with a shelter for cover in bad weather. When the 'bobby' saw Peadar photographing his pretty girlfriend, he gave him a big grin and willingly agreed to pose with her by the shelter. Peadar took the shot with an especially wide angle lens which ensured an excellent photograph of the house behind. He had, by this time, discovered that the room where the Cabinet met was on the ground floor of the building and was only ten to fifteen yards away from the wall. It seemed incredible that in a war situation, Ministers could meet in such an exposed place with only one unarmed London bobby to protect them.

The week went extremely well. Peadar and Ingrid did other sightseeing, went to the Tower, St. Pauls, Madame Tussauds, and to the theatre to see The Mousetrap. Peadar's interview with the machinery exporters was also successful: the glowing reference they had received from a Mr. Collins of the Penn Tubular Stacking Company of Philadelphia, had helped considerably.

Within a few days Peadar was reporting to Rick at a rendezvous in Paris – being ultra-cautious they had decided not to meet again in Ostia – and Maloney flew in to join them.

At last, after all the months of preparatory work, the plan was beginning to take definite shape. The Libyan Colonels were prepared to be very helpful and recommended the team to two German armament specialists who had, for some years been seconded to the Libyan armed forces. They were said to be entirely reliable politically, anti-Israeli and anti-English, and the Arabs were full of praise for their expertise.

Rick decided to waste no time. Maloney 'phoned the Germans and, after giving the pet name of the senior Libyan Colonel, was accepted immediately. They arranged to travel to Essen early the next morning, hiring an Avis car for the trip.

The journey took them out of Paris past Le Bourget

airport towards the North East of France. It was a beautifully clear day with the smell of spring in the air. The motorway cut through the rolling countryside like a scythe and they made rapid progress.

'Couldn't drive as fast as this in the States,' confided Rick.

'Why's that?' asked Peadar.

'We have a rigorous speed limit. Fined on the spot in most States.'

'Are you so worried about accidents?' said Maloney.

'No, it isn't that. The restrictions were brought in to save gas. It's a way to keep down oil imports and beat the Arabs. Money is more important than lives.'

They skirted Cambrai. The area was new to Rick but he had read about it in the history books.

'Look out for cemetaries,' he said. 'This is where the dead of the first world war are buried – millions of them. A war to end all wars and look where we are now! Wars still going on – Ireland, Middle East, Argentina.'

'Think of the useless sacrifice of all those young men,' said Peadar, thinking of the stupidity of Irishmen fighting Germans in two world wars.

'Yes,' said Rick, 'all those big wars could have been avoided if the leaders had been dealt with early on. Take 1939 and 1940, the assassination of Hitler would have stopped all that aggression.'

'I think you're right,' said Maloney. 'The leaders take the decisions but seldom pay the price for their madness. Hitler paid but too late.'

'If someone had worked at the elimination of Hitler, Goering, Himmler and Goebbels in the same scientific way in which we are operating our plan, a great deal of misery would have been prevented,' said Peadar. 'The Germans are good people really and suffered themselves from Hitler's brainstorms.'

Still on the motorway, they passed into Belgium, flicked over the border without even a glance by the guards on both sides at their passports, and drove around Namur and Liège, crossing into the Federal Republic near Aachen. The traffic had been steadily building up after Liège and now, down to two lanes of autobahn, they were forced to slow down.

Even so, after skirting Cologne, they soon reached Dusseldorf, on the edge of the huge conurbation which is the Ruhr. It was now only minutes to complete the journey to the heartland of German industry at Essen, just over six hours after leaving Paris. They were in good time for their appointment.

Chapter Twenty-Two

Chinese Food in Essen

Their German contacts in Essen had told them to go to the Folkwang Museum and to stand at the main entrance at three-thirty. At the appointed hour, the three men were waiting. Patience was necessary.

For twenty minutes Rick watched every person in the vicinity. They were mostly tourists visiting the Museum and battling for a place against the high-spirited school parties, who were on their way out. There was no sign that they were under surveillance which might have been the case if the Germans' 'phone was bugged.

Then Rick saw two tall blond and athletic-looking men, hair cropped short, and dressed in well-cut gray suits. They came directly towards the American and the two Irishmen.

'Good day,' said one. 'Mr. Maloney we presume?'

'No,' said Rick. 'My name is O'Coiléain or Collins and these are my two colleagues Mr. Maloney and Mr. MacSwiney.'

'Very glad to meet you,' they both said in unison and in perfect English, but with clipped precise accents. 'We think you will like to see the Museum, Yes?'

'Yes,' said Rick, hoping that it would not take long as he was anxious to get down to business.

As they strolled from room to room one of the Germans, who seemed to have the most initiative, spoke to Rick, having confirmed that he was the senior of the three.

'Sorry to be late Mr. Collins, we have been trying to telephone Tripoli all day. Nothing seems to work over there despite all that Siemens telecommunications equipment we sold them. However, we spoke to our friends a short while ago. They speak very highly of Mr. Maloney and your excellent work. Let us show you our works of art – we have one of the most excellent collections in the whole of Europe here in Essen.'

Between the Van Goghs and the Gauguins, the German spoke again.

'We understand from Libya that you are intending to improve your war against the English – correct. Yes?'

'Yes,' said Rick, 'we want to deliver a master blow which will bring victory without any more senseless bloodshed.'

'All generals from von Clausewitz to Rommel have dreamed of such things, but few achieve it,' he said with a whimsical look.

Between the Renoirs and Kokoschka, Rick replied:

'We believe we have the plan which would devastate our enemies.'

The German slapped Rick on the back and said:

'Anything you can do to the English will have our support. We have not forgotten their brutality to the German people. My friend Helmut and I were both born during the war but our fathers never lived to see us.'

'Terrible,' muttered Rick thinking of all the parentless children from countless wars.

'And yet we never went to war on England. The Germans could have co-operated with England. That stupid Chamberlain declared war on us for no good reason and Churchill, the warmonger, carried on. Together we could have defeated Russia, but now the Russian puppets are in Berlin, Dresden and Leipzig. But we know our friends and we are glad Ireland stayed out of that war.'

Peadar MacSwiney had joined them and overheard part of the conversation.

'We Irish are grateful for past help from Germany. One of my own relatives was working with you in 1916,' he said in faultless German which surprised the blond man.

'Where did you learn to speak such good German?' the German asked quickly, relieved that he had not made indiscreet remarks to his friend which the Irishman would have understood.

'I lived in Hamburg.'

'Good, very good. German connections with Ireland have always been close. Germans have had to fight most countries in Europe during our long history, but never Ireland. And now you can see some of our Beckmanns. Are they not beautiful?'

The five men left the museum after half an hour and walked the short distance to Kahrstrasse.

'Now you see why we choose Folkwang as our meeting place. It is so near. Yes?' asked Jorgen, who had by now introduced himself. 'Here we have our office.'

They were shown into a tall building with smart but heavy furniture displayed in a huge shop on the ground floor. Rick made a mental note of the sign Möbel-Hessen in case he had to find this place on his own.

The elevator took them to the eighth floor and to leave it the Germans had to activate an iron grill which they did with a small key. They were then able to step into a large opulently furnished room with soft low settees in the centre. The lights, which had come on as the grill opened, were subdued but showed up the delicate colours of the decor. Here and there were brass coffee pots and other souvenirs of the Arab world, but the room was dominated by a massive sculpture depicting Icarus.

Jorgen went to a cabinet and turned a switch. Within a flash the place was filled with music coming from four amplifiers concealed in the four corners of the room.

'You like it, yes? Quadraphonic, I think you call it. Now make yourselves comfortable here. Drink, yes?'

Rick was impressed. 'Your security is good.'

'Yes,' said Helmut, taking up the conversation as Jorgen dispensed drinks, 'we have to be very careful about Israeli agents. They would like to know about us. See this.'

He turned another switch and a panel on the wall opened up to reveal a television screen showing people walking along a crowded pavement.

'That is the street outside,' he explained. 'Now if I adjust the camera you can see the entrance to our building. Anyone coming here can be scrutinised without their knowing it. We only admit people we know.'

'It is good, yes?' said Jorgen. 'We are the most effective representatives for sophisticated arms in the whole of the Federal Republic. We have been helping our Arab friends for five years now, and the Israelis do not like it, yes?'

'Yes,' said Rick sipping a whisky.

'How can we help our Irish brothers?' asked Jorgen.

Rick explained the type of equipment required. It had to be highly mobile and yet completely destructive of a limited area, which could be a conference room in a big building or the whole of one house.

'I think I understand,' said Jorgen. 'Your master plan is to destroy a number of very important people, yes?'

'Yes,' said Rick.

'They are the enemy's generals, yes?'

'No.'

'Ah, they must be the politicians then. A good plan. Is this to be executed in London?' said Jorgen.

'Yes,' said Rick, all caution abandoned. It seemed pointless to deny information to these highly intelligent Germans who could not be fooled like the Arabs. At this stage it would probably be more dangerous not to trust them than to take them into confidence.

'You Irish are very clever,' said Jorgen, with more respect in his tone. 'I did not realise that you meant such serious business against our English friends. It is very interesting, yes?'

They talked generally for an hour and agreed to continue discussions on the plan next day.

'We shall book you into the Kaiserhof Reichshof or the Vereinhus,' said Jorgen. 'But I think we have dinner somewhere else, yes?'

'That will be fine,' said Rick.

'Do you eat with chopsticks?' The three Irishmen looked doubtful. 'Well then you must learn. There are eight hundred million Chinese and we must know their ways if we are to be their allies against the Russians,' said Jorgen.

'Shall we take them to the Yuen Yong in Viehtofer Strasse?' asked Helmut.

'Good, very good,' said Jorgen.

After perfect Chinese food, washed down with cold Riesling, sleep was no problem to the visitors. Their image of the Ruhr heartland had been of industrial squalor and grime, but instead they had found a clean, attractive city with the living and social arrangements as good as anywhere. For Rick and Maloney, it was an eye-opener; Peadar knew his Germans better.

Helmut collected them at eight the next morning, after they had eaten breakfast of coffee and rolls in their rooms.

They found Jorgen was ready for them with manuals and charts spread around in the sitting room office.

'Good morning. Now we can show you what is available,' he said in a very business-like voice.

For two hours he and Helmut demonstrated to the Irishmen an understanding of weapons which was totally impressive.

'It is like this,' said Jorgen, 'we can use either very simple devices like grenades which can be fired from the shoulder.'

'What range do they have?' asked Rick.

'Take this one, the M203 grenade launcher. It will throw the projectile up to four hundred metres.'

'Held on the shoulder?' asked Rick.

'Oh, yes – very simple to use. But it has only up to one hundred and fifty metres range for a point target.'

'What is the projectile?' asked Rick.

'Well it can be high explosive or buck shot. If you want to kill a lot of people the buck shot projectile would be best,' said Jorgen, warming to his theme, 'there are more sophisticated techniques if you want to blow up a whole building and everyone in it.'

'Such as?' asked Rick, who had some doubts about the effectiveness of a grenade attack.

'If we knew the exact location of the building in question it is possible to programme a robot to fly a helicopter to it and release a high-explosive bomb immediately overhead. Do we know the place we want to attack?' asked Jorgen.

'It is in the middle of London where the Ministers meet,' said Rick.

'You cannot mean to blow up the whole Houses of Parliament. That would mean a very big bomb indeed,' Helmut now intervened.

'We think another place might be better,' said Rick.

'I see,' said Jorgen, 'Number 10, Downing Street, very interesting, yes?'

Peadar now spoke: 'I have the exact position of Number 10.'

'What is it?'

'Latitude 51° 31.15 North and Longitude 0° 07.50 West.'

'Is that absolutely accurate?' asked Jorgen, now very intense.

'Yes, I double checked it on the largest Ordnance Survey maps. I have the numbers of them here. TQ 37 North West and TQ 27 North East. It's as reliable as you can get I suppose,' said Peadar.

'Good, very good,' said Jorgen. 'It would be possible to launch the helicopter from somewhere North of London, say here in Hertfordshire,' he pointed at a map of Southern England, 'and have ground units stationed here in Hampstead Heath and south there just over the Thames.'

'What would the ground units do?' asked Rick.

'Provide directional beams for guidance. The helicopter's flight would be adjusted according to the air currents so that it came to exactly the position we had pre-determined,' said Jorgen

'Then it would release the bomb?' asked Rick.

'Yes, then it would release the bomb,' said Jorgen. 'And your mission would be completed.'

'How about radar; isn't all air traffic over London controlled?' asked Peadar, pleased that his detailed researches had been of value.

'The helicopter would fly below radar,' said Jorgen. 'Anyway they would not dare to shoot it down. It would look like an ordinary civilian helicopter flying off course. Isn't there a landing pad near Westminster?'

'Yes, there at Battersea,' said Peadar, pointing to a spot on the London map. 'By the Thames along from Westminster.'

'There you are, they would think the helicopter is going there,' said Jorgen triumphantly.

Rick was fascinated, but also sceptical. His active mind could see all sorts of snags to this sophisticated scheme. It involved too many uncertainties. There would be the problem of obtaining the helicopter and programming it, and the dangers of detection by the police in Hertfordshire, even before the helicopter was off the ground. It needed a lot of thinking about.

'What are the other possibilities?' he asked.

'In between the grenade and the airborne bomb there is all this,' said Jorgen, pointing to the diagrams spread around the room.

Maloney and Helmut were looking at one.

'This is a free flight rocket launcher made in Sweden, called the Carl-Gustav MS,' said Helmut, holding up an illustration. 'It has a range of one thousand metres, needs only two people to operate it and can be fired from a shoulder. It can blow up a tank at four hundred metres and the missile takes only one and three quarters seconds to get there.'

'That weapon is in service with your Irish Government army,' said Jorgen. 'It is good, very good. But we have a missile developed here in Germany which can be guided by beams straight to its target.'

'What is that?' asked Rick, taking his cue.

'It's the Mamba,' said Jorgen, 'made by Messerschmitt-Bolkow-Blohm, and named after an African snake with a deadly sting.'

'What's its range?' asked Peadar, now realising the full significance of his detailed surveys around Whitehall.

'From three hundred to two thousand metres,' said Jorgen, 'and its very, very accurate.'

'That company makes more simple devices also,' said Helmut. 'For instance the Armbrust 300 which any man can carry.'

'How much does it weigh?' asked Rick.

'Only six kilos and it can blow up a tank at three hundred metres,' said Helmut.

'Can we discuss the actual target in more detail,' said Jorgen. 'Believe me, there is the appropriate weapon for every purpose. I understand you need to pick off a number of people who will probably be together on some occasions.'

'Yes,' said Rick.

'At Number 10 Downing Street?'

'Yes.'

'Do we know much about that building?' asked Jorgen.

'Yes, Peadar has photographs and drawings,' said Rick.

Peadar opened a briefcase and displayed the results of his week's work in London. Jorgen looked at the photographs.

'Pretty girl, pretty enough to be a German,' he said. 'Pity she's blurred, but the buildings come out beautifully.'

He paid particular attention to the photographs taken from St. James's Park and Horse Guards Parade.

'This is excellent,' he said at last. 'The rear of this building is completely unprotected. There is nothing to prevent a missile fired from the park from penetrating the window of that conference room at the back and destroying everything inside it.'

'That room is the Cabinet Room. I myself stood only a dozen or so metres from it, as you can see from this photograph,' said Peadar, pointing to a photograph of Ingrid standing with the policeman.

After some seconds Jorgen spoke again and with a tone of determination. 'This operation will be easier than I thought. We will not need the helicopter or anything so expensive and complicated. Number 10 can be penetrated from the rear with great accuracy, using relatively unsophisticated weapons.' The three visitors looked at each other in stunned silence as though they had just experienced a religious revelation. This was the solution they had been groping for over many months. Jorgen soon broke the tension with a curt comment, 'We hate the English, you know that very well, yes, but still we are professionals; our fee for our services on this project will be two hundred thousand dollars paid into a Swiss Bank account. You understand, yes.'

Rick, sensing support from Maloney, said confidently,

'Don't worry, the Libyans will take care of that.'

And if not, he thought, O'Halloran and Noraid always could.

Chapter Twenty-Three

The View from Scotland Yard

Early in the Summer of 1976 after James Callaghan had become Prime Minister, it was decided to split the responsibilities within the Bomb Squad at Scotland Yard to ensure a tight line of control in case of local emergencies. Chief Superintendent Bosworth, in addition to his other duties, was given overall control of the South West One area of London. He regarded the appointment as a mark of approval because the area included the Houses of Parliament, Downing Street, the Prime Minister's home and most of the ministerial offices.

It had been a tense and bitter year with little evidence of a solution being found to the Irish problem. Bosworth could not understand why the Protestants and Catholics could not get together and avoid bloodshed. He blamed the politicians on all sides. They had messed up the economy, increased unemployment and ruined Britain's reputation abroad. Thank goodness he thought, the British policeman was still regarded as a figure of honour and competence, despite the nasty *Daily Mirror* reports about policemen accepting bribes from porn kings. Nevertheless he was somewhat concerned that those inquiries might be coming a little too near home.

On his office wall he studied the large scale Ordnance Survey maps of his area of responsibility. He looked at them often to judge whether there could be any obvious weaknesses in the pattern of security. Trafalgar Square and down Whitehall to Parliament Square was secure enough; Ministry buildings had put grills on the windows to protect them from bombs thrown from passing cars. Downing

Street itself had a permanent barrier at the entrance, stopping all but official cars from entering the side street. The pedestrians' right-of-way through to St. James's Park had been maintained, which was fair enough: the tourists must be allowed access to take their photographs.

No one could get into the Home Office, the Treasury or the Foreign Office without a pass. Bosworth was a little concerned about some Arab Embassy officials with CD plates on their cars, who insisted on driving into the Foreign Office courtyard without having their vehicles checked. The issue could not be pursued without a diplomatic row and he had left it alone.

The Houses of Parliament were the most worrying from the security point of view. Everyone on the staff, even MPs, had to have passes to get in, but with five separate entrances there was always a chance for someone to slip through. The public had to be let in, which was a pity as sometimes they were most difficult to control. Some constables had been injured when mass demonstrations against unemployment had taken place. But, still, it was impossible for anyone to get a bomb into the place. That explosion in Westminster Hall had brought everyone to their senses and they had, at last, cleared out the Irish workers on the underground car park.

He looked at the map again. We forgot the river approach, he thought. Supposing someone in a fast boat came along the Embankment wall at high tide and threw a bomb through the Commons Library window. The consequences did not bear thinking about. Nevertheless, he made a note to ask the River Patrol to check up on the situation.

Buckingham Palace was like a fortress. Nothing to worry about there. Since the attempt to kidnap Princess Anne on The Mall, better arrangements had been instituted for Royal Family travelling.

Bosworth lit another Players No. 1. He could not give up the habit and by the end of the day the ashtray was full of stubs. Must find a substitute, he thought, but maybe enough have already been smoked in my lifetime to give me lung cancer, so what does it matter? Anyway, how could he be expected to stop smoking when he had one of the worst jobs on the Force. Constant tension and never knowing when the guerrillas were going to strike next.

He pulled up the bulky files on past incidents to refresh his memory and to see if any discernible pattern emerged. Fortunately, they had managed to jail some of the terrorists responsible for the earlier crimes – the twenty-five year old girl who had been infiltrated into the Army and, after discharge, had blown up an army coach to murder twenty people. Thirty years for her. Other known supporters of Provisional Sinn Fein had been thrown out of England like John Rafferty, McGarrigle and Sean Greely, who was at one time its chairman in Britain.

All the same, the toll of incidents and of lives had been bad. Harrods and Selfridges in Oxford Street, bombed during the Christmas rush of 1974, the terrible explosion at the pub in Birmingham when seventeen people were killed and a hundred and twenty injured, three telephone exchanges blasted and a telephonist killed, the two attempts on the life of ex-Premier Heath, the bombs in the Army frequented pubs at Woolwich Arsenal and Caterham, the restaurant bombings and the assassination of McWhirter. It was a sickening story.

Bosworth surveyed the reports and wondered how it was that the British people could stomach all that violence without hitting back. It was surprisng there had not been demands for Britain to pull out of Ireland. It just went to show how resolute the British people were when put to the test. They could take a certain level of violence in their stride. Strangely enough, the constant exposure of terrorism in the media had helped in conditioning the public to it; most people would not remember last year's incidents under all the layers of newspaper stories pumped out since that time.

Bosworth was still confident that the terrorists could be beaten back. Constant vigilance, he preached to his men, is the price we must pay for security. In his own Whitehall area he maintained patrols of uniformed and plainclothes

men to watch for any suspicious movements. The bombers
would have a difficult job to attack where he had
responsibility.

But in his personal life George Bosworth was far from
happy. Despite her avowed intention to move to London,
announced months before, Mary was still stuck in
Brighton. It had turned out to be impossible to sell the
shop. Being off-season did not help and the estate agent cut
the asking figure by half, saying it did not stand an earthly
of fetching the original figure they had in mind. The
hanging-on irritated Bosworth. He was annoyed because he
did not have enough money to bring Mary back to Chelsea,
and say to hell with the shop. Sometimes he wished he was
back in the vice squad, where he could collect a little extra
on the side. There was no money in the bomb squad – only
headaches. Well it will not last for ever, he said to himself,
preparing, after an incident-free day, to slip home to
Angela. Tomorrow he could plead work and catch the late
afternoon Pullman to Brighton; it would be a soothing relief
to have Mary in his arms again.

Just as he was leaving, an assistant came running in with
a telex. 'Today, at a press conference held in Belfast within
yards of the British troops, the leader of the Provisional
Sinn Fein, declared that the struggle against the occupying
army would go on with renewed bomb attacks in London.'

'Well,' said Bosworth in anger, 'they're still shouting
wolf.'

Chapter Twenty-Four

Journey to Libya

After the meetings with the German arms specialists in Essen, Rick and the two Irishmen drove to the international airport just south of Cologne, well pleased with their progress. They arranged to divide forces: Maloney was to fly back to Libya to fix the orders which the Colonels would place with the various German firms on behalf of the Libyan Government; Peadar would fly to Dublin to report progress to O'Connell; and Rick himself was to return to Rome, Luigi and the Italian project.

They checked the car in at the Avis desk, where Peadar signed for the hiring charges on his American Express card. Rick, cautiously, did not use any of his credit cards knowing that it was the practice of the Company to obtain the vouchers of their personnels' card accounts every month, and cross-check on the transactions. When operatives were discovered to have been in countries or staying in hotels where they were not supposed to be, according to the reports sent to the Company, then the alert signals went up and close surveillance was ordered. Rick could take no risks: CIA surveillance was the last thing he wanted at this stage.

After his four days away, nothing had changed: Italy was still in a political and economic mess, but at least the airport was working and he got to his apartment without difficulty. The most disturbing aspect of the situation was the increasing cooperation between the Communists and certain Roman Catholic Bishops and priests, following the lead set by Cardinal Michele Pellegrini, the Archbishop of Turin. In January he had held a service at the parish church of Leoni for two thousand strikers from the Singer factory, quoting from the book of Isaiah: 'Woe upon them that decree unrighteous decrees and turn aside the needy from judgement and take away the right from the poor of my people.'

The link between the Communist Party and elements of the Catholic Church was a new dimension in Italian political affairs. Rick expected that the American Ambassador to the Vatican would make strenuous representations to the Pope about it and was pleased not to be directly concerned in this mess of pottage; his reports to Intelligence in Virginia had been very well received. It was up to them to use the information to advantage, and he was sure they had done so during the general election in June. Even so the C.I.A. must have had an almighty scare when the Communists increased their seats in the Chamber of Deputies from 179 to 228 and polled 34.4% of the votes. But at least U.S. help had enabled the Christian Democrats to remain 4% ahead of the C.P. which was something to show for his efforts. But without a clear majority there was bound to be even more political uncertainty and economic decline. He was glad he would soon be out of Italy as well as the Company: he was surprised to find he was looking forward to the prospect, especially after remembering his earlier commitment.

On his last trip to Philadelphia he had talked over the coming resignation with Kathy, and she had been ecstatic. As a result some of the old warmth had come back into their relationship: their lovemaking had been much better. They both felt a terrible blanket of stress was being lifted from their lives.

Rick was uncertain what he would do after resignation. He certainly could not stay with Tube Stack: Hal would never allow it. Perhaps he could get an assignment with an American company representing their interests in Europe, perhaps even live in Ireland. He touched the slim, green Irish passport which he always kept in a hidden inside pocket of his jacket. It was both a talisman and a comforter.

He had promised Kathy to resign from the CIA at the

end of November – as soon as the job for Ireland was completed. She still did not know what it was but fortunately, she never pried; he was grateful for that. It was a long summer with Rick impatient for the final act of the drama. He knew though that nothing should be rushed: the piecing of the jigsaw had to be painstakingly correct.

By late August most of the equipment had been delivered to the Libyans and the Germans were in Tripoli to test it out. Rick joined them, travelling on his Irish passport, so the Arabs would regard him as a friend and not as a spy. United States support for Israel had made Americans very unpopular in Libya which, of all the Arab states, with the exception of Syria, was the most hostile to the Jewish homeland. It would also be far too dangerous from the Company's point of view to be identified as an American. If word went back to Virginia, some extremely awkward questions would be asked. A project on the Italian Communists could hardly include covert trips to unfriendly North Africa.

Libya was hot, certainly the hottest place Rick had ever experienced, and his discomfort was increased by the arid wind blowing off the vast Sahara to the South. Oil had given the country a superficial affluence. Newly constructed concrete buildings – some starkly beautiful, but mostly ugly – were everywhere, superimposed on the ancient suk. Rick marvelled at the transformation being wrought in this barren land. Hospitals and schools were being provided on a scale which would have been unthinkable before the liquid gold had begun oozing out of the wells twenty years before. Medical care and education were free for all Libyans, but the welfare state did not include alcohol, forbidden – to his chagrin – under the strictest interpretation of the Koran.

The population of two million people were among the wealthiest in the world in terms of per capita income, but the wealth had obviously not percolated to all the ordinary people. Rick studied the faces of the men, invariably weather-beaten and taciturn, wrapped up in brightly coloured scarves and sometimes thick greatcoats on the hottest days. He soon realised the reasons for this protection: sand dust-storms could be wounding to the ill-clad and the nights could be bitterly cold.

Rick wondered if these simple people, dragged through two centuries of experience, within the past two decades, realized the immense strength they wielded in the world.

There was no doubt that the Colonels understood their power. They were mostly in their late thirties and early forties who had been thrown up by the revolution which had deposed King Idris seven years before, and having chosen the winning side, had stayed to ride the desert tiger. The majority had been educated in the military academies of Cairo, a few in Damascas and one or two at Sandhurst. They were united in a loathing for Israel, with compromisers with Israel, like the Egyptians, and a dislike, mixed with disdain, for the English.

The Germans were ebullient. Rick was surprised to discover they had both spent five days in London studying the exact location of the Cabinet room and checking Peadar's figures. They had discovered one or two minor discrepancies.

On their second night in Tripoli, sitting on the hotel verandah, looking out to the dark Mediterranean with a moonless sky showing the intensity of a myriad of stars, they talked about the coming debacle in a country hundreds of miles away. Considering the enormity of the conception, the conversation was strangely matter-of-fact. It was as if the scheme, having been launched months before, had now developed an internal logic and momentum of its own, and as if the mere human hands to the drama were not unthinking servants to it.

The Germans had decided on the most effective, as well as relatively simple, technique for the destruction of the vital room in Number Ten Downing Street. The helicopter plan was rejected as too sophisticated and requiring too many participants. The positioning of anti-tank missile launchers in St. James's Park would require time, perhaps ten to fifteen minutes, and detection from plain clothes patrols might be effected within that crucial period. The solution was to mount two launchers in a sturdy estate car. At the exact point for the appropriate trajectory, the projectiles would be released.

The calculations the Germans had made were perfect and Rick admired their application to detail: even the camber of the road had been studied to ensure that it would not affect the accuracy of the missiles. The route had been paced out many times. The estate car, with two launchers mounted in the curtained off rear, would be driven along Constitutional Hill around the Queen Victoria Memorial, facing Buckingham Palace, and down The Mall. Before Admiralty Arch the car would turn right, keeping to the road encircling St. James's Park. Ahead would be the wartime bunker, built at the back of the Admiralty, where Prime Minister Winston Churchill had had his underground office.

By turning right at this point, the driver would be able to ensure an uninterrupted drive towards Birdcage Walk with Horse Guards Parade on the left. The road had been observed on weekday mornings and it was always clear of obstruction and traffic. It was an ideal road for their purpose. When the car drove off from the marking bollard of the T-Junction, the mechanism of the launchers would be activated to release the missiles seconds later. The car would be driven at a steady twenty miles per hour, which would mean that the missiles would emerge through the now opened car window at a point two hundred .and ten metres from the junction. The target would stand ninety-eight and a half metres to the East, exactly at right angles to the position of the moving vehicle.

The missiles would crash through the window at the end of the long Cabinet Room, straight on to the Cabinet table. There would be no possibility of failure. All the problems of sighting and aiming would have been dealt with and the two men in the vehicle would need only to think of three actions:

1) Open the window as the vehicle slowed to stop at the bollard

2) Activate the mechanism as the car drove from that marking point and
3) Drive at a steady twenty miles per hour.

The plan had the merit of simplicity and was foolproof against accidents, apart from sudden car engine failure.

Rick congratulated the two Germans on their efforts and asked: 'What do you propose the missiles should contain?'

'We thought long and hard about that and decided high explosive would not be sufficient in itself; there might be some survivors,' said Jorgen.

'We want no survivors; they would become heros and defeat our purpose entirely,' said Rick.

'Don't worry, all the people in that room will be eliminated within seconds. Special missiles are now being developed which will ensure that,' said Helmut.

'Good,' said Rick.

'They will contain explosive, buckshot for body and brain penetration and lethal gas which will be released to fill the room as soon as the missiles enter the window,' explained Jorgen.

'When will they be ready?' asked Rick, elated.

'September 13: air freight delivery into Tripoli from Munich,' said Jorgen. 'The rest is here and we will test it with dummy missiles.'

Next morning as the bright dawn was breaking over the sand dunes and the sea to the East, they drove out of Tripoli to the secret training and testing unit the Libyans had established inland between Gharyan and Yafran. As soon as they left the capital, the land looked inhospitable with occasional peasants, eking out an existence with scrawny flocks of sheep and goats. Rick speculated on the problem of passing the country's wealth down to these people. The automated oil industry could run on ten thousand people or less and all the food and supplies the country needed could be imported at half – or even less – of the revenue from oil. How could people be paid for work which was not necessary?

On the road leading to the unit, their convoy of three cars

was stopped at a check-point by soldiers carrying machine guns, but they were soon waved through, as the Libyans accompanying them had priority passes. Beyond the barbed wire were other men with guns, firing at a practice range and conducting other exercises.

'Palestine Liberation Army,' Maloney said quietly to Rick, 'they come here from Jordan and the Lebanon for training.'

They reached another road block and here again they were saluted and waved through. After a mile the road changed to tarmac and the cars ceased throwing up irritating clouds of sand. Rick eased the window down to get some fresh air, but quickly closed it as the blast of stinging hot air hit him. It was barely two hours since dawn, but the heat was already intense.

After another mile they reached a cluster of buildings.

'This looks like it,' said Maloney.

They got out of the cars and joined the Germans who were in the first vehicle.

'Good journey, yes?' said Jorgen. 'Now we can have some refreshments with our friends and show you the test.'

In a reception room with surprisingly comfortable armchairs, they sat and drank iced orange juice, tasted sickly sweet cakes and ate large lucious dates. The fans of the air conditioning whirled with an annoyingly shrill noise.

Jorgen whispered to Rick: 'Our friends have prepared things well for us. I gave them sketches of the target area – without, of course, telling where it was – and they have produced a mock-up for us. We go there now, yes?'

When they reached the site, Rick was amazed to see the extent of the preparations for the test. Jorgen pointed to a marker on the road and to a plan he held in his left hand.

'That is the bollard on The Mall and this track leading from it has the same curve as the road around St. James's Park. This is where the vehicle with the missile launcher will drive. And see that wooden structure over there, that is the simulation of the rear of Number Ten Downing Street. Now here is the vehicle. Would you like to come with me?'

The Libyan soldiers had driven up an estate car to join the group. Two neat launchers were mounted in the rear compartment with two projectiles ready in position for firing.

'Now you will see for yourself how it will work,' said Jorgen. 'Come.'

They climbed into the car, with Rick taking the right hand passenger seat.

'This is a left-hand drive car,' said Rick. 'You do realize, I hope, that in England it will be right-hand drive and there you keep to the left hand side of the road?'

'I am glad you have such an eye for detail. We do not neglect it either,' starting up the engine. 'Now watch, I will press this activator just as we drive away.'

Rick checked the speedometer and saw that after they reached twenty miles per hour, Jorgen kept the car steadily at that speed.

Exactly as Jorgen had predicated, 33·12 seconds after leaving the marker point, the car shuddered as the two missiles, almost simultaneously, blasted off through the car window. With a chilling thrill, Rick saw both of them hit the wooden structure dead on target.

Chapter Twenty-Five

Courtmacsherry

In Rick's mind the countdown to the ultimate was accelerating; like a metronome picking up speed. It was now September and all his other interests were becoming increasingly submerged as the fateful weeks ticked by. Even Philadelphia was shrouded in the mists of his consciousness like a far away dream. He still loved Kathy very much but she belonged to another life, another time. She did not share and could never share this temporary extension of himself. The man now travelling from Rome to Cork as Ristéard O'Coiléain was a unique creation: physically identical to Richard Collins but mentally another man.

The missiles had arrived in Tripoli from the Munich firm on time. It was now only necessary to finish the planning for the transfer of the equipment to the United Kingdom itself. Error at this stage would be fatal.

Rick had concluded his main report on the Italian Communist financial situation and had handed it to the courier, who had flown in especially from Virginia to collect it. He was quite proud of it. The information up-dated the position since the election in June and gave fascinating details of certain Communist controlled companies. One called Restitulal, based in Milan and operating a subsidiary Sorimpex, used a valuable concession with the U.S.S.R. to trade in diamonds, gold and manufactured goods. And in another case the non-C.P. firm of Marelli sold half a million dollars of radio equipment to Czechoslovakia using the good offices of the Italian Communist Party which in due course collected a commission on the deal. He had told headquarters that he was going to Switzerland and Luxembourg to tie up the odd ends of the Communists' external banking connexions. It would be a plausible excuse for an extended absence from Italy.

He changed planes at Le Bourget Airport in Paris, to the direct flight 823 to Cork. Peadar was there to meet him.

'I've arranged a cottage for you. It's on holiday rental to tourists and, as its the end of the season, it's available for the next six weeks if we want it,' he said, as they drove away from the airport.

'That sounds very suitable,' said Rick, breathing in the sweet fresh smell of Ireland like a man coming up for breath after weeks underground.

'Rome is stifling, Peadar. It's good to be back in the home country.'

They turned right on to the main L42 road towards the South.

'Are we missing Cork?' asked Rick.

'Yes, we are going to a place just over twenty miles from here. We don't need to go into Cork at all. Pedraig and Patrick are waiting for us at the cottage.'

Within half an hour they had passed through Kinsale and across the long bridge over the Bandon River. Ireland looked prettier than ever, incredibly green, relaxed and relaxing and epitomising the ideal Rick hankered after: calmness and absence from the tensions afflicting Italy and, to a lesser extent, America.

Their destination was Courtmacsherry, a tiny place with gaily painted cottages on a quiet road on the shore of a beautiful estuary. Behind the village were deep green hills rising to four or five hundred feet. It was idyllic and Rick loved it at first sight.

O'Connell and Maloney were drinking tea in the front room looking out on the water twinkling in the twilight.

'Welcome home,' O'Connell said, 'how d'you like it?'

'Couldn't be better,' Rick replied, feeling more Irish than the Irish. 'You'll be having me forgetting there's work to do.'

'To be sure, you'll not be forgetting with things going so well,' said O'Connell.

The four men reviewed the progress on the plan, which they agreed, should still not be revealed to anyone else, including the High Command. The need for tight security was paramount. But they needed some help to get the equipment into England. It would not be the easiest task to bring it from Libya across Europe into London. Any airfreight by commercial flights out of Tripoli would invite careful customs examination and to ask the Libyans to include it in Embassy stores, would lead to them getting too deeply involved.

Maloney knew the Libyans would provide the money needed for transport costs as well as all the other expenses. 'It could be put down as part of their testing programme,' he said. 'Development of new weapons.'

The import into Ireland would produce no particular difficulty as arms were being brought in all the time under the noses of the Irish coastal patrols. Transfer from Europe or Ireland into Britain needed more careful attention. Using the Queen Elizabeth II on the Cherbourg to Southampton route had to be ruled out since the recent arrest of Irish sympathisers involved in the route and the new rigorous searches of the liner.

O'Connell suggested a light aircraft. There were, he said, several short take off and landing Cessna 182s on the Irish register, which could be hired for the job – at a price. It was agreed that Rick should study the various options and the transport plan should be formulated before he left Courtmacsherry to return to Tripoli.

For the next three days Rick wrestled with the problem. The 'ultimate' was like a jigsaw puzzle. The first pieces had fitted together very easily, then there was a run of luck when the Germans came into the picture with one piece following the other almost without conscious effort. But now the final pieces had to be put into position exactly. One false placing would shatter the whole edifice.

In the mornings he went walking around Ramsey Hill to Broadstrand Bay. The weather was delightful; after the dry heat of Libya and the stuffy, sultry atmosphere of Rome, it was refreshing to breathe in the clean and still warm air of the Irish fall. At Barry's Point he stood on the cliff to look towards Britain, the enemy, across one hundred and fifty miles of sea. After ten months he felt even more convinced that his concept of the 'ultimate' had been right. The arrogance of the English had to be cut down to size. After centuries of ruling colonial countries, they had been forced to disgorge their Empire. Even tiny islands like the Seychelles, with only sixty thousand people, had secured complete independence. But in a throw-back to a colonial past the English still clung to Northern Ireland. It was a disgrace which could only be remedied by extreme measures: the end would surely justify the means.

With Peadar's help Rick checked the performance of the Cessna. It would suit their purpose admirably for carrying the equipment into Ireland. The plane had a pay-load of 608 kilos or 1340 lbs and a range of 885 miles at economic cruising speed. Even allowing for the pilot and one passenger there would still be 800 lbs capacity available for the equipment which only weighed a total of 248 lbs.

The aircraft could pick up the consignment in Britany in North West France, landing on one of the long straight roads which could be blocked off for half an hour with diversion signs. Without refuelling the plane could then make the return trip of 310 miles back to Ireland with gas to spare. Radar screens would be no problem as far as Eire was concerned, as they were only effective in the few miles around Cork, Dublin and Shannon airports. In France the pilot would need to keep fifty miles away from the naval base at Brest, which was well equipped with radar, and fly in over the coast at less than five hundred feet. On the return to Ireland there were dozens of fields where the Cessna could land, even at night with help from flares. It would be better to return in daylight, which should be possible, as the return trip could be accomplished within six hours. It would be too dangerous to attempt to fly straight into Southern England as the whole area was too well patrolled against illegal immigrants and drug smuggling.

'It's a lovely little plane,' said Peadar. 'It can land in

three hundred feet and has a stalling speed of fifty-five miles per hour. Any fool could fly it.'

The other two legs of the journey – from Libya to North West France and from Ireland into Britain, needed more thought. Flying the Cessna into other parts of Britain was hazardous. British radar surveillance was more comprehensive, particularly in Cornwall and Devon, which were the obvious places to land and the country police, if they got wind of an unauthorised landing, could easily block roads leading out of this toe of England. The police were also vigilant against Pakistani immigrants flying in. Flying up the British Channel at four hundred feet under the radar screens might be the way to bring the plane to land in Somerset, from which the load could be dispersed into the Bristol area. But the risk in this case was of observation by shipping, particularly coastguards, operating in the busy sea lanes to Barry, Cardiff and Avonmouth.

Central Wales offered a radar and observation free area. But hours poring over the one-inch maps Peadar had brought could produce not one suggestion of a suitable landing spot. There were only a few military airfields in the whole Principality and no abandoned airstrips, as was the case in Eastern England. It was impossible to find a hundred level feet of field, let alone the three hundred necessary for landing and take off.

They decided Peadar would look at other more reliable means of delivering the equipment into Britain, whilst Rick and Maloney would return to Libya to escort it as far as North West France. Meanwhile, they recruited the pilot, a Republican supporter, who had often flown into France on clandestine missions, and they agreed with him the place where the pick up would take place. It would be at a point near Pontrieux which had the great advantage, from the pilot's angle, of being easily located. From Cork he would fly South East for two hundred miles, turning due East over the English Channel. At precisely three degrees longitude West, he would head directly South, reducing height to four hundred feet. He would then fly visually over the landmark of the Ile de Brehat and slightly to the West up the estuary of the River Trieux.

It was agreed that Rick and Maloney would carry a VHF radio in their vehicle to enable communication to be established with the plane when it came into range over the French coast. They would plan to arrive at the appointed rendezvous by the last week of October and wait at the place from noon each day until weather conditions allowed the plane to fly in. A signal on the radio would enable the diversion signs to be put up in good time to effect a safe landing.

Regretfully, Rick had to leave Courtmacsherry by the end of September to ensure that he met the strict timetable. By the time he returned in a month, the ultimate equipment would be safely with him and the jigsaw would be almost complete.

Chapter Twenty-Six

The Men in Virginia

In a large darkened office in Virginia three men were sitting in easy chairs studying photographs thrown up on a screen at one end of the room. One other man was standing at a projector inserting slides and talking at the same time.

'We have these photos from our man in Tel Aviv. He got them from Israeli intelligence. They can't unravel the significance and they've asked us to help. We may be on to something. But on the other hand it may be another bum steer. You never know with the Israelis.'

He inserted another slide; it was rather blurred.

'This shows the three men arriving at Tripoli Airport. This is a routine shot of passengers arriving in Libya – Israeli agents, as far as possible, take a record of all arrivals. They've thrown up some interesting information as a result, particularly on Germans, but that's by the way.'

The next slide was clearer.

'This shot shows two of the men entering the hotel in Tripoli. They were brought under partial surveillance by the Israeli agents because they had spent the day visiting the training camp operated for the Palestine Liberation Army. At that time the Israelis thought they were military advisers to the PLA – probably Germans too.'

He inserted the third slide, which was in good focus.

'This shows one of the men getting into a car outside the hotel. The Israelis bribed the hotel staff to get at the mystery men's passports, and discovered to their surprise they were all Irishmen – at least they were travelling on Irish passports.'

'What were their travelling names?' asked one of the men lounging in the easy chairs.

'Reported as MacSwiney, O'Coiléain and Maloney,' he replied, slipping in the fourth slide, 'and here is a clear shot of the three at Tripoli airport just before they caught a plane for Rome.'

'Say, hold it there,' said another of the men. 'I'm darned sure I know that face.'

'Is he one of the KGB agents you've been working for?' asked another.

'Nope, he doesn't look like a Russian does he? His head isn't square enough – or thick enough,' he added with a chuckle.

'Well, who is it then?'

'Must be someone I met once in Europe.'

The other man in the group now exclaimed: 'I know him too and I've never been to Europe. Let's see those shots again.'

The slides were shown, slowly, one by one until their features were as familiar to the four men as those of Kojak or Ronald Reagan. Suddenly the last man exclaimed again, 'I've got it. He's the double of someone on my course at Camp Peary.'

'Maybe I saw him around the Company too,' said the other.

The senior of the three was talking now: 'This could be serious if he's one of those who's defected from the service. Check up on the passing-out photos of the classes in '65 and '66.

They met again within an hour, during which time computerised records had come up with all details of the graduates of ten years and earlier.

'The man travelling under the name of Ristéard O'Coiléain has now been positively identified as Richard Collins,' reported the projector operator. 'The Israelis had obtained his fingerprints off a glass and they match up with our records on Collins.'

'O'Coiléain must be the Irish spelling of Collins,' said one of the others.

'This could be a false alarm if he's engaged on Company business,' said the senior man. 'According to records he's still in the service under DDI. It may all be legit but to be on the safe side will someone do a memo to DDI. Meanwhile, where were we on the PLA dispositions?'

When the memo reached DDI he was more than perplexed. He buzzed the Deputy Director Plans.

'I have a report on one of my men who has been seen in Libya, apparently on unauthorised activity. You haven't recruited him for some super-clandestine job have you? If so I wish you'd tell me these things.'

DDI could not believe Collins could be acting as a double agent. All the records confirmed the operative's competence and reliability; the last LCFLUTTER examination revealed no retrograde tendencies and all the polygraphs taken since he joined the service showed the same stable pattern. Collins was one of the best men he had.

DDP was back on the line:

'We checked with Western Europe, Near East and Africa Divisions and there's been no change in Collins' mission. He should still be on the Italy job and his last report indicated he'd be in Switzerland and Luxembourg.'

'Well there must be some explanation. We can't suddenly have our key men popping up in PLA training centres. I'll instigate a complete check on his wife's movements and put him under twenty-four hour surveillance just as soon as we can locate him,' said DDI.

Within a few hours the Director was reading a priority memorandum: *Emergency procedures have been activated in respect of Collins, Richard, currently operating under DDI in top secret WE mission (country: Italy). Operative is suspected of defecting or acting as double-agent for unfriendly power. Immediate location unknown but search being instituted by local stations in Switzerland, Luxembourg, Libya and Italy. All other WE and NE stations alerted.*

Chapter Twenty-Seven

Across the Mediterranean

The two packages looked so innocent in the back of the truck. It was difficult to imagine the power compressed into those containers. As they drove along the hot dusty coast road West out of Tripoli, Rick was philosophising again: power or strength to be useful had to be applied at the most sensitive point. To blow off these missiles in this desert would be useless, but at the right place and at the right time the explosion could change the course of human history like the assassination at Sarajevo. It was an awe-inspiring thought for an early morning in October, with Maloney still half asleep in the next seat and an Arab swathed in a red-checked scarf driving recklessly over the bumpy road.

They were soon entering Al-Khums, an undistinguished town hugging the shore; Rick pointed to the map for Maloney to see.

'Half-way, we'll be there before long.'

'Good, I don't like this fellow's driving. They treat vehicles like dodgem cars.'

'Yes,' said Rick. 'He'd be a bit more careful if he knew more about the load.'

As they drove on the heat came up; not as bad as August but still very hot.

Maloney said: 'Another scorcher today. Imagine living here, or worse still, fighting a war in these conditions like the Germans and the English did.'

'Yes, those soldiers had guts,' said Rick. 'Rommel forced the English right to the gates of Cairo. Fancy fighting over this God-forsaken land, no oil discovered then. Hardly worth it.'

'Strategy I suppose,' said Maloney. 'Wasn't the English General Montgomery their best man? Didn't he beat Rommel?'

'I believe he was an Ulsterman,' said Rick.

'You don't say,' said Maloney.

At the Misratah Marina the Germans were waiting.

'Success, success,' said Jorgen. 'The boat is all arranged. The Captain is from Naples and he knows the Mediterranean like a pool in his back yard. You'll have to pay him six thousand dollars in nice clean notes before he'll take you. I have given him my word of honour that you are not carrying drugs. He's terrified of the French police who arrested him once in Marseilles, with a load of cannabis resin.'

'Has he understood our cover story?' asked Rick.

'No doubt,' said Jorgen. 'He's done it before. You two gentlemen of leisure are simply putting in to pick up your girlfriends who are flying down to Perpignan to meet you.'

The ship was a large high-powered cabin cruiser which, usually, was leased by the month to prosperous holiday makers. The Captain enjoyed an income on the side by smuggling. The journey, calculated to take between four and six days depending on the weather conditions, would take them first to Cagliari in Sardinia for refuelling and supplies and on to Canet, a tiny seaside resort on the South coast of France, just North of the Spanish border. The Captain had already been there several times.

'This is Victor,' said Jorgen, introducing a very fat Italian wearing a sort of uniform with large buttons.

'Bon Giorno,' said Victor.

'Bon Giorno,' said Rick.

The other members of the crew, who looked even more dishevelled than the Captain, were the mate and a chef, both also Italians. Rick did not fancy a holiday on this ship, which must have known better times but beggars could not be choosers on occasions such as this.

Maloney and Rick loaded the equipment into the cabin; they agreed one of them would remain with it at all times. They did not want inquisitive Italians poking their fingers into it. Jorgen carried in a long container like a violin case. When he was alone with Rick, he opened it up.

'I have a present for you,' he said. 'This is the nine millimeter Walthier – the MPK version with the short barrel. It also has a silencer. It is easy to use. Better than the Sterling. You may need it in emergencies.'

Rick, in gratitude and surprise said: 'That's great.'

'See you in a few days at Canet. Bon Voyage!' said Jorgen.

'Have a good trip yourself,' said Rick.

'Don't drink too much Campari, it will rot your gut,' said Jorgen, as he jumped back on to the quayside.

The ship slid smoothly away from the marina with the Libyans apparently paying no attention; but in a white concrete building overlooking the entrance to the harbour, a Libyan Army officer made some notes quickly in a flowing script. Anyone who understood Arabic could have deciphered the words: Allah be praised. The Enemies of Englishmen commence their journey as the sun is at its highest; the weapons safely on ship.

Both Rick and Maloney peeled off their sticky clothes, covered in dust and permeated with sweat, and put on shorts. After explaining to Maloney about Jorgen's gift of the sub-machine gun, Rick climbed up the narrow steps to the deck. The cruiser was already well out to sea; the villas and palm trees on the shore were taking on a romantic look. They were not nearly so pleasant seen from the landward side. The waves sparkled in the midday sun; Rick thought maybe he would enjoy the trip after all.

The voyage to Cagliari was without incident except that the mate got tipsy on a revoltingly-sweet Italian vermouth. Rick dozed much of the way, letting the hum of the engines and the whooshing of the water act as a soothing lullaby. Once Maloney aroused him with the news that they were passing the most northerly tip of Africa just east of Tunis and they stood together watching the disappearing land shimmering in a haze of bright hot light like a mirage. Apart from that one occasion, they were careful to man the cabin at all times.

At Cagliari they tied up at a quay near the Agostino Wharf, where dirty coasters were discharging coal, and Victor went ashore to arrange fuel and supplies. Rick and Maloney stayed on board so as not to invite inquiries from the Sardinians.

To their surprise, Victor, after an absence of nearly two hours, brought back a swarthy looking squat man called Alberto who, he claimed, was recruited as an extra crew member. The man gave them a sinister toothless grin which implied that he knew another role had been planned for him. Fortunately, there was no problem with the harbourmaster, nor with the officials in the customs house, who did not ask to see the ship's manifest. Victor had reported he was simply cruising from Palermo in Sicily en route to Civitavecchia on the mainland.

Soon after they were safely away from the busy, noisy harbour, Victor came down to the cabin. Rick suspected trouble when he saw Alberto with the Captain. There was a smell of grease and greed in their attitude. The Captain's avuncular personality on the first day of the voyage from Libya, had evaporated in Italian territorial waters.

'Mr. Coiléain, we think we need a little business talk,' he said, his toothless companion grinning and saying nothing.

'What about?' asked Rick.

'In our trade we take risks, That is the business. But some risks are greater than others.'

'Well,' said Rick.

'We think you are carrying a dangerous consignment. We could have big trouble if the coastguards stopped us and searched the ship. My friend Alberto has come on board to protect my interests.'

'What do you mean by that?' said Rick, playing for time and hoping Patrick Maloney would return soon from the deck.

'He is, if you like, my Trade Union representative. He tells me I should have an extra five thousand dollars danger money, Mr. Coiléain.'

'But you agreed the figure with the Germans,' said Rick.

'That was before we knew you were carrying contraband.

It could be bad, very bad, for me. I could lose my licence and my ship could be confiscated. Very bad, Mr. Coiléain, you see, very bad.'

The toothless man grinned in an even more menacing way, but Rick was disinclined to give in to blackmail. One concession might not be the last with such men. Their cunning minds had understood that the two packages were very valuable, but they did not know whether they contained drugs, gold or arms.

'You see, Mr. Coiléain,' Victor was saying, 'if I suspect you of smuggling I can take you to the nearest Italian port and report you. The authorities would praise me for that. It would do my business good.'

'I don't think your other customers would like it.'

'I don't think they would know, Mr. Coiléain. You could hardly advertise your experience from an Italian gaol. Anyway, who would believe you?'

'We agreed on a figure; you've been paid and I'm not paying any more,' said Rick, getting more irritated.

'It's not as simple as that Mr. Coiléain. My friend and I will have to examine the packages. Under Italian maritime law, I am responsible for all cargo.'

On instructions from the Captain given in some Sicilian dialect, the ugly squat man came forward to the bunks; Rick lunged forward to stop him, but his agility was not as good as the Italian's. Rick took a blow on his stomach which knocked out all his breath and he collapsed to his knees.

As he attempted to get up the little man applied a vice-like grip to the back of Rick's neck and held him like a chicken ready for plucking. The Captain was speaking again, but the words were indistinct to Rick as his head was aching from the shock of the sudden assault.

'Mr. Coiléain, perhaps you now understand we mean business. I have authority on my own ship. If you do not behave, I shall put back into Cagliari and have you arrested for attempting to smuggle.'

Rick could only grunt because the grip on his neck was holding him paralysed and as he could not get off his knees, he was in a position of obeisance to the Captain. It was very undignified. He made a sign with his arms of compliance and on a signal from the Captain, the Italian slowly released his grip.

'My friend Alberto is tough. They train them well in the Sicilian hills, Mr. Coiléain. What do you say in English? "Survival of the fittest".'

The Captain was bending down to open the packages when Maloney came in to see, to his surprise, Rick kneeling powerlessly on the cabin floor.

'Stop him,' said Rick, turning to punch the Sicilian in the crutch.

Maloney brought a karate chop on the back of the Captain who went out like a light. The Sicilian tried to pull a pistol out of the inside pocket of his jacket, but Rick saw his movement in time and knocked the gun out of his hand. It fell to the floor; Rick picked it up. It was a neat Beretta. After that there was no fight left in the squat man and Rick motioned him to lift his friend Victor on to the bunk which he did, whimpering to himself in Sicilian.

'What happened?' asked Maloney, still shocked by the incident.

'They tried to blackmail us for another five thousand dollars. I don't think we would have got to France at all under their auspices. They're gangsters who wouldn't hesitate to slit our throats if they thought it worth their while.'

'Wow!' said Maloney. 'What do we do now?'

'You and I must take turns to stay awake. That's all. We'll have to hold the machine gun on these rascals.'

Alberto, clearly could not understand English, but his eyes opened wide when Rick took out the Walthier and slowly and deliberately filled the 32 rounds.

After a few moments the Captain came round and Rick sat both Italians on the bunk with the Walthier trained on them. He kept the safety catch on.

'Now the situation is clear,' Rick said. 'We hired this boat to get to Canet. We paid you the agreed price and that's where we're going. And no more nonsense,' he added firmly. 'We will not hesitate to use this if there is any more trouble.'

After the whack on the head, the Captain was subdued.

'Just as you say, Mr. Coiléain.'

Rick searched the Captain's cabin and the mate's quarters but did not find any more guns. They probably had them well hidden, but he could hardly tear the ship apart.

For the rest of the voyage he took turns with Maloney to keep watch on the Captain, the mate and the Sicilian. The Walthier was a great asset and he was grateful to Jorgen. His position would certainly be perilous without it.

When one of them slept, which they did for only three or four hours at a time, they kept the cabin door locked and the Beretta under the pillow.

Early one morning just after dawn when Rick was on guard, the Captain pointed ahead through the mists.

'Look Mr. Coiléain. You can see France now. You should be very glad you did not shoot us. I do not think you could have found Canet.'

Keeping his hand firmly on the machine gun, Rick stood up and looked ahead. Above the rolling waves he could pick out land. During the preceeding days he kept a check, as far as he could, on the navigation of the ship and hoped, as he thought, that this was in fact Canet and not some Italian port. If Victor had tricked him he could expect an Italian coastguard vessel to draw up fairly soon.

But all was well. As the mists rose in the slowly warming October sun, Rick saw a large motorboat heading in their direction. It came nearer and with relief, he recognised the heads of Jorgen and Helmut just visible above the spray, with Jorgen apparently steering.

Within seconds they were alongside, Jorgen calling: 'Bring all the gear and come for a joy ride.'

With the help of the mate and the Sicilian they stowed the packages away on the motorboat under tarpaulins, and jumped into the boat themselves.

Jorgen revved the engine and took off in a wide circle at a rate of knots, waving goodbye to the Captain who was standing on the deck in an attitude of disconsolate relief. Jorgen turned to Rick and said:

'You look pale. Have you been seasick?'

'Oh! no, thank God. Just lost a lot of sleep keeping the guns on those criminals.'

In shouts over the noise of the outboard motor and the bump on the waves, he explained the experience of the journey to the Germans.

Jorgen smiled nonchalantly and said: 'You should have told me that earlier. We could have taken back the six thousand dollars they didn't deserve.'

Chapter Twenty-Eight

The Approach to Wales

Rick and Maloney were exhausted by the strain of the voyage and decided to stop overnight at a hotel just outside Toulouse with the Germans. The rest would help them to recover and allow time to review the final stages of the plan. Rick was excited at the prospect of its early implementation, but tried to suppress his emotions. The Germans were cooler and although he knew they hated the English, their attitude to the project was dominated by complete professionalism with personal feelings wholly excluded.

Secretly, Rick was relieved at the Germans' objectivity; their strength sustained him when he felt stress, which had become more frequent. In no way had his resolve or his faith in the project weakened, but he had to recognise his deficiencies with regard to its execution. It was one thing to conceive an assassination plan, and to accept intellectually all its implications, but it was quite another to do it personally. He had never been a gunman and had never killed anyone directly in his life.

Harry Truman, the gentle haberdasher from Kansas, would never personally have harmed anybody, but he authorised the bombing of Hiroshima and Nagasaki, which killed countless innocent people. If Harry Truman had been given a machine gun and asked to shoot a dozen defenceless Japanese mothers and children, he would have flinched with revulsion from the task. Destroying two cities was easier. Richard Collins stilled his qualms as the moment came closer by equating himself with all the Harry Trumans, the wise leaders who made great decisions on the deaths of others, but never once participated personally in the killings. He remembered the Merle Miller biography of Harry Truman who made 'a simple, necessary military decision'.

'Simple, necessary military decision' was it in a nutshell. Merle Miller had also written, that to justify the decision, or in any way apologise for it would be repugnant. The Ultimate was in exactly the same category. Truman had relied on his Air Force pilot and bombadier, Rick would rely on the Germans. They had, fortunately, volunteered to be the executioners.

After a two hour sleep – the first for days away from the humming of engines and the fear of the Sicilian – Rick felt refreshed and ready for the final conference. They met in a large old fashioned bedroom with the faded comforts of yesteryear. But the walls were thick and they felt secure.

'The British Cabinet meet on Tuesday mornings at Downing Street,' said Jorgen.

'So we shall now confirm twelve noon on the second Tuesday in November as the time of execution,' said Rick, 'unless something extraordinary happens we should keep to that date.'

'Agreed,' said Jorgen.

'Before we leave here, I'll send a cable to Peadar so he knows we'll be at the rendezvous point near Pontrieux in three days time,' said Rick. 'He'll line up the Cessna flight.'

'You should be safely back in Ireland with all the equipment by the end of the week,' said Jorgen.

'Yes,' said Rick. 'I think we'll keep the packages for a week or so safely in Ireland and deliver them to you in the first week of November. Before that you should travel to England as tourists, and hire a suitable estate car, fix up the curtains as though you are sleeping in it, and be all ready for the great day.'

'Did you give up the idea of flying the Cessna into England?' asked Jorgen.

'No alternative,' said Rick. 'The chances of being located by the radar screens are too great. The best plan is to repeat the Canet landing and come ashore from a fishing vessel somewhere in remote Wales. We could land a plane there if you could find three hundred feet of level grassland but I don't think you can.'

'We shall do a final survey of the Whitehall setting and then set off for Wales to fix the best place on the coast for the boat to come in,' said Jorgen.

It was agreed that Helmut and Jorgen, after collecting the equipment from Peadar, would drive from Wales to London. They would return to the Hilton Hotel where their rooms would have been booked through until the day of execution. On that morning they would wait until 11.35 for any message from Rick and, if none were received, would then leave for the drive along St. James's Park. The missile launchers would have been mounted beforehand and cased in the kind of plywood boxes which could be dismantled in seconds.

'Good,' said Rick. 'Phone us from Wales as soon as you have located a landing place. Peadar and Patrick will come over with some of our Irish fishermen to deliver the equipment to your hands. Do you want either of them to come with you to London?'

'Not necessary,' said Jorgen. 'The English policemen are vigilant and if we are stopped at a road block, they may search the car if we have an Irishman with us, yes? Better just two German tourists, yes?'

'I think you may be right,' said Rick. 'The police over there have made so many mistakes. There was a case when they let an Irishman go without searching his hired car. It was driven around by other drivers for two years full of explosives. I suppose they must be more careful now.'

That evening, their last together, the four men had a fabulous meal in the hotel dining room. For a small provincial hotel it was a creditable performance. Rick learned, to his pleasure that, in Toulouse, as in nearly all French provincial towns, food comes first in life and the great traditions of French cuisine survive best in them, especially when they can be afforded on the wages earned by the engineers working on Concorde.

The next morning the Germans caught a taxi to the

airport to fly to Paris and on to London. Rick and Maloney prepared for a leisurely drive to Brittany. They had two nights, possibly three, to sample further the delights of French cooking. Maloney was in favour of driving into Paris for a day, but Rick vetoed that idea with a stern admonition on the need to safeguard the packages. They would drive cautiously at all times, stay at small hotels and out of trouble.

By the end of the week, by this time quite refreshed, they had reached Pontrieux, a small market town on the Trieux river. Maloney who had not been in the region before, was struck with the similarities to Ireland. The Bretons are celts too, Rick explained.

Apart from some early mist, the day of the rendezvous had perfect weather conditions. It would be ideal for the Cessna to fly in. From eleven onwards they kept the VHF radio tuned to the agreed wavelength. At half-an-hour after midday, the crackling started and they heard a faint Irish voice saying:

'This is Paddy requesting permission to come to the party.'

They drove the car to the other end of the designated landing road to put up the diversion signs, which they had obtained in Rennes, and placed the marking sheets on the road. The stretch was perfect for a landing at this point – straight with hardly any trees about. Some peasants were in a field some distance away, but it was unlikely they would take any interest in the landing.

After some minutes the plane appeared overhead at about two hundred feet wagging its wings in a signal. It circled and landed without problems.

'That was good,' said Rick.

They drove to the plane, loaded the packages, and within seconds were airborne again with Rick in the passenger seat. The pilot turned the Cessna towards the North and Rick, looking down, saw Maloney already rushing to pick up the diversion signs. It was his job to return the car to the rental agency in Paris, and catch the Aer Lingus plane next day to Cork.

Once over the rocky coast they headed West, and then North West towards Ireland. That evening, Rick was in the cottage at Courtmacsherry, drinking whiskey with Peadar to celebrate his safe return and the arrival of the equipment. It only remained for the Germans to 'phone them with the Welsh contact point and the transport problem would be virtually licked. There was a lot to celebrate. They had come a long way.

Three days later they heard some bad news: Maloney had been arrested in Paris for drunken driving, causing an accident and assaulting a gendarme. They had locked him up to await trial in a few weeks and informed the Irish Embassy. It seemed not too serious and the likely penalty would be expulsion. However, they would have to manage without him. Peadar arranged to get another reliable Republican to sail with him to Wales but he would be told no more than the minimum about the delivery.

Several days later the Germans telephoned. The line was bad but Rick got the message clearly enough. They were staying in Aberystwyth, had found an ideal place for a boat landing and would wait there with headlights shining out to sea at dawn on Friday the fifth of November. The place was between Borth and Aberdovey and the position four degrees three and a half inches Longitude West, and fifty-two degrees thirty and a half inches Latitude North. If storms or bad weather delayed the vessel's arrival, they would wait at dawn on the subsequent days. The plan seemed foolproof: the coastal patrols would be non-existent at this time and at this place.

Chapter Twenty-Nine

The CIA Moves

At the Virginia headquarters of the CIA, a special team had been set up to find Richard Collins. Despite their efforts he remained completely elusive. Men posted on surveillance duties at Tripoli, Rome and Zurich airports, reported no sightings and Immigration Control in Switzerland, France, Belgium and Italy made nil returns, although there were false alarms involving several American businessmen. One, at Zurich, was discovered to have fifteen thousand in US dollar bills in his luggage, but was allowed to proceed after questioning as the importation of any quantity of currency into Switzerland is not an offence. Richard Collins, Tube Stack representative and covert CIA operative, had completely disappeared.

There was one minor clue which was uncovered in the exhaustive search of his apartment on the Viale A. Manzoni. The address of someone called O'Connell living in the Crumlin district of Dublin was discovered in his papers. The name and the address had no apparent relevance to the assignments of Richard Collins and DII ordered a full check on O'Connell and his connections. Assassination at the hands of left-wing groups was feared but DDI could not accept this theory as no explanation had been forthcoming for Collins' apparently voluntary appearance in Libya.

Mrs. Kathy Collins was interviewed in Philadelphia. She could only say that her husband had telephoned her regularly until two and a half weeks before. He had said he was going on an extensive trip and would telephone again in mid-November. Under cross-examination she admitted

that he intended to resign the service. She also remembered
a Mr. O'Connell in Dublin at a New Year's Eve party.

Within twelve hours the message came back to the desk
of DII. *O'Connell: positive identification as leading Republican
campaigner belonging to the Provisional non-Marxist wing stop
Believed active in importation of arms supplied by sympathisers in the
United States.*

To the trained senses of DII there were too many
ingredients in this cake to make good eating. He instructed
one of his senior assistants to fly to Dublin to investigate.
Collins was at fault in not reporting his Irish connection.
Possibly it was innocent but everything pointed the other
way. The British Government, who had already talked to
Kissinger about CIA men in London, would be extremely
angry if it came out that one operative was actually
personally involved with the Provisional IRA.

As soon as he arrived in Dublin, the assistant contacted
the Garda special branch; he was convinced the Irish
Government would, in the interests of good relations with
the British, co-operate to the full with his investigations. He
was correct in this assumption.

Chapter Thirty

The Holocaust

Peadar brought the ship into Courtmacsherry and berthed her almost facing the cottage. In the early morning, before the other residents were about, they loaded the packages, wrapped in tarpaulins, in the tiny hold which often on other occasions was filled with herring or mackerel. The crew were reliable. After five years of smuggling arms Peadar knew his men.

Time and time again Rick had gone over with Peadar the instructions he was to follow. The beach just North of Borth was the off-loading point and at dawn on Friday the Germans would be waiting. Peadar was to row into the shore in the small rolling boat they carried, drag the packages over the mud and the sand on a rubber wheeled trolley and deliver them to the Germans, then sail away quickly in the half-light. In the event of any questions, they were blown off course and if any inquisitive officers looked as if they might board the vessel before the delivery, then the fresh herrings carried should be thrown over the tarpaulins in the hold. At the worst, they still had the Walthier and Peadar would not hesitate to use it.

As they steamed away towards Wood Point and the open sea, Rick could only hold his fingers firmly crossed: six days to go.

He turned back to the cottage to clear up his things. Next day he would drive to Dublin to be with O'Connell and await the news of the holocaust and its aftermath. Taking his last look at Courtmacsherry, he promised himself to bring Kathy and the kids back to this delightful corner of unspoilt Ireland, perhaps to the same cottage which had meant so much during the last weeks and the climax of his plan.

He stayed in Dublin at the Gresham Hotel, for he could see no reason for any caution in Ireland, and as soon as he arrived he rang O'Connell.

'I'm glad to say …' he began.

'Don't, my 'phone is probably tapped. Wait until I call you,' said O'Connell, anxiously.

Fifteen minutes later the 'phone in his bedroom rang.

'Leave your hotel now, walk around the block, make sure you are not being followed and when you are sure, come to the front entrance of Trinity College,' said O'Connell. 'I'll see you there.'

Rick was curious, as this cloak and dagger stuff was not in character for O'Connell, but he did as instructed. O'Connell was late in coming, twenty minutes or so, saying breathlessly that the traffic through Dolphin's Barn had been very heavy.

'We're in some trouble. And I don't know how serious it is yet,' he was saying as soon as they found a quiet corner. 'But what is certain is that your friends in the CIA know about you.'

'Know about me?' said Rick, incredulously.

'Yes, and I think a senior CIA man is in Dublin at this very moment. If he's not staying with the Ambassador in Phoenix Park, he may be in the Gresham next door to you,' said O'Connell, looking concerned, his usual twinkle much subdued.

'My God, supposing I bump into him,' exclaimed Rick.

'You won't. I'm arranging for you to stay with some of our friends in Ballsbridge. It's a bit out of town and you should be safe there. 'Phone the hotel later and say you've gone on a trip for a few days.'

'Will you be able to find out more of what's going on?'

'Yes, rumour has it that the High Command are calling a special meeting for the day after tomorrow and I'm being summoned. Something's brewing and I don't like the sound of it. Big pressure from the United States Government, I suspect,' said O'Connell.

Rick stayed the intervening days with the family at Ballsbridge. They gave him the tiny box room. He felt cut off with only Irish papers and RTE and no telephone. He could only assume that Peadar had made a successful landing and meeting with the Germans. If anything serious had gone wrong, Peadar would have contacted O'Connell.

On Sunday he went to early Mass with the family in the church on Heddington Road. It was so peaceful and domestic he could not believe it was real, a contrast with the raging inferno inside his brain, trying to piece together the elements of the mystery. A CIA man in Dublin, apparently looking for him, and the High Command in almost permanent session: it did not make sense unless somewhere there had been a breach of security.

Then he remembered. Maloney. He must have talked to the French police when he was drunk, and been put under intense interrogation. And with the French it was very intense. Perhaps they had discovered the secret and passed it on to the Americans and the British. If so, all was lost.

After Mass he excused himself from the family and went walking along Mesdil Road along the canal, on and on past three bridges for about a mile. Then he saw the barracks: Cathal Brugha Barracks and recalled the conference in Cork months before and the revelation – to him – of the Cathal Brugha plan. Now it was only two days before the plan would be implemented, provided Maloney had not leaked it. And providing the High Command did not cancel it, which would be a strange repetition of history.

Perhaps he was unfair to Maloney. Perhaps Peadar and the Germans had been caught. The uncertainties began to resolve themselves. O'Connell came to the house after midnight, banging demandingly on the door. Rick dressed, and shuddering against the November cold, went with him into the streets which were the only safe places to talk.

'I am sorry, very sorry,' said O'Connell, when they were away from the house. 'I've spent two whole days with the High Command and I had to tell them about the plan. My life would not have been worth living if I hadn't told them. It would have been considered treachery. My Command is allowed some initiative but this is regarded as much too big.'

'What did they decide?' asked Rick, the pit falling out of his stomach.

'It's not easy to tell you this. But I must. The majority instruction is that the plan must not be implemented,' said O'Connell.

'Why, oh why?' said Rick.

'There's been big pressure from the American Government. Somehow they've got wind of something and whatever it is they want it stopped. They've told the High Command that Republican associations in the United States will be declared illegal – like the Klu Klux Klan – if the plan is not called off,' said O'Connell.

'Do you think they have any details at all?' asked Rick.

'No,' said O'Connell.

'Good, that means Peadar got through,' said Rick.

'But you must stop it now. I am under military instructions from the High Command,' said O'Connell. 'I must give you the order to stop it.'

Rick was devastated that after all the months of thought and preparation, and now only sixty hours before implementation, he was receiving such orders. It was unfair and unjust.

'I know how you must be feeling,' said O'Connell, 'but we have no alternative. I think one of the problems for the Americans is your own connection. They are really concerned that the British authorities may suspect CIA involvement as you are a key figure. They want the plan killed in such a way that the British need never know it ever existed.'

'I thought you said they didn't know about the plan?' said Rick, still perplexed.

'They don't yet know the details, though that is only a matter of time, now the whole High Command know. They are only too well aware that you are the king-pin in a very big enterprise, and that if they stop you they stop the plan, and with it any suggestion of CIA involvement,' said O'Connell.

'What do the High Command hope to gain from abandonment of the plan?' asked Rick.

'The Americans are putting out suggestions that if we co-operate they will be willing to put pressure on the British both directly and through NATO, to make peace in Northern Ireland. You know, the line Senator Edward Kennedy has been plugging for years,' said O'Connell.

'So you think we may achieve our purpose anyway?' asked Rick.

'Yes,' said O'Connell, 'there is a very good chance of that.'

'What should we do now then?' asked Rick, somewhat pathetically.

'Well, I don't know how far you have gone with the final stages of the plan and frankly, I don't want to know. I told the High Command I didn't know and we should leave it at that. This whole business is dynamite, and it's better if the High Command go on thinking it's unauthorised private enterprise by you and the Germans. But my instructions to you are: "Go over to London fast and stop it".'

Rick knew he had no choice. After a tortured few hours of sleep, he left the Ballsbridge house to catch the first available direct flight from Dublin to London. As he did so, the two Germans, driving a large estate car, with its rear windows obscured by curtains, were setting out from a motel on the outskirts of Birmingham on the last stage of their journey along the M6 and M1 to London. It was twenty-eight hours to deadline; although they had been delayed they were still in good time to meet the agreed schedule. Due to bad weather off the Welsh coast, Peadar had been two days late in coming ashore at Borth, but on Sunday morning the delivery of the equipment had taken place without incident. Now the missile launchers were securely mounted in the rear of the car.

The CIA man in Dublin had submitted desperate coded reports to Virginia. *Collins alerted by associates has gone to ground in Dublin stop Whereabouts unknown stop Provisionals High Command ordered mission to be aborted stop However strong suspicion Collins is deranged and unwilling to co-operate stop*

Further instructions awaited END.

In Virginia a top level meeting considered the reports in the light of American interests. It was agreed that the plan, whatever it was – and reports had not yet clarified its details – must be stopped at any price. Furthermore, it was imperative that any association of a CIA operative with the plan must be denied. The image of the CIA was already bad enough without adding to the scandals. To keep the CIA out of it, the British should not be informed. The plan could be stopped without involving them. It was clear that success in influencing the Provisional High Command had been achieved. Richard Collins was the prime mover, and might still be acting on his own initiative. If it appeared he was about to execute the plan then every possible action must be taken to stop him.

The signal went out from Virginia to the CIA team in Dublin: *Top security essential on Collins stop If he is sole mover and cannot be stopped by associates you are hereby authorised to activate the E instruction stop Repeat if necessary in your judgement E instruction on Collins stop Imperative Collins does not reach England in view of need to stop execution of plan and avoid United Kingdom being made aware of any Company involvement END.*

Sitting in his office by St. James's Station on the same Monday morning, Chief Superintendent Bosworth was reading intelligence reports supplied by informers within the Provisional IRA. He buzzed his assistant.

'Get Special Branch. We need to get more information on these leaks from Dublin.'

The Special Branch people could supply few further facts. The Provisionals had planned a further escalation of violence in London, probably involving bombs in strategic places, but latest reports indicated the plans had been cancelled or shelved. Bosworth decided to take no further action at the moment.

As Rick was booking on the London flight at the airport north of Dublin, two men were watching him.

'It sure looks like Collins,' said one, 'ask one of the officials to check his passport during the gun frisk.'

After ten minutes the second man came back. 'Passport

checked out as Ristéard O'Coiléain – that's Collins' Irish name. It's him alright. He has no luggage: not even a brief case.'

'Well here I go. This is it. I'll fly straight on to Paris from Heathrow to get the hell out of there. You stay on here in Dublin.'

The first man booked a seat economy class and ascertained the plane was two-thirds full.

Rick settled down in a window seat at the rear of the Boeing 737 and fastened his seat belt. The stewardess was speaking into a microphone: 'Welcome aboard this Aer Lingus flight to London. Flying time is sixty-five minutes and we shall be flying at twenty-five thousand feet.' Rick was still in a stunned state. He could hardly believe his presence in this seat going to the England which he had vowed never to visit until Ireland was free. He felt disembodied, as though merely a witness to his body going on a journey to stop a plan which was to have been his life's fulfillment. He was tortured with doubts and anguish.

When breakfast was served, he asked for a whiskey instead and then had a second and a third. The alcohol cleared the mists in the dark recesses of his mind and he felt better. There was, he now recognised, no alternative to the course he was taking. He would go straight to the Hilton Hotel from Heathrow, meet the Germans and carefully explain why the plan had to be abandoned.

There was no need for the British, or anyone else, to know any of its details. It would fade into the obscure pages of history like the Cathal Brugha plan, fifty-five years before. If the United States Government honoured its promise and put pressure on the British, then it might achieve its purpose without being implemented. Perhaps history did repeat itself. Perhaps the Brugha Plan, although aborted by Michael Collins, had frightened the then British Government into listening to sense over Ireland. His plan might have had the same effect on the State Department.

It did not really matter to Rick that the Company had discovered his association with the Provisional IRA. He was not engaged in activities against America. Anyway, he would be resigning the service within a week or so. Kathy would be pleased. It would be a new life for her and the kids. Kathy, he thought, poor neglected Kathy, whom he had not even telephoned in weeks. He would telephone her from the Hilton, as soon as he had dealt with the Germans, and tell her the Irish job was all complete and everyone could relax.

The plane was flying over Central England and through the patches of cloud, Rick could pick out the towns below. Soon they would be descending to Heathrow. A man was standing in the aisle beaming all over his face.

'Say, aren't you Rick Collins from Philadelphia?'

'Yes,' said Rick, a bit nonplussed to have such a greeting, which he could hardly deny. The man, obviously an American, slipped into the spare seat and leaned over to face Rick.

'Well I'm sure glad to meet you,' he said, gripping Rick's right hand firmly and, at the same time, holding the upper part of Rick's right arm with his left hand, as if in a gesture of exaggerated friendship.

Rick felt the pressure on the arm growing and something in his suit – a horse hair perhaps – was sticking into him. He was annoyed with the stranger's boisterousness, but he could hardly object to friendship.

'Well, sure hope you enjoy the rest of your trip,' said the man going almost as soon as he had arrived.

Rick was drowsy. The cabin noises were slipping away from him. 'As we are about to land at Heathrow, will you please fasten your seat belts and extinguish all cigarettes,' the stewardess was saying, but Rick only heard part of it.

The steward checked that all passengers' seat belts were fastened, including that of the passenger in the window seat who had gone to sleep after three whiskeys.

The other American, who was travelling without baggage, quickly passed through transit and within forty-five minutes was airborne on a flight to Paris.

Later that Monday afternoon, Bosworth was intrigued to receive the account of the incident on the Aer Lingus flight to Heathrow.

'This may be the breakthrough we've been waiting for,' he said to the Inspector. 'This man O'Coiléain was clearly a top Provisional IRA terrorist and his murder on that aircraft is part of the growing quarrel within the Provisionals. He was killed by his own people. I understand they used a sophisticated poison.'

'Yes,' said the Inspector. 'We don't have the full autopsy yet, but he died through a poison introduced into the blood stream either through food or injection.'

'We must capitalise on this quarrel within the IRA,' said Bosworth.

'How?' asked the Inspector.

'I want this man's death mask splashed over all the papers tomorrow. Do a Margaret McKearney publicity job on him. I want the works,' said Bosworth. 'Top terrorist, leader of the Provisionals, most dangerous gangster and all that stuff. The papers will lap it up. But we want anyone with information about his contacts over here to come forward. We can break the gang if we can get to know where they operate from.'

'Shall I open a special line for telephone calls from the public to come in direct?' asked the Inspector.

'Yes, advertise it. We want anyone who knows this man or who has rented him rooms to phone in. There will be hoax calls but just one good lead will be worth all the effort.'

'Right, Sir,' said the Inspector.

Most newspapers made it the main story on Tuesday morning: MYSTERY TERRORIST FOUND DEAD IN IRISH PLANE. BIG SPLIT IN IRA. BOMBER ASSASSINATED. POLICE CLAIM SUCCESS IN BREAKING GANG.

The two Germans had slept well after the long drive and a late night watching a mystery movie on the colour TV in the bedroom. They had a leisurely breakfast of coffee and rolls served on a trolly in the room. At nine o'clock, Helmut took the elevator to the lobby, which had been restored after the bomb outrage of a year before. He sauntered to the newstand, bought *Die Welt*, *Der Spiegel*, the Paris printed *New York Herald-Tribune*, and returned to the bedroom.

'Any news?' asked Jorgen, in German.

'Not much,' said Helmut. 'Be more tomorrow. Only two and a half hours to our deadline. That should wake them up.'

Valerie Commin was shocked. She was sitting at breakfast with Graham, who was talking about the police success in breaking up the IRA gangs.

'We're really licking them,' he said.

The words stuck in Valerie's throat. She was sure the face staring out at them from the front pages of the *Telegraph* and the *Mail* was that of Rick Collins. It was not just a case of recognition; she felt his death instinctively. It was him, no doubt. The police appealed for any information and she wondered if she should tell Graham about Barbados. But it was all past; it would not do any good to rake over those embers. What possible use would the information be to the police? Better not say.

Bosworth was pleased with the press publicity. 'That should bring in the calls,' he said to the Inspector.

Bosworth had agreed to meet Mary that morning at Victoria and go with her to see some flats in Fulham. He was glad to be resolving that problem. It would only take a couple of hours and he would be back in the office just after noon. Nothing much could happen in that time. The Inspector would monitor all the incoming calls on the O'Coiléain case.

At eleven thirty, Graham Commin, stockbroker MP, was in the City and Valerie was consoling her doubts at the hairdressers. The Inspector at Scotland Yard had dealt with forty-two calls of which at least half were hoaxes.

There could be value in the information given by five or six of the callers and he had given instructions that they were to be followed up urgently. A new signal had arrived from the Garda in Dublin, which referred to the Irish police uncovering a big plot against British Ministers, details uncertain. The Inspector decided not to act on it, as Irish intelligence was often unreliable, until the Superintendent had seen it. He would be back before lunch. It could wait until then.

At the same time Helmut turned to Jorgen and said, in German: 'Shall we go then, it's half past eleven?'

'We promised Collins we would wait here until eleven thirty-five. We'll wait another five minutes and if there's no news from him, we will go then,' said Jorgen, precise to the last minute.

No call came so the Germans left the room and, having already paid the hotel bill, quickly walked out the back entrance towards the underground car park.

At eleven forty-seven, Helmut eased the car out of the driveway and turned it around the Mayfair roads heading to Hyde Park Corner. Jorgen leaned over the seat to push off the plywood case coverings. The missile launchers looked magnificent, ready with the projectiles, like crouching beasts of prey.

They drove along Constitution Hill down The Mall, stopped and turned right. Jorgen pressed the button and Helmut drove on at a steady twenty miles per hour. They heard the explosion as they turned the car along Birdcage Walk to make their getaway from St. James's Park tube station.

The devastation in the Cabinet room was total. There were no survivors.